23:23:23

POWER SHIFT

TOBY STEELE
BOOK 2

ADAM ECCLES

LITTLE BIT STRANGE PRESS

ABOUT THE AUTHOR

 Adam Eccles is a cynical tech-nerd hermit, living in the west of Ireland for the last twenty five years.

With a long career in technology, and being an avid time-travel fan as well as having a life long love of comedy, you can find elements of all these things in his novels.

If you'd like to read more, and let's face it, why wouldn't you?

You can sign up for infrequent zero-spam news here:
https://www.adamecclesbooks.com/subscribe
But, most of all, he hopes you enjoy his stories.

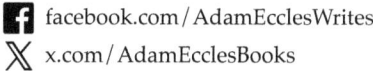 facebook.com/AdamEcclesWrites
x.com/AdamEcclesBooks

For Robin & Willow

AUTHOR'S NOTE

This is book **two** in the Toby Steele series. Ideally, you would have already read book **one**:

22:22:22 Frequency Shift

Available on Amazon, before starting this book. In fact, there's a wonderful audiobook narrated by the talented Mark Rice-Oxley, so you can save your eyes and indulge your ears if that's your thing.

— Adam.

CHAPTER
ONE

I FADE INTO THE NIGHT, merge with the surroundings, and become invisible amidst the urban jungle.

The darkness is my friend. She coddles me in velvet arms, and I lean into her cool embrace. An old familiar companion, a confidante, a buddy. We go back a long way, the darkness and I. She's always been there, lurking in the shadows, tempting me to her side. I'm easily beguiled by her sultry siren wails echoing into the night.

A fine drizzle mist silently and subtly permeates everything, just enough to hurry people but not completely keep them away — ideal for my needs. I nod to myself in approval. Move along, nothing to see here.

The perpetual toxic taint of smoke and fumes hangs acrid and sinister in the air. It's a wonder anyone can breathe at all, yet the place teems with life during the day.

At night, there are fewer people around, but never none. Those that linger in the darkness differ from the day folk.

Streetlights cast their dim sodium glare as I plod along the final few steps of my route. Headlights dazzle, and red brake lights flicker. Shadows multiply and stretch out over the wet ground. My world is desaturated into a gritty black and white and then tinted sickly yellow, as if through a poignant photo filter. A fitting diorama.

I find my spot and flop down in the semi-shelter of a shop doorway, getting myself together. A thick blanket insulates me from the cold pavement, and a filthy, torn sleeping bag drapes over me, providing some warmth in the long night. A scrawled note on a torn-off chunk of cardboard box vaguely propped up against my crossed legs. 'Homeless and hungry' next to an empty coffee cup. I drop a few shiny coins into it to add to the effect.

A stupid joke from a meme comes to mind and tickles me — an army sergeant addressing a private, 'I didn't see you at camouflage training this morning, Murphy?'

'Thank you, Sir.'

I snigger, but only internally. My face is steadfastly set in a mix of apathy and pain to remain invisible.

I hide in plain sight. In fact, people actively go out of their way to avoid me. This is the perfect cover.

My clothes are disgusting, threadbare and greasy from food stains and rubbish, but that's part of the disguise. I'm not here to be noticed, far from it. My mission demands stealth. I stink like hell and try as I might, I can't get used to it. Sour puffs of foul air rise on my body heat, crinkling my nose.

Opposite where I sit and about thirty yards down the road towards the canal, a building looms dark and quiet. I don't look directly at it; instead, I face vaguely towards a bar a few doors along. The tiny camera nestled in my dreadlock wig, invisible and twisted into a row of beads, is trained on the door I'm interested in. Behind that door and somewhere deep inside the building, there is suffering and pain that I intend to stop.

· · ·

I check my burner phone under the cover of the sleeping bag. Nothing yet. I slip it back into a pocket, hidden from view, and set to silent mode.

I check the screen of my little video recorder, again hidden under my sleeping bag, brightness turned down low, checking the position I need to keep myself angled to get the best view of the building I'm watching. I shuffle into the corner of the doorway and tilt my head down a little. The recorder is adapted from a car dash-cam and records a two-hour loop onto a tiny memory card. Perfect for my needs.

I haven't heard from Jenny for a few days. I wonder if she's in trouble or dead in the Thames somewhere. No. Unlikely. The burner phone I got her probably ran out of battery. Hard to find a USB power outlet on the streets of London. She'll be okay. She's a tough one.

Jenny approached me a few weeks ago outside Camden tube station, asking for a favour. Begging.

Obviously, the favour was money, but she said not for drugs or booze. She was hungry and wanted a shower. I gave her twenty quid, and her face lit up with genuine joy or relief. Both, probably. She smiled, showing a heartbreaking lack of teeth; those remaining were gnarled and blackened. I knew I couldn't save her and pull her back from the underground world of London's homeless, but I had to do something. I offered her a shower in my hotel room. She was reluctant at first, assuming I meant sex rather than just a shower, but she took the risk. The thought of hot water, soap, and maybe a clean bed to lie in was too tempting to resist. Of course, I didn't mean sex. I just wanted to help the girl and only wanted information in return.

I'd been casually keeping an eye on the place for a few days. In my meanders and coffee shop window glances, I'd noticed that Jenny — I didn't know her name then — often lingered near the same building, stopping to look up at the barred windows, but never for more than a second before being distracted. She clearly knew something.

After an unsuccessful night of my typical vigilante wandering, I'd heard about the place in the stinking toilets of a nearby pub. Two blokes at the urinals sharing a story of debauchery only a short walk away from this very hostelry, and some 'Fucking dirty bitches that are worth the cash.' His words. I stood on a closed toilet in a cubicle, listening, then peered over the thin chipboard laminate door and got a look at the tops of their balding heads.

'Word has it that a copper runs it.' The first bloke whispered to his piss-hole compadre.

'Oh, yeah?' The other fine, upstanding gentleman looked over and swayed as he urinated.

'That's what they reckon. So, no chance of being nicked.' He tapped the side of his nose, steadying his still-draining trouser snake with the other hand.

'Good to know. Cheers for the tip.' The other man was balancing a half-empty pint glass in his left hand as he held his cock in the other. By way of thanks, he held up the glass towards the nonce next to him, sloshing a few slurps over the edge as he did.

Drunk as shit, both of them, but as I shrank back down out of sight and waited for them to leave, I formed a plan to investigate.

An illicit brothel run by a bent copper. Should keep me busy for a while, I thought.

"Are you polis?" Jenny sat down on the edge of the bed and looked up at me after she had showered. Glasgow accent, I reckoned. She looked in her early twenties with blonde hair and blue eyes, short and petite. Gaunt and hardened. She would be pretty, under different circumstances. Life on the street had drained her of youth and beauty. Whatever put her there in the first place lingered in her eyes. Ever moving, untrusting.

Hair wet from the shower, she hadn't bothered to style it, just shoved it back from her face. She smelled better after the wash, but she had put the same filthy clothes back on. There was nothing I could do about that immediately.

I got the hotel room as a base of operations for a few days while I scoped out the area. My native patch at home had run dry of jobs that needed doing, and I was also getting a bit paranoid about my operation being shut down by the real cops. No sense in becoming complacent. A change of scenery was needed, so I shifted south a little, assuming the big city smoke would have an abundance of gobshites that needed putting to bed. I was right, and I had a bit of fun with a nasty little scrote selling dodgy vape liquid to kids. His lockup garage stash somehow went up in flames. Funny how that happened when no one was anywhere near. I didn't know vape liquid would be flammable, but it turns out it most certainly is.

"No." I laughed. "Far from it."

"What are you then?" She looked around the room, eyes darting, lingering on anything that could be robbed. My laptop was closed on the little desk. Then she looked back at me, sizing me up, pausing on a scratch on my arm that I sustained in a recent struggle with one scumbag back home. A little hooded turd with a big knife in an underpass, robbing anyone stupid enough to try for a shortcut. He got lucky with a swipe before I smashed it from his hand and fractured his ulna.

"Just a dude." I shrugged. "I'm Toby."

"Jenny." She smiled thinly and reached out a hand to shake.

"Hungry?"

"Aye, fucking starvin'."

I pulled out my phone and scrolled for a while, found a place nearby, and ordered pizza and soft drinks to be delivered to the room.

"Why are you being nice to me?" Jenny paced herself. I thought she would scarf down half the pizza in one gulp, but she was calm and slow. Savouring every bite. She took a sip from a can of Coke and peered at me over the top.

I shrugged, "Why wouldn't I be?"

"What do you want?" She accused. "Everybody wants something."

"Nothing. You can go anytime you want, but I can't eat all that pizza on my own."

She hesitated, looked towards the door, but stayed sitting.

"You must want something." She fixed me with a stare.

I took a deep breath. "Okay, yeah. Information."

"Aye, I fuckin' knew it. You are a cop." She stiffened, almost dropping the current slice of pizza.

"No, seriously, I'm not."

"What then? What information?"

"I think you know what's going on in that building down the road." I didn't need to give the address. She knew which one I meant.

Her poker face was good, but I noticed a change in her pulse rate, a flicker in her frequency. Anger, adrenaline, and sadness.

She paused for a moment, then looked up. "Aye,"

Jenny told me how her friend, Oleksandra, had vanished one night, and that she knew she was being held prisoner in that building with who knows how many other girls. She'd seen a face at a window once before it was quickly pulled away. Kept drugged, dulled, unable to think straight, never mind escape. Forced into being a prostitute for the lowlife of London. She couldn't help her. Bouncers or henchmen at each entry kept her at bay, bars on the windows kept the girls in.

"She's only fifteen." Jenny pleaded. "Her family is all dead. She trusted me, and I let her get taken."

"I'm going to get her out. All of them."

Jenny, almost in tears, looked up at me, hopeful for a second, but then shook her head. "How? They have guns, I've seen them. Big bastards, too."

"Good to know. This is the kind of information I need. What else can you tell me?"

"Men go in and out all night. In the front and out the back door, and there's mebbe three security guys in there. Could be more."

"I heard something about a copper running the operation?"

"Aye, I heard that too." She nods. "I've seen him."

"Do you know a name?"

She shakes her head. "Nah. But he's around sometimes. Doesn't come every night, just every so often, mebbe to collect the money."

"How do you know it's him?"

"I ken a copper when I see one." She eyes me up and down again, then shrugs. "He's the main man, anyway. No doubt."

I nod. "Tell me about your friend?"

Oleksandra was a refugee from Ukraine. Her family was all slaughtered, and her home was destroyed, along with many others. She managed to escape and found herself in London, penniless, with only the clothes on her back, frightened and with very few words of English. A laundry room at the back of a hospital became her makeshift bedroom, accessed through a small window. She was tiny, lithe and desperate. Venturing out only for food when absolutely necessary, hiding most of the day. Jenny saw her running away from a baker's shop with a loaf of bread clutched in her hand, so she distracted the chasing baker, letting the little girl escape. She found her after, hiding in a park, squishing the bread into balls and chewing. She was thirsty, and Jenny gave her a bottle of water. They became friends, despite the language barrier, and Jenny took her in, as much as she could, being homeless herself. They were inseparable and slept most nights tucked into the same sleeping bag in their little cardboard city under a bridge. 'Nothing lesbian about it' Jenny was keen to point out, but she felt responsible for the girl. Needed to keep her safe and close. She had no one else, after all. It wasn't fair.

"One night, Sandy never came back from going for a pish. I heard a van drive away, and that was it. She was gone. Taken." Tears filled Jenny's eyes as she spoke. "She's just a kid!"

I reached over and offered a hand. Jenny held it and gripped it tight. "I'm going to get her out of there. I promise."

I feel a buzz in my pocket. A text on the burner phone. I don't react immediately. The dim street scene unfolds around me as a couple hurries by across the road, the man shielding his glasses from the rain with a hand, and another man stomps past me without acknowledgement. I'm invisible, just the way I like it. I slowly slide my hand under the sleeping bag and slip the phone out under the cover. A message from Jenny.

blue@red2N

A thud of adrenaline courses through me. Someone has seen the cop on his way here or maybe heard something on the grapevine. I want to jump up and burst into action, but I pause. Take a deep breath and stay sitting on the cold ground. Tonight is the night, but I need to stick to the plan. Jenny had spread the word amongst the homeless community that she wanted to know when the brothel cop was going to pay his girls a visit. I don't know who or how, but it doesn't matter. The streets have ears and eyes. Amazing what loyalty a fresh, hot cheeseburger can get you in the depths of starvation.

I tried to teach Jenny a cypher, but as she only had limited resources, and we would be short of time in these situations, instead we came up with a simple colour code system. Blue for the boss cop, red for the brothel. Not up to Evelyn's standard of encryption, but if Jenny was caught, it is obscure enough that it can't be tied to anything that might go on.

The phone buzzes again.

15m

Jenny is on her way to the building and should arrive in fifteen minutes. I want to reply and tell her to stay away, that it will certainly be dangerous here soon, but I know she won't listen. She will be the backup camera. I have another small camera in a pocket that wirelessly connects to the same video recorder. We need as much footage as possible.

I send a text back.

Copy

Jenny will meet me at my fake begging spot, disguise herself with a brunette wig and clothes that are stuffed into the bottom of my sleeping bag, clip the camera into her jacket and then go a long, obscure way around to the back of the building, lingering in the darkness. She'll hide behind a bin or low brick wall, staying in the shadows, poised and ready. She's not to venture into the building. I was very clear about that.

. . .

"Hey." A whisper. Jenny kneels down next to me. Sweat on her brow despite the chilly night air. She's soaked from the rain and shivering slightly. Perhaps that's more nerves than cold.

"Hey. Are you okay? Did you eat?"

"Aye, I did earlier."

"Good. You ready?"

Jenny nods. "Aye."

"Do you know when it will be?"

"Nah, it could be anytime. But it will be tonight." She bites a cracked dry lip with broken teeth.

"Right. I don't need to know how you heard."

She nods. "Best get ready, yeah?"

"Yeah."

I delve into the sleeping bag and pull out a worn supermarket carrier bag that's stuffed with Jenny's disguise. I find the spare camera in my pocket and slide it into the bag along with the clothes and wig. We glance around for anyone watching, but the coast is clear and I hand her the bag. She takes it quietly and vanishes around the corner to change and prepare. Can't do anything about her dental profile, but I've told her to keep her mouth closed as much as possible. I don't want anyone to identify Jenny, or me, for that matter, if anything should not go to plan. Speaking of plans, there isn't really much of one. I'm going my usual route of making it up as I go along. That has served me well so far. Hopefully, it keeps delivering.

Now, all we can do is wait.

I've done a whole lot of waiting recently. Sat in this cold spot, staring into the distance and keeping one eye on the doorway. Thoughts swirl and repeat in my head, and on more than one occasion I've almost given up and left this post to go home for a hot soak in a bath and a cold beer. But then I think of Jenny grieving for her friend Oleksandra, who's tortured and raped repeatedly, probably drugged to within an inch of her life to keep her dulled down. She and the other girls are in the same situation. There's more than one in that building, for sure. All of them need help. The system has failed them. The people who should keep them safe are responsible for this depravity. Who else is going to come to the rescue? This realisation fuels my rage and keeps the adrenaline coursing through my veins. By accident or perhaps coincidence, my brain was reprogrammed to be a Flash Gordon or James Bond or something. I was given skills to right wrongs, to save the innocent, and to bring justice where society won't deliver. I didn't ask for this, but regardless, here I am. Maybe it wasn't a coincidence, and maybe the universe chose its champion with purpose.

Entropy, chaos, serendipity or divine intervention, doesn't matter, in the end. Shit is going down tonight.

A buzz from my pocket signals that Jenny is in place. The message is a single emoji. A red balloon. She chose this one. Signifies imminent freedom.

I ready myself under the cover of the grotty sleeping bag. The street is quiet now, the odd taxi passing, occasional people who pass in a shadowy blur more than reality. They don't exist in this scenario. NPCs who will never know of the events of tonight. I'm jealous of them. Living their normal lives, going about their business. Then I remember everyone has a story, a problem, a drama, maybe even a secret. I shake my head to be rid of these thoughts and focus on the task at hand. I check my video feed on the dash cam device, then flip to Jenny's camera. Just at the edge of its wireless range, but a dim grainy image appears. She's where she should be, and judging by the darkness, she's well hidden. Good.

I breathe in the night air, letting it swirl into my lungs,

become a part of me, and then exhale and watch the mist dissipate into the world again. Calmness fills my mind, and I focus on the building and all the blacked-out windows on the ground floor. Like an Olympic diver slipping into a pool with barely a splash, a plan thrusts itself into my mind and dives deep into my consciousness.

"Spare change?" I croak out occasionally as passers-by hurry to get away from me. Most of them don't even glance in my direction, but the odd one will drop a coin into my cup. I've made about thirty quid over the last week. I save it up and give it to Jenny when I see her.

A man in a long dark coat approaches and bends down, dropping a ten-pound note into my cup. He looks me in the eye as he does and I nod a thanks, offering a smile for his generosity. "Get yourself a hot meal, yeah?" He winks at me and a sickly feeling flows through me.

"Yeah, cheers, mate. Thank you."

He's clean-shaven, with groomed hair combed to the side. A waft of aftershave hits me in his wake when he stands back up, I keep up the smile and look into my cup of cash, picking it up. The man lingers and waits for me to make a move.

"Go on, then. No time like the present, eh?"

My throat tightens, my stomach churns and the sickness spreads in me, amplifying, twisting my guts, throbbing in the back of my head. This man pours out hatred and evil. His frequencies are all wrong. He's dangerous, chemically unbalanced, and toxic. Every molecule of my body wants to get away from him. I move to stand up and the man backs away, nodding slightly.

"There's a place up the road still open." He points back from where he came from, hinting that I should piss off in that direction.

I've never met the man before, or seen his face, but I know

who he is. He's the brothel cop.

"Cheers, right."

I gather my stuff up and ball the sleeping bag under an arm, then plod in the direction the dodgy copper pointed. He smiles and carries on walking towards the building.

Thirty seconds later, I dare to glance back, but the man is no longer on the street. Presumably, he went into the building, unhindered by his security guards. I duck into an alleyway, drop my bags and blanket behind a bin, then crouch down, peeking out onto the street. I need to get back to the building, and quickly, but I can't risk walking along back the way I came. Obviously, he wanted me out of the way, so he would have told his henchmen to make sure I don't come back. I spring up and back through the alley, which leads out into a passage behind the shops on this side of the street. From here, I navigate back towards the building I'm interested in, out of sight. At the end of the row, there's a small gap that leads to a fire escape on the side wall, almost directly opposite where I need to be. Perfect. I climb up the first flight and crouch on the metal landing. From here I can clearly see the brothel. The door is closed; the windows barred. Only a dim light is visible from behind the upstairs glass. The cop is inside. He has to be.

I check my phone. No message from Jenny. I check the video recorder and I can see she's still in place. I send her a message.

blue@red. Ready.

A flicker in the video feed from Jenny's camera suggests she is moving. A moment later, a text from her.

ready.

Here we go.

Propped up on my elbows, I lie flat on the metal landing, facing the building. I breathe in, out, in, out. I brush away a few itchy dreadlock strands from my face and focus on the windows. The panes of glass, double thick and blacked out. I learned something new about my abilities recently, but I've never tried it on a scale like this before. I focus, pushing everything else out of my mind, broadcasting a stream of energy out across the cold, dark street. A wave reflects at me. I adjust my frequency, amping up the power. My head feels light and my fingers tingle like pins and needles. I ignore it and blast out the waves with everything I have for what feels like ages. There's a deep bass vibration in the air, like standing in front of the speaker stack at an Iron Maiden gig. A loud crack, a ripple, and then an almighty smash as all four ground-floor windows and three upstairs windows implode into the building at once. Glass rains down and smashes further on the pavement, scattering into a tinkling shower of sharp chaos. Light pours out of the ground-floor rooms now the blackened glass is gone. I breathe and shake my head. It worked!

I get up quickly and run down the metal stairs and into the street in front of the building. By the time I arrive, there are two henchmen already outside the building looking at the mess of glass and up and down the street for the culprit. They probably assume that someone attacked the building with rocks or guns. It couldn't be me, alone, with no weapons visible. Just an innocent homeless dude, trying to chill out and get some sleep. One of the big bastards looks at me, accusing.

"You!" He bellows.

"No, it was a car. I saw them. They slowed down, and the windows went down, then smash! What the hell?"

"What car? Where?" His accent is Russian, or certainly Eastern European. Hired thug number one.

I point up the street. "A black car. They went that way.

Sorry, I didn't get the number."

Thug One weighs up his options, pauses for a moment, and then runs off towards a side street. Thug Two is still standing at the door, stunned. He pulls out a phone and starts tapping on the screen. He ignores me completely. Good.

A motorbike roars into life and Thug One promptly zips by and up the street where I indicated the drive-by shooting car had gone. Nice one. One down, two to go.

Thug Two taps at his phone some more, then clamps it to his ear, turning his back to me.

I quietly approach him, careful not to step on any of the broken glass that litters the pavement. Then I flatten myself against the wall and focus once more, this time on the phone in the henchman's hand, pressed up against his head. Resonant frequencies cycle in my mind, and a surge of energy pulses from my body. The henchman flinches and takes the phone away from his head and I hear a stream of garbled words come from the speaker. He tentatively puts it back to his face and grunts out something I can't understand. Not Russian, then.

I concentrate, boosting my signal and directing it towards the thug. A spurt, then a fizzle sound comes from the doorway, followed by a pained yell as the thug stumbles out into the street, crunching on broken glass. He drops the phone — now burning and spewing out a thick acrid stream of smoke — to the ground, slipping and racing forward to try to balance. What little hair the thug had is now sizzling in flames. He lunges forward, smacking and clutching at his burning head, blindly staggering out into the road and straight into the path of a black cab that turned from a side street. He's knocked down with a solid thud and lies motionless like a beached whale on the wet road as the taxi driver gets out of his car to help. Over the stink of burning electronics is the unmistakable smell of burning hair. The scene is like a carefully orchestrated slapstick comedy routine, and I can't help but chuckle. Two down.

I pull on rubber gloves from my back pocket, sneak in through the brothel door and quietly close it behind me.

I know there is at least one more guard here, and I'm guessing he's closer to the action, possibly upstairs.

Inside, I quickly scan the large room off from the hallway. Empty of life now, but there's a table covered in beer cans and ashtrays on one side, with various couches around the other edges, pointing vaguely toward a TV that's silently blaring out some kind of sport. Probably the guard room. The air is damp and cool because of the sudden lack of glass in the windows.

The third guard was probably the recipient of the phone call that Thug Two was having before his phone spontaneously combusted in his hand. It won't be long before Thug Three comes to investigate. I need to be quick.

There's a flight of stairs at the back of the hallway. Carpeted in a tasteless dark red, filthy and covered in oily black stains. The middle of each step has worn threadbare. I'm guessing the cleaners haven't been for a while. Under the stairs is an old iron coat stand with someone's long woollen jacket hanging on it. I recognise it from a few minutes ago. This is the policeman's coat.

I dart back to the front door and open it again, then silently race back to the coat rack, crouching behind it with only seconds to spare as footsteps now trudge down the stairs above me. As predicted, Thug Three has come looking for his friend, and as he steps off the bottom stair into the hallway, he sees the scene outside. A group of people now surround the fallen man on the road. I can't see much more from here.

"What the fuck!" A London accent from Thug Three, and he barges outside to see what is going on. I move back to the door and again quietly close it. This time, turning all the lock mechanisms and sliding over the thick, heavy deadbolts.

Three down.

Sticking to the edge of each step, I climb the stairs, avoiding the creaks that I heard when Thug Three lumbered down moments ago. At the top is a landing with three doors leading off. One at the back of the building is wide open, revealing a small room, dimly lit, with another TV and a couple of rough chairs. I try the other landing doors, but they are locked. Another set of stairs going down is at the other end of the landing. Narrower and bare wood this time. The servants' stairway. That must be the back doorway out.

I turn back to the open room and go in. The room is tidy. There's a coffee table with a few motoring magazines strewn over it and a small glass-door fridge under a counter filled with Polish beer bottles. A waiting room. It could be any take-away, but behind the solid door, I know there won't be any Chinese food.

Here we go. There can't be many more obstacles now. The copper must be behind that door, possibly doing his accounts, or maybe indulging in a quickie with one of his unpaid staff members.

I try the door. It isn't locked and opens with a stiff pull. The door itself is thick as a whale sandwich. Could be sound-proofing. It pulls itself closed behind me as I step inside. Another narrow stairway is in front of me, leading up to what must be the attic floor. This area is dark, lit only by small red lights that are flush with the ceiling. Music floods down quietly from above. I check the door is still operable, then climb up the stairs again.

The stairs come out into a large space with a low ceiling. It looks almost like a hospital with three curtained-off areas to one side, and a large dormer window that looks out onto a steep roof and down to the backyard. There's no one visible, but I can hear murmurs of life coming from behind the curtains over the music. This is not a hospital. Dim lights shine into each of the curtained areas, lighting them up from inside like lanterns. This is it.

As quietly as I can, I unclip the camera from my dreadlock wig and find somewhere to plant it so it points at the cubicles. A shelf unit against a wall does nicely. I check that the video is still being recorded on the dash cam in my pocket, and once again flip to Jenny's feed. All good. I pocket the device again and ponder my options.

"Oi!" a voice yells out above the music, catching me off guard. I was looking around for some kind of weapon but found nothing of use. "How the fuck did you get in here?" The cop exits from one of the hospital cubicles and quickly slides the curtain back after him. He walks towards me at the window, but then changes direction and over to the door. "Damo, what the fuck is going on?" He yells down, presumably to Thug Three.

He turns back to me after a second and has no answer.

"Who are you? How did you get in here?" He walks over to me before I can answer. "You!" His face lights up in recognition. "Homeless twat. What is going on here?" He turns back to the stairs. "DAMO!" He screams out. "I told you to bugger off."

Behind him, I can see the curtain moving in one cubicle.

"What's going on?" A female voice calls out, barely audible and spaced out.

He turns to the voice. "Stay there." Then turns back to me.

"Answers, now. Who the fuck are you, and what are you doing in here?"

I put my hands up. "Calm down, pal." I put on a mock Liverpool accent. "All right, all right."

He looks bewildered for a second, then lunges at me with

a fist. I block it, but he's ready and swipes again with his left hand. He catches me in the side of the head, but not full force, as I roll with the punch and away from him. I drop to a crouch as he punches again with his right hook, and he hits nothing but air. I'm behind him in a flurry of movement, and he turns to face me again. Now he's up against the window. "You're fucking nicked, mate. I'm Old Bill!"

"So I heard," I say in my normal voice. "And honestly, that doesn't make me feel very good about the world."

He moves to punch at me again, but I'm ready this time. Time slows down, and I watch with a grin as his fist slowly comes towards me. I grab his wrist and pivot on the spot, using his momentum to twist him around a full three-sixty and release as he's facing the window. He flies forward full force into the dormer window. Another cacophonous crash of crunching glass and wood, and he's through and out onto the roof in a hail of broken shards and splinters. There's a hideous scraping as he thrashes around, sliding down the roof tiles, but even if I wanted to, which I most certainly don't, I couldn't help him. He reaches the edge of the roof and vanishes from sight. A crash and thud come from below moments later as he hits the ground.

"Well, that's a shame."

I reach into my pocket and grab the phone, sending a single emoji text to Jenny. The ambulance symbol. Not for the copper. I assume he's already too far gone after that drop. No, the ambulance is for the girls.

I run over to the cubicles, unsure of what I will find. Inside the first one, I see a girl sprawled on a bed in nothing but a pair of knickers, with sweaty sheets and pillows around her. A cuff secures one of her arms to the bed rail. Shit. A quick check of the other cubicles reveals a similar scene. All chained in place. An empty syringe is next to the first girl on a small bedside table.

"Key?" I shout out to her. She's barely aware of my existence. Her eyes are far away. I gently shake her shoulders. "Where's the key for the cuffs? You must be able to go to a bathroom sometimes."

She seems to wake a little and points out of the cubicle to the shelf unit where I stashed my camera.

Sure enough, on a hook next to the shelves is a keyring. I grab it and pick up the camera while I'm there, then try the various keys in the handcuffs until they spring open. All the girls are equally comatose, drugged and almost naked, but at least they are now free of bonds. With no sign of clothes anywhere, I yank the sheets from the beds and, with a lot of encouragement, get the girls to stand up, then wrap the sheets around them.

"I'm rescuing you, okay? We're getting out of here. Can you walk?"

Looking like some kind of scene from Sodom and Gomorrah, the drugged-up girls wrapped in sheets vaguely nod at me. "We don't have much time. Come on. Hold hands." I don't know if any of them are Oleksandra, Jenny's friend, but one girl seems young enough that it could be her.

I take the first girl's hand and lead on, making sure the others are following. We make it down the first set of stairs, and I pause, tentatively opening the door in case there's anyone on the other side. There isn't and we creep out and through into the landing area. I can hear thumps on the front door now. Presumably, Thug Three is trying to get back in. I lead the girls down the back stairs and through a small kitchen area, then out into the backyard. The cop lies in a heap near the door and I steer the girls well away from him, out through a gate into the passage behind.

"Jenny," I call out. "It's done."

Jenny rushes out of the darkness over to us.

"Sandy!" She finds her friend and grabs her in an embrace. Her eyes are wet with tears. Sandy doesn't seem to acknowledge her but stands motionless in the chilly night air.

"Did you call for help?"

"Aye, ambulance on the way."

"Okay, good." I take a deep breath and try to calm myself, but my blood is pumping with adrenaline. "Take them to the pickup point. I need to disappear."

"Aye. I know." Jenny grabs the girls' hands and leads them the other way down the passage, out into another street where the ambulance will arrive shortly. She turns back to me with a wet face. "Thank you, Toby."

"No problem at all. Get them safe. I'll see you soon."

CHAPTER
TWO

COMA KARMA COP IN LONDON SEX TRAFFICKING SCANDAL

In a spine-chilling revelation that has left the nation reeling, a police officer once hailed as a hero now stands exposed as the sinister mastermind behind a despicable sex trafficking ring. Detective Inspector Ryan Turner, a name once synonymous with courage, now finds himself at the centre of an unimaginable scandal that has shattered the trust of an entire community.

The Dark Underbelly - A Cop's Secret World

Unbeknownst to his colleagues and the public, the very man sworn to uphold the law had been leading a double life, delving deep into the murky underworld of human trafficking. Shocked investigators, with evidence from an anonymous source in hand, unveiled a web of deceit so vile that it sent shivers down the spines of even the most seasoned officers.

"It's beyond comprehension," Chief Superintendent Robert Daniels said, struggling to find words to describe the betrayal. "We never saw this coming."

The Fall from Grace - A Rooftop Tragedy

As the walls closed in on his wicked empire, D.I. Turner

attempted a desperate escape, leading to a heart-stopping rooftop chase. In a grim twist of fate, karma caught up with the corrupt officer, and he tumbled from the rooftop, leaving him in a coma from which he may never recover, doctors say. The irony of his fall from grace was not lost on the public, who now grapple with the revelation of his sinister crimes.

Unravelling the Web - Exposing the Trafficking Ring

Through painstaking investigations, law enforcement uncovered the seedy network that D.I. Turner had so callously orchestrated. Innocent lives were tragically shattered as young victims were lured into the clutches of a sex trafficking ring that operated right under the noses of those sworn to protect them.

"Every effort will be made to bring all those involved to justice," vowed Detective Inspector Olivia Harper, who leads the team determined to dismantle the sordid operation.

"We trusted him to keep us safe, and he betrayed that trust in the most horrifying way," a distraught resident lamented.

Three young women who cannot be named at this time escaped from the den of crime on the same night, and are now resting in a secure hospital where they are expected to make a full recovery.

———

I HATE NEWSPAPERS, especially tabloid ones, but it is nice to see my handiwork getting national attention. Albeit slightly exaggerated. There was no rooftop chase, and I'm not sure if it was strictly speaking sex trafficking, but I'll let them have their drama. As far as I know, I'm not mentioned, implicated or suspected. Police are undoubtedly looking for a homeless man with dreadlocks to assist them with their enquiries, but that line of investigation will likely go nowhere. They have more important matters to attend to, as eloquently noted by the press.

Detective Inspector Ryan Turner didn't die in the fall from the roof, but he's in a coma and may never recover, which is more or less the same thing. I was only acting in self-defence, and I had no intention of throwing him out of the window. It just sort of happened. I won't shed a tear for the scumbag either way. Who knows how many girls suffered and were disposed of before I shut down his operation? Homeless and already invisible, according to society, no one cared if they were taken off the street and used as sex dolls. Well, now they do. One more scumbag was removed from the rota.

After editing out anything that could identify me, Jenny, or the girls, the video footage I captured was delivered anonymously to the Chief Superintendent. Wiped clean of fingerprints, sent with a note that clearly stated that backup copies were stored in safe places around the globe in case they decided not to act on the evidence. One more copy landed on the tabloid reporter's desk, hence the scoop. Somebody must have shot the video of the copper in that attic, so questions will be asked. I have to hope that they don't find out who.

If the newspaper had been silenced, I was ready to upload the whole thing to YouTube and kick off a viral spread of the video. Thankfully, that wasn't necessary.

After the rescue, I disposed of my disguise and burner phone by burning it, quite literally, then I picked up my bike from a nearby locker and cycled home in the early hours of the morning; it took about four solid hours, but I had been training for it, and the workout was welcome after sitting on my arse on the cold ground for so long. It also helped to use up all that adrenaline my body had poured into my veins.

I took a day off after that. A long soak in a hot bath to ponder on the nature of the universe. The evil that is everywhere will keep coming no matter what I do. I can't fight it all, yet I think I have done some good. I have rescued three innocent girls from a fate worse than death. They won't make a full recovery, as the newspaper claims, far from it. Even if their bodies somehow shake the need for whatever drug was being pumped into them, the psychological damage will persist forever. The trauma will never end for them, and I can only hope that their suffering is eased with time.

I haven't dared to contact Jenny yet. We have a fourteen-day cooldown period, agreed upon in advance. No contact and no mention of each other's existence. No doubt the police will have asked her numerous questions about how she found the girls after they came out of the knocking shop, but all she will tell anyone is that she was walking there by coincidence as they came out and promptly called an ambulance.

She would have destroyed her phone afterwards. Removing any connection with me. That was the plan, and it seems to have worked so far.

If the cop dies, then I suppose I could be in the sights for murder or manslaughter. But in light of what he was doing and the embarrassment he has caused the force, I reckon I'll have at least some advantage in court. I should probably care more about all this, but it doesn't bother me. Strange.

The feelings become numb after a few days. The elation, the anger, the worry. They all dissipate like steam from a cup of hot coffee. It's all just a memory now. A deed that was planned, patiently waited for, enacted and done. Game over for D.I. Turner and me. I defeated the final boss on that level, and now onto the next.

I should be thinking about my next job, and, come to think of it, the next job I do better have some kind of financial element to it because I've also come to the end of the money I accumulated when I was paid off from my old job. They caught me shagging a colleague in a dodgy video made illicitly by my nemesis of old, Steve Twatly. Evelyn paid me handsomely to rescue her granddaughter from the clutches of the Department, but sadly, that lump sum is more or less depleted after six months. I'm skint, and the forces of evil are barely scratched.

The world may have to do without my services for a while because Flash Gordon / Toby Steele needs to find a proper job, or he may find himself sleeping rough in a cardboard box next to Jenny.

About six months ago, something unusual happened to me as I was performing maintenance on the data servers at BioDigi Pharmaceutical. I worked as the night shift IT tech support dude, which was mostly as tedious as you might imagine. I rebooted the odd machine, swapped the laser printer toner, and ensured the network was functional. That sort of thing, on repeat every night for years.

But on the night of the twenty-second of February, 2022, at precisely 22:22:22, the servers froze up. A program was waiting to run, an accident. It should never have survived all the decades it was waiting for just this moment, but fate and circumstance meant that when that code ran, my life was forever completely changed.

In the sixties, the British government requested, no, summoned Evelyn Greenwood, one of the codebreakers who worked with Alan Turing on the Enigma machine at Bletchley Park, to work on Project Flash Gordon. This was a top-secret project to investigate the possibility of turning any simple man into a Superman overnight by means of brainwave frequency shifting. Evelyn worked on this project for decades, squirrelled away at the Porton Down research facility in Wiltshire. The project was cancelled and shut down before she could finish her work, but what nobody knew was that Evelyn did manage to make it work, and she hid her program in a database halfway around the world. Many years later, that code still lingered in the dusty realms of a mainframe that was no longer used, but when BioDigi Pharmaceutical bought the company that owned the mainframe, it also inadvertently bought that hidden code.

It flashed my brain. I'm the new Flash Gordon. I have skills I couldn't even have imagined before this. I'm fast and strong, and I can somehow broadcast energy in the form of resonant frequencies. I can manipulate people's emotions, and I can speak many languages. I'm smooth and confident. I'm driven to make the world a better place, and above all, I have absolute loyalty to Evelyn and her granddaughter, Cassie.

Of course, there was a nefarious element involved. A branch of the government that simply called themselves 'The Department.' We later discovered that was a shortening for 'The Department for the Prevention of World Changing Technology.' Another paranoid knee-jerk reaction government plan to interfere with the running of the world. They feared anything that could drastically change the nature of society, for better or worse, and they saw Evelyn's Project Flash Gordon as a major threat. In reality, it turns out that they just wanted the technology for themselves, and in some weird and twisted way, they got it, albeit a different version.

The Department was always small and underfunded, and they found themselves hiding out in a house in the west of Ireland, deep in the Gaeltacht area of county Galway, miles away from anyone. They carried on their plan to keep the world dulled down, and it seems that when they found someone who could really make a difference, they would abduct them, destroy their records, and then, by using the same brainwave recording technology that Evelyn developed all those years ago, they would wipe the memories of those poor folk.

They did this to Evelyn's granddaughter, Cassie. Well, they tried, but it didn't work. Cassie sent an encrypted message to her gran, and I was sent to rescue her, which I did, with some efficiency, if I do say so myself. It was quite fun, in the end, and I torched their facility, destroying their computers and equipment and leaving the Department in tatters.

I don't know what I expected after I brought Cassie back to her gran, but what happened left me a bit deflated.

Of course, there was an emotional reunion when Cassie and I walked into Evelyn's care home, and we talked for hours about exactly what happened and how we managed to escape. I had to edit my story slightly to leave out anything that might sound a bit too supernatural to Cassie because I remain under strict instruction from Evelyn that I must never reveal what happened to me to anyone. Too dangerous, too complicated and too ridiculous. I had trouble believing it until the evidence was at the tips of my fingers.

I took Cassie home afterwards, and I slept on her couch for a few nights, keeping guard in case the Department tried to retaliate. A bit awkward, and when nothing happened and Cassie wanted her privacy back, I went home. Simple as that.

Cassie is beautiful, smart, and funny. Perfect, in fact, but she told me before that I'm just not her type. Still, I thought saving her life and rescuing her from the clutches of evil might change her mind. But, no.

I do my thing, and she does hers. She's thankful for the rescue, naturally, but when she started asking too many questions about how exactly I knew her gran and what I did to start the fire at the Galway Department headquarters, I had to make my excuses and change the subject. Cassie knows I'm bullshitting, but she also seems to know when to stop asking. She has Evelyn's DNA, and there's no better woman in England to keep a secret.

Evelyn celebrated her one-hundredth birthday on the same day that I was transformed. She saved the program code with the filename 22:22:22, which we think triggered the process at that exact time.

She had no way of knowing that one day, decades after she put her project to bed and long forgotten about it, it would run on some unsuspecting night shift IT support man.

Evelyn is as sharp as a pin, even with her old age. She puts that down to the fact that she also ran the Project Flash Gordon code on herself. Her brain was stimulated with the same frequencies and tones that mine was. There's no denying she's an old, frail woman, but her brain is as sharp and capable as a supercomputer.

The Department found out about Cassie's work on her home computer. She had somehow found a way to amplify a resonating frequency and generate much more heat than the input amount of energy. An over-unity device. Perpetual motion, of sorts. Something that the science world continues to believe is impossible, but Cassie thinks she's found a way while not breaking any laws of physics. I'm not privy to the technical details, and they would be lost on me anyway, but Cassie has a model of the system. She had hidden a backup of all her data on a tiny memory card behind a photo of herself in a locket around Evelyn's neck. The Department didn't destroy it, and they were unsuccessful in erasing Cassie's memories.

They tried the same technique on me briefly, and it was quite a horrific experience. I destroyed the system before it could destroy me. It's a shame because they were running it on an original Cray-1, a rather nice piece of vintage kit. Worth a fortune.

Cassie was rescued with no harm done. Her desktop computer was destroyed, but her data was all backed up. Her fake relationship with Brian from the Department is over, and things mostly returned to normal. Cassie went back to work at her day job. I don't know if she will keep working on her energy device, but it will be in absolute secrecy this time if she does. All her searches online will be done anonymously, and she won't make the mistake of posting technical questions on forums again. That's what got her into trouble in the first place.

Outside of Evelyn and me, no one else knows about the incident in Galway, and that's how we intend to keep it.

This brings me to what I've been doing for the last six months. I can categorise that quite easily.

- Putting scumbags out of business.
- Building up my strength and agility at the local gym.
- Honing my Flash Gordon skills and exploring new things I've discovered I can do.

I'm particularly fond of the glass smashing thing as it makes a very satisfying sound. **Psshhh**. Messy, though.

And that's about it. I don't have a real job anymore, but short of finding some kind of super-rich sponsor for my vigilante work, I'll need to do something about that very soon.

CHAPTER
THREE

"FOR SECURITY PURPOSES, please confirm your full name, date of birth, mobile phone number, email, and home address, including postcode, please?"

These words are meant to bring us peace and safety, but to me, they bring the opposite. Paranoia.

A couple of months ago, I decided to cut costs at home and cancel a few services I could do without. Television channels that I never watched were high on the list of things to delete.

The girl asking the question had no idea of the danger the information she so casually asks people all day, every day, is capable of in the wrong hands.

And almost all hands are wrong if you ask me.

"No."

"Pardon?" The voice on the phone sounded surprised.

"No, you can't. You rang me. How do I know you are who you say you are?"

"Sorry, sir. But for privacy and security reasons, until you can confirm your security details, we can't proceed with the call."

I had asked for a callback because I didn't want to wait with their awful hold music for hours, so I was expecting the call, but still, I had no proof that she was from the TV company. She could have been a scammer. Granted, she didn't sound intelligent enough to be a scammer. I'm sick of handing over data when any random stranger asks with the lies of 'protecting my privacy and security' thrown around without understanding what that means.

I know she was reading from a script, but in that case, let me talk to a computer or do this online without any humans involved. Computers do what they are told. Humans lie.

I had already decided to cancel the direct debit and cut them off at the source. I couldn't be bothered with the hassle; no doubt she'd have tried to keep me as a 'loyal customer' by offering six months of discounted service or some such bollocks, but I was annoyed and decided I may as well have some fun.

"For my privacy and security purposes, can **you** confirm your name and address, including postcode, phone number and email, please?"

There was a pause. "I'm sorry, sir. We're not allowed to give out personal information."

"Oh? So you don't like giving out personal information to strangers on phone calls?"

Another pause. Awkward silence.

"Well, neither do I."

"Sorry, sir. But we can't proceed with the call until you can confirm your security details." She repeated.

"I've already confirmed my security details on your website and answered the phone number that's registered to the account. What you are asking for is utterly irrelevant."

"I'm sorry, sir …" She started the same diatribe again, but I didn't wait to hear the rest of it. I hung up.

It's the same story with every big company you call now. The same lies, the same fake patter that sounds official enough to get through most people's barriers. The same kids are employed who aren't paid enough to give a shit and have no authority to do anything. That's why they are the front line. They are powerless, and the companies hide behind these canon fodder customer support agents. It's always 'I'm sorry, there's nothing I can do.' Well, enough is enough. There is something I can do. If someone doesn't make a stand, then it will forever perpetuate, and it is this very proliferation of bullshit and urgent need for rebellion that lead me to my current mission.

I went north this time, guided by a digital breadcrumb trail I pried from the invisible grip of the internet.

Like a flat stone skimming across a perfectly still lake, each touchdown of every packet of information online leaves a ripple in its wake before it hops away again to the next flip. An ephemeral drop in the vast ocean of billions, trillions of other similar drops, all on their own targeted paths to deliver information from one machine to another. Perhaps a single pixel of a funny cat video sent between friends, a text message between distant lovers, or a millisecond of a voice conversation routed through various foreign lands, then back again and into a fake landline number before ringing my phone. A skip of data leaves a trail, and if you know how to see it, you can follow it back to the start. A traceroute ping that leads a chaotic path from a computer operated by a scammer, then halfway around the world to obfuscate the source before exploding into sound energy, delivering lies and deceit directly into my ear.

In this case, the start was a grotty office above a laundrette in Birmingham. A grotty office that I am currently sitting in my car outside, waiting for the right opportunity.

It wasn't even especially innovative or intelligent a scam. A phone call from what seemed like a charity begging for donations. People were starving and in need of shelter urgently after some made-up natural disaster. They didn't have time to form a national advertising campaign to find funding, so they were ringing around to generous people who had previously donated, asking if they could spare a few pounds for this very deserving cause. The chap was very convincing. Persistent, too. He knew how to manipulate and get his message across quickly and eloquently. For that, you have to give him some credit.

Of course, it was all a lie. The charity didn't exist; I checked. And I've never donated any money to them before or given my personal details for follow-up. They dial randomly or extract data from unguarded repositories. Once you have entered your data onto the Internet, it lingers in many directories, legitimate or not. Data is harvested and then exploited.

They don't personally call every number, obviously. That would be impossible. Computers do the bulk of the work, whittling down to a set of numbers that meet whatever criteria they are looking for. My number could have been extracted from LinkedIn, the 'professional' social network, or any number of other places that I couldn't even remember using. We think our touches are fleeting, but in reality, every brief encounter is written in permanent ink.

I've been getting many fake text messages lately, saying I need to reset a password by following a link. Clearly, a fake if you look for more than half a second. I've also had a few bogus robot phone calls claiming that I've won some prize and just need to give more details to be able to receive it.

I haven't fallen for any of the scams, but because I answered the phone a couple of times absentmindedly without first checking the number, the system is aware that my line is active.

I'm on someone's list of potential prey, so I was targeted for the charity scam.

What the slimy shit didn't know, of course, was that I am not your average punter who'll hand over credit card details, lose a fortune and roll with the punch. No. What this, and many other bastards, are going to learn very soon is that Toby Steele strikes back.

I was taking a day off when the call came in — relaxing after a long bike ride. I've taken up swimming in the last couple of months. I don't know why I never did it before, but I'm loving it, and I seem to be quite good; another of the skills that Evelyn's benevolent program granted me, no doubt. So, I biked to the swimming pool, did a good few laps, and then topped it all off with a long bike home. I'm still in the blackout period with Jenny, and I haven't heard how the girls I rescued are doing. I need to burn the energy away to take my mind off pondering and worrying. It worked, too. I had a well-earned beer and was about to sink into the depths of a hot bath when my phone rang. A number that seemed to be local. The last time that happened was when Evelyn called me to tell me her granddaughter had been kidnapped. I answered.

It was obviously a fraudulent money extraction call two seconds after I did. The man was overly jovial and asked me if I had a nice day like some kind of American. What the bloody hell has it got to do with anyone if I had a nice day or not? I let him talk, and while he did, I looked up the number he dialled from.

It was a strange number, landline format, but something unusual about it. The pattern of digits wasn't as it should have been, so obviously, I dove deeper. People never answer withheld numbers these days, so the scammers have got smarter.

It was a VOIP to landline forwarding service. A call made through the internet, not the phone network, and then routed back to the copper telephone cables, before being disintegrated into bytes of data again and broadcast over radio waves into my mobile phone. A long way for a signal to go in less than half a second. It was deeper still. Before it reached the forwarding service, the packets of data had been sent through Romania, the Czech Republic, Sweden, China, Malaysia and then somehow Antarctica and an equally convoluted route back to England. I thought the traceroute was wrong at first, but I checked again, and the second data set returned the same. A ridiculous mess of redirecting darknet routers that operate out of sight, invisible and unfathomable to most. Presumably, an attempt to hide the origin of the call. But you can't ever be completely invisible.

I had an endpoint. A building where the person making the call was sitting. He tried so hard to hide his location that, of course, I needed to narrow it down. I needed to be sure that was the real address, so I kept him talking. "Can you give me some more background details on how the charity will use the money?" He started rattling off a pre-written script about sending food trucks, medical aid, clothes, blankets, and water purification systems. He was almost convincing, if I didn't know it was all generated from an AI bot asked to create just such a script. I let him deliver the spiel, all the while digging for more information. I had recorded the call, of course, and it was when I played the audio back I noticed the background sound. Distant and very faint, but in between his bullshit yapping, there were tiny snippets of church bells.

I ran the audio through various filters to enhance the tones and dull down his annoying voice to almost nothing. Then I listened, over and over, until the gaps of missing bells became irrelevant and I could hear the church tower in my head as well as if I was sitting on a pew. The tones were clear as … bells. From there, it was a simple process to write down the notes of each bell, then look up and compare against a database of church tower chimes around the country, and then find a YouTube video of each of the matching bells until I found the exact match: Our Lady of the Rosary and St Therese, Saltley, Birmingham.

What you can find online is really quite impressive.

This confirmed my endpoint address. Got him.

The guy was either faking a southern accent or not from the area. Another level of obfuscation. The wonders of the United Kingdom; the accent changes every few miles and gives away your origins to those who can hear the collo-quialisms.

I tried calling the number back from my new burner phone, but it didn't accept incoming calls. Instead, I formed a plan, partly to put an end to his con and partly to keep my mind off wondering about Jenny and the girls.

While I'm staking out the premises, I should do something I've been avoiding for a while. Something that's been causing me stress, worry, sleepless nights and trepidation. Something far worse than being hunted by the police for the murder of a detective, worse than a slash from a scrote's wildly swinging blade, or the numb arse of sitting on a cold pavement all night, pretending to be homeless.

I take a deep breath, glance around me and then tap the screen of my phone to wake it.

At arm's length, I open the app tentatively, as if it might bite at my nose.

It doesn't. It waits for my input.

I tap in my details, tap again to continue, and then squeeze my eyes closed before the screen can refresh.

I let out a breath. This is ridiculous. I open my eyes and scan the data on the screen.

"Shit!"

It's worse than I thought.

"Bloody hell. How?"

I scroll up and down, looking for some mistake, but no. It adds up, or more accurately, down.

"Fuck. Well, that's that then."

I close the bank app, lock the phone and try to account for

how I'm down to my last three-hundred and sixteen pounds, fifty-seven pence, with no income, no savings, and no way to pay the rent at the end of the month.

"Shit," I repeat because the situation certainly warrants it. "Suppose I'll have to get a real job," I mutter to no one.

I've been thinking I should move on for a while, anyway. I can speak various European languages fluently. It would be simple for me to blend in anywhere on the continent, further afield even. Somewhere where no one knows me, won't know my history or my talents. Won't be connecting me with any of the recent spate of vigilante-type retaliations that have occurred over the last six months. I could easily bluff and schmooze my way into any job interview and demand a salary of my choosing. But that does sort of admit defeat. Corporate worlds are prisons of our own making. You'll never get rich or be genuinely appreciated by working for someone else. You are a cog in the machine to earn money for the people at the top. They pay you just enough to keep you alive, keep you going so you can work more every day, drowning in tasks and arbitrary deadlines that make no sense in the grand scheme of things, but they reward you with tokens and trinkets. Occasional free drinks, trips away. Don't be fooled. You are expendable. A human resource that is irrelevant when cost savings are needed.

And yet, here I am, scrolling my phone again on a list of IT jobs.

"Shit."

Moving country would cost money, and my bank balance confirms that is a resource I don't have. Besides, I'm nervous about being too far away from Evelyn and Cassie. The Department may still be lingering, waiting to strike back after I destroyed their stronghold in Galway. There hasn't been so much as a peep from them over the last six months, but they could be playing the long game. Biding their time, ready to pounce.

My loyalty to Evelyn is strong. A part of her programming, I know, but nonetheless, I am powerless to change my mind. I need to be close enough that I can come to her aid should she need it. That rules out going too far afield for work. I filter on jobs that are tagged with 'remote work', meaning I can work from home. That might mean I can still carry on my extracurricular activities and gym training. This is a downgrade, though. I've got used to doing what I want when I want. The thought of conforming to a routine again gives me a nasty feeling in my gut.

A man walks towards the door I'm watching. He's overweight and carrying a flat pizza box in one hand then fumbles for keys in his pocket with the other. Struggling, he balances the pizza on his chest, pushing it up against the door, then uses both hands to extract the keys and open the door. He looks around sheepishly, shakes his head, then goes inside and kicks the door shut behind him. A few moments later, a light turns on in a room upstairs.

Target acquired.

I pull out my phone and find the location of the pizza place, recognising the logo on the box. It isn't far, so I hop out of the car and set off towards the restaurant.

Pizza is a door opener. If you carry pizza, you have the authority to go anywhere and bang on any door. Food carriers are granted access and are almost as invisible as homeless people. Someone orders food with an app, and someone else brings it to them. This happens countless times a day in every town. Nothing strange.

Mix-ups happen as well, as my scammer friend is about to find out.

I ring the bell and stand back. I hold the pizza box flat like he did not long ago.

I wait for too long, so I ring again and knock.

I wait.

I'm just about to ring a third time when I hear a thudding down a set of stairs from behind the door. I stand back and hold the pizza in front of me.

"Yeah?"

The chap is out of breath and sweating. He was either knocking one out or squeezing one out. Either way, I hope he washed his hands.

"Pizza delivery for Robert Donnelly." I cheerily chirp, affecting a mild and vague Midlands accent, and offer him the pizza.

After I found his location by backtracking through the internet, I researched the building and found some basic details about the 'business' he runs here. His cover is a market research consultancy, with scant few details on his website. I found a phone number and called it a few days ago asking for some prices. He answered, and I could confirm his voice matched the scam call I had received from him asking for charity donations. I put on a thick Brummy accent and called from my burner phone. He was keen to get rid of me and, no doubt, get back to his real business of conning gullible people out of money.

Now, a look of confusion spreads across his face, and he looks down at the pizza box. "No, I already collected it."

"Hey?"

"Yeah, I ordered to collect and picked it up about twenty minutes ago."

"Oh." I pull out my phone and pretend to look for information about the order. "Well, it must be a mistake, then. But it says it's paid for, and I can't take it back. Do you want it?"

His greedy eyes light up. Free pizza? Who can resist? I took a gamble and ordered him the 'mighty meaty' topping.

"Yeah? Well, I might as well, then. Cheers!" He grabs the box from me, smiling.

I take the opportunity to focus some influencing wavelengths of energy in his direction. Trust, happiness, safety. Everything is fine and dandy. He's got double dinner, and luck is on his side. I blast out the frequency and watch as his cheeks flush.

"Sorry, mate. Could I use your toilet quickly?"

His smile falters, and he hesitates. So, he was caught during a download. "Err."

"I wouldn't normally ask, but I'm desperate." I boost the wavelengths again. Trust and safety, friendly feelings.

He nods. "Yeah, yeah. Course you can. It's just upstairs."

He steps back, beckoning me in, then makes sure I shut the door before scampering off upstairs, clutching his free pizza. He drops it down on a desk in one room, then flits over a landing, ducks into another room, sprays some air freshener and then nods towards the door. "Just in there, help yourself."

"Cheers, mate. Won't be long."

The toilet is barely bigger than a broom cupboard, and the air freshener does nothing to mask the stench he left in his wake. I pull my T-shirt over my nose and try not to breathe. I did need a bio break, as I've been staking him out for hours now. I flush and wash and exit back into the relatively clean air, daring to breathe again.

Robert, the scammer, hears me and appears in the doorway of what is likely his office.

"All set?"

"Yeah, thanks."

"Right, I'll see you out."

I switch the frequencies back on and blast out another wave of trust and safety wavelengths. He seems to relax. I peer over his shoulder into the room.

"What is it you do here, mate?"

"Oh, erm, very boring, really. Market research, you know. Phone surveys and whatnot."

"Yeah?" I step forward towards him, and he retreats back into the room. His new pizza is open now, and one triangle has been removed already. I glance around the room. Not big, but cluttered with three desks and shelves in every corner. On one desk is an ancient tower PC hooked up with multitudes of cables that lead off behind. There's a monitor attached, but it is showing a screensaver. On another, there's a laptop open, but the screen is dark. A headset is on the desk next to it. There are books, magazines, junk mail and clutter on every surface. A router flashes tiny LEDs on one of the shelves. A faded rug on bare wooden floorboards is dull and filthy. A TV up on a high shelf shows a CCTV camera feed from the door below. There's one window that could really do with a clean, and the walls are texture-papered and painted in a sickening creamy yellow. The last coat was likely applied in the early 80s and has never been touched since. The room is quite disgusting, much like its occupant.

I turn back to the pizza and raise my eyebrows. "You going to eat all that?"

"Hey?"

"Spare a slice? You know, since it was a mistake. I'm starving." I grin.

"Oh." He pauses, but I blast out the frequencies once again. "Yeah, sure. Why not? Go for it."

"Nice one." I rub my hands together and grab a slice of the pizza I paid for. I'm reminded of my dismal bank balance again, and a cold feeling flows through me. "Any money in it?" I motion towards the tower PC that I assume is his scam server. "The market research stuff, I mean." I take a bite of the pizza.

There's a flicker of a grin across his face before it sags into a grimace. "Nah, not really. Just about pays the bills." He shrugs, but his eyes briefly land on a desk drawer before meandering back to the pizza. He's lying, obviously, and there's something interesting in the drawer. I turn, pretending to cough and grab an eyeful of the drawer. There's a lock on it and no sign of a key. It won't be tough to yank open or pick the lock. I scan the room briefly for anything that could be a weapon. There's an ancient-looking fire extinguisher by the door, which probably doesn't have any fizz left in it, an umbrella, flimsy but spiky, and a heavy-looking glass paperweight on the desk that would do some damage.

"Tell me about it," I scoff between mouthfuls of the pizza. "Barely scraping a living myself. Was thinking about doing some online work-from-home stuff, you know, like surveys or whatever. You see those ads on Facebook. Get paid to take surveys, they say." I play dumb, easing him into giving up his secrets.

His eyebrows raise a fraction, and he opens his mouth to say something but then stops. Instead, he nods in sympathy. "Yeah." He glances at his watch, willing me to leave, but I'm not finished.

"So you reckon not worth it? You're in the business, yourself. You should know, right?"

He fidgets, and I sense I'm losing his interest. He probably wants to get back to his pizza and a nice juicy wank before he starts his evening of conning people out of their hard-earned. I flick the wavelengths back on and boost the signal. Focus on safety and trust. I'm betting he's dying to tell someone about the real work he does and spill the beans about how much money he's hiding in that drawer.

"There's easier ways to make money, let's just put it like that." He grins and very nearly gives a knowing wink.

"Oh, yeah?" I look straight at him, eyes wide. "I'm always on the lookout for ways to part a fool from his wallet."

He shakes his head with a smug, shit-eating grin. "It's like taking candy from a baby, only you don't have to hear them screaming."

"What is?" I play into his weakness. I was right; he's desperate to be the big man and tell someone how cool he is. I take another slice of pizza from the box, and he doesn't even flinch.

"What I do." He chuckles. "I ring people up, and they give me money. It's so bloody easy that I sometimes pinch myself to check I'm not dreaming."

"Heh? How do you manage that?"

He taps his nose. "It's all in the charm."

"Yeah?"

"I've got quite good at it if I do say so myself."

"I'm not with you, mate; what exactly is it that you do?" I sit down on the edge of the desk so I'm looking up at him. He's the big man, the winner, the dude who knows the secret, and he's been waiting for this moment to show off for years. I'm the trusted friend with whom he's always wanted to share his secret.

"It varies, depends on my mood, or what the profile says, or just on the vibe I get from them, but basically, I ring up, ask them to donate money to me for one reason or another, and they mostly do."

"Just like that?"

"Yeah. Just like that." He shrugs.

"Bloody hell." I puff out my cheeks. "I'm in the wrong game!"

He chuckles. "I mean, not everyone does, of course. I get a lot of piss off's and people hanging up, but it pays to be persistent. Literally."

I hang my mouth open, aghast. I take a gamble and decide to ask the big question. This could go badly, and he could freeze up, in which case we can always resort to violence, or he'll just spill the beans, high on his confession endorphins. I take another bite of pizza, focus on the frequencies and spit it out with what I hope looks like an awestruck glint in my eyes. "How much have you made?"

His eyes flicker to the drawer again, and then he focuses on me, looking down from his portly stature. "A hundred and thirty-five grand this year so far."

"Fuck me!" I exclaim, genuinely taken aback. The scamming little shit. I suppose he's right. He is good at this.

A sickening grin spreads over his chops, revealing mouldy-looking teeth. From the state of this place, him, and his clothes, he hasn't spent a penny of that money. He must be saving it up for something, and I'd bet my bank balance that a good chunk of it is in that desk drawer.

He hasn't quite admitted it, but he's guilty of fraud. The sort that could land him jail time. That gives me the edge.

A plan forms itself in my mind like architecture. Scaffolding, then structure, then interior design and carpet. All laid out and built within a split second.

I spring to my feet, and before he can flinch, I'm behind him, his arm yanked up his back, and he's flat against the desk, yelping in pain. "Robert Donnelly, I'm Detective Inspector Steve Thompson of West Midlands Police. I'm arresting you on suspicion of fraud. You do not have to say anything, but it may harm your defence if you do not mention when questioned something that you later rely on in court. Anything you do say may be given in evidence."

He freezes, his struggling stops, and there's a quiet sob and a splash of liquid on the floor below me. He goes limp and passes out on the desk. I stand back, and the nasty little shit has pissed himself. Good grief.

I poke him, but he's out for the count. He's fainted. I check he's breathing, then back away.

I try the drawer, and as predicted, it's locked tight. I could force it, but the noise might stir him from his pissy slumber. I notice his jacket hanging on the back of a chair. I check the pockets and, sure enough, find a bunch of keys. Scanning through them I find one that looks right and slide it into the drawer keyhole. Bingo. It opens with a clunk, and my mouth drops open once again. There are thick wads of cash bundled up with rubber bands. Ten grand each by the look of the girth. At least a dozen of them, too. "Holy crap."

I glance back at his unconscious lump and raise my eyebrows. "Some business you've got here, mate. Shame I'm going to have to take some tax off you."

I grab the pizza box, empty out the remaining slices, then drop six of the bundles of cash into it and close the lid. I'm skint; he's a fraudulent scammer. It's only fair, isn't it? I'm some kind of modern-day Robin Hood, robbing the rich to fund my ongoing activities. I don't have time to ponder on the morality now. If he wakes up and starts to question my legal authority, it could be a problem.

I make for the door, then glance back at the room and the tower computer case on the desk. I reckon that's what he uses to gather his data. I walk back over to it, rest my hand on the top and burst out a wave of chaotic frequencies. The screen flashes into life but then quickly turns to a blue screen of death. I keep up the energy flow, wiping the disk inside the case, filling it with spurious data, garbage ones and zeroes to make it unreadable. The scammer begins to stir, so I yank the power plug and then head for the exit, pizza box held in front of me and down the stairs as quickly as I can.

Outside, I call back in. "Sorry for the confusion, mate. I'll get you a refund." I pull the door quietly closed; then I head back towards my parked car, pizza box held flat in front of me in broad daylight.

CHAPTER
FOUR

"THIS IS the first drink I've had in months!" Philippa raises her glass of wine for me to clink against. I do.

"Cheers."

After my little windfall, I decided it was time to catch up with Philippa. My ex-girlfriend, now just 'friend' who had a baby recently by another scrote that I had to deal with when he got drugged up and violent. What is it with these arseholes everywhere? I can't keep up with all the twats that need sorting out.

Philippa looks stunning. She's lost her preggo belly and gained some delicious-looking mummy boobs that she's proudly displaying with ample cleavage in a long blue velvet dress. I think she's grown her hair out, too. Temptress.

I haven't seen her for a while. I didn't want to bother her when she had a new baby to take care of. I have no experience with children, let alone babies, so I doubt I would be much help.

Taking her out for a drink and a meal while granny babysits is another story. I have ample skills and experience needed for such a venture.

"Don't let me get drunk, okay?"

I turn to her with a grin.

"No, I mean it, Toby. Baby needs mummy to be sober and alert."

I nod. "Fair enough."

She pokes me in the ribs. "You haven't asked …"

"Asked what?"

"Well, anything, now I come to think of it. But mainly, his name."

"Oh. Yeah. Sorry," I feel my cheeks blush. I've been so wrapped up in my own life of dealing with scumbags that this kind of thing didn't even occur to me. I knew Philippa and baby were doing well, and that's how far I got. "What's his name?"

She looks at me coyly, takes a sip of wine, and then grins at me. "Toby."

"Yeah?"

"No, I mean, his name is Toby."

I pause for a moment, realising what she means. "Oh! Really? You called him after me?"

She nods.

"Wow. I don't know what to say. Thank you." I lean over and give her a hug. She pecks me on the cheek.

"Well, you were so nice and may have saved my life that night… I just felt like … sorry. When he was born, it was the first name that came to mind."

"Don't be sorry. I'm flattered. That's lovely of you."

She smiles, and it's her turn to blush. She hides her face with her glass of wine.

"So," She changes the subject. "What have you been up to? Haven't seen you for ages."

I knew this would come up, and what could I possibly tell her? I've been righting wrongs, dealing with bastards who need to be dealt with, saving young girls from sex slavery. Changing the world as much as I can for the better. I try to use my talents for good, fighting the constant torrent of evil everywhere I look.

Not to mention skimming a nice sixty grand from a scamming prick in Birmingham.

When I got home, I counted out the wads of notes. I was right, and they were ten grand each — used notes, non-sequential, perfectly sorted and legit. No fakes. Should keep me going for a while. I could have totally cleaned him out and taken all of it, but there's no need to be greedy. Yes, he stole it from thousands of people, but something about him made me think he had a good reason for it all, aside from being a lazy scammer.

He hadn't spent any of it. He was saving up for something specific. Maybe that was a medical thing. Maybe he wanted to pay off his mother's mortgage. I'll never know for sure. I'm not likely to go back there to ask. As it is, he's been robbed, but he can't exactly go to the real police and report it, as he robbed the money himself. He has evidence of me being there, and I expect I'm on his CCTV tape, but I doubt he'll come after me. He literally pissed himself and fainted when he thought he was being arrested, so he's not the hardened criminal type. Just a bloke with a talent for extracting money from people. I wiped his computer, but there is nothing to stop him from starting all over again.

I did ponder about tipping off the cops anonymously about his venture, but then I could end up implicating myself. They'll find out about the missing money and chase up the CCTV footage. I'm already arse deep in potential trouble for all the things I've done lately. I should try to keep a low profile.

I'll have to live from cash for a while, which is inconvenient in the modern world. I can't exactly deposit sixty grand in cash into my bank account without drawing attention to myself, even if my bank manager is sitting right next to me at the bar.

I can't explain my life without giving away my secret, and

the words of Evelyn forever ring in my mind. *'You can never tell anyone about this, Toby.'*

"Oh, you know. This and that." I take a sip of beer and flash a smile.

"Did you find a new job?"

"No, not yet."

"I could maybe have a word at the bank. We always need IT staff."

"Oh, thanks, Pip. But …" The last thing I want is a job in a bank, even if it is on the technical side. I can't think of many things that would be more boring. Plus, I think I would be too tempted to hack in and figure out ways to deposit millions of pounds into accounts around the world I control. That can only end badly. "I'm thinking about maybe moving away. Europe, you know?"

"Are you? Whereabouts?" She raises her eyebrows.

"Dunno yet, maybe France or Germany. Somewhere I can speak the lingo."

Her eyes widen. "I didn't know you could speak French and German?"

Shit. "Oh. You know, school language classes. I did really well. Probably a bit rusty now."

The reality is that I can speak many languages fluently, all from one night of Evelyn's FSMI process. *Frequency shifting memory implantation.* A lifetime … no, many lifetimes of knowledge and skills were downloaded into my brain overnight, and my life was forever changed.

One day, I was a boring night shift IT support dude; the next morning, I was a secret agent, Flash Gordon, with super-powers that I still struggle to understand.

"I'll miss you if you go."

"You could come visit. Always welcome."

She smiles. "Thanks, Toby, but travelling with a baby isn't much fun."

"Ah. Yeah. Fair enough."

"Would you really leave England?"

I scoff. "Yeah, in a heartbeat. I mean, what have I got to stay here for?" She flinches. "Sorry. I didn't mean you."

"No, it's okay. We aren't an item. I've got little Toby. You have to do whatever makes you happy." She smiles that beautiful smile again, and I wonder if … could it work? No, how could I continue my vigilante work if I had a relationship? There's no way I could explain my absences and occasional scrapes. And I wouldn't want to implicate Philippa if the cops finally caught up with me.

I should leave, start fresh and keep moving. The cash I grabbed could be my opportunity to up and leave.

"I'm still pondering on my options." I change the subject again. "You ready for some grub?"

"Yeah." She smiles and swigs the last of her wine. "Ooh, I shouldn't have done that. Feel a bit lightheaded."

"Take it easy, Mummy." I grin.

Philippa pauses for a second, then pokes me in the ribs and gets up off her stool. "It's okay now. Come on then, I'm starving."

We couldn't decide on a restaurant, so we chose the same Italian as the last time we went out. They do a decent lasagna, so I'm happy. The walk is short, just along the high street, and we take our time, ambling without purpose. Philippa takes my arm, and we walk in silence. Maybe she's thinking about what I just said, that I might move away. Would she really miss me? I know she's been busy lately with the baby, but she hasn't contacted me.

The evening air is cool. A gentle breeze carries the smell of cigarette smoke from someone out of sight. A thought occurs to me.

"What happened to whats-his-name? Monkey-boy."

She blurts out a giggle. "Monkey-boy?"

"Yeah, you know. The speed freak."

"Oh, you mean Jason." She rolls her eyes.

"That's the one."

"Three years' suspended sentence for possessing illegal amphetamines."

"Suspended?"

"Yeah." She pulls a face. "Given his 'stature' in the community." She makes air quotes with her fingers in front of us and shakes her head. "Don't worry, though. I've got a restraining order."

I nod. "Good. So, he hasn't seen the baby?"

"Pff." She scoffs. "Bastard wants nothing to do with him, and I don't want him anywhere near."

"Right. Good." How anyone can abandon a baby like that, I don't understand. A human life. Innocent and real. I don't think people realise that this life we have is the only one we get. This isn't a test or a rehearsal. You can't rewind and start again, and you can't change the damage you do along the way. Makes me shudder to think of all the gobshites that litter the planet, spreading evil and hatred anywhere they go. Philippa is one of the good ones, though. She'll be a great mother, and she's right. They are better off well away from that turd. "Nasty piece of work, he is."

Philippa nods and grips my arm.

"Here we are." I open the door of Angelo's and motion for Philippa to go ahead. A blast of heat and delicious smells wafts out at us, making my tummy rumble.

"Thank you, Toby." Philippa smiles and leads the way.

We wait at the door until a waitress comes over. "Table for two?"

"Yes, please."

We are seated at the back at a dimly lit table; a candle in an elaborate raffia chianti bottle is the main source of light. The restaurant is busy, and there's an ambient noise level of chat, laughing, cutlery on plates, and glasses clinking.

"Fancy a bottle of Chianti?" I smile at Philippa as the waitress hovers.

"Oh, go on then. But I mean what I said earlier."

I nod. "Bottle of your best Chianti, please, and a jug of water, too. Thanks."

The waitress nods and flits away.

Soft music, dim lights, beautiful woman and the lingering scent of good grub. This is what it's all about. The Italians know the language of love. The word romance, after all, has its roots in Rome.

I reach over the table and gently take Philippa's hand. "Sei così bellissima stasera."

"Ooh, I didn't know you could also speak Italian?" Her eyes widen, and a rush of colour flashes over her cheeks.

"I can't, not really. But I have a few phrases." Again, from Evelyn, but Italian isn't one of my fluent languages. Shame, as it is a beautiful tongue.

"You are a man of mystery, Toby Steele." She grips my hand and smiles.

I nod and feel a grin spread over my face.

The waitress returns with our wine and water and pours me a taster.

"Never mind that. I'm sure it's fine. Pour away." She smiles and pours a glass for Philippa and then for me.

"Someone will be over soon to take your order. Enjoy."

I raise my glass. "To a wonderful evening with a wonderful friend."

Philippa clinks her glass against mine with a coy wink. She takes a sip of the wine. "Oh, that's lovely."

I take a sniff and then a deep drink. "Ahh. Layers of flavour evolve on the palate, complex and inviting, warm and leathery. Crushed red berries and violets. A distinct personality encapsulating the timeless region of Tuscany's rolling hills and Mediterranean climate. A classic Italian elixir of passion."

Philippa snorts a laugh. "Where did that come from? Are you a wine buff now? Thought you were more into beer?"

"Erm, well, you know. I like to broaden my horizons sometimes."

"Hang on, didn't we go to Italy once?"

"Yeah. Milan, as I recall." We went to a gig and then stayed a while after. I think it was that trip that triggered our break up.

"I don't remember you speaking Italian or being into wine back then?"

Shit. I'm rumbled. "No. Well, you know. Remember, I was on the night shift for ages. I had to do something to keep me busy all night. Ended up doing some Duolingo course thing on my phone."

She seems satisfied with my answer and looks down at the menu.

"What you getting?"

"Lasagna, I reckon."

"Good call."

"Hello, are you ready to order?"

I'm distracted from staring blindly at the menu, not really reading, just mesmerised by the words. My mind is parsing all the possible ways that maybe this beautiful woman across the table from me could be a good thing for me, but the cons always outweigh the pros. I look up towards the voice.

"Oh." My good mood falls away like a bucket into a well. "Hi, Steve."

The man stands at the side of our table, clutching a pen and pad. His friendly smile evaporates into a look of shock and horror.

"Toby. Oh, err. Hey."

Philippa glances between Steve and me with a quizzical look. I shake my head slightly.

Steve Twatly, once my arch-nemesis at work, bringer of constant torment and bullying for years, until I changed, put an end to his bullshit and broke his finger in the toilets. Well, he did it himself. He was trying to punch me. I just stepped out of the way. Fucking idiot.

"Well, what are you doing here?" I flash a fake grin.

He vaguely motions with the waiter pad. "Working." The air between us is filled with tension and awkwardness. He almost visibly vibrates with it. I'm the last person he ever wanted to wait on. The feeling is mutual.

"Right, obviously," I smirk. "Not at Bio-Digi anymore?"

"No." His eye twitches slightly. He clears his throat. "Sorry, Toby. We are quite busy tonight. Are you ready to order?" He looks towards Philippa.

My appetite has somewhat waned since I saw the repulsive turd, but I won't let him ruin any more of my time. I'm here with a beautiful woman. My life has changed for the better since I left Bio-Digital Pharmaceutical. His has obviously gone downhill.

Karma in action?

Waiting tables is a worthy and important profession, but this prick is the type who would have made a waitress's life horrible at every opportunity. He doesn't deserve even this.

Philippa senses the situation and takes the lead. "We'll have two lasagnas, please. Oh, and a side salad to share."

"Yes, madam." The fop jots down the order and gratefully runs away.

Philippa points at the retreating bellend and raises her eyebrows at me. "Who's that?"

"Steve Twatly. We used to work together at Bio-Digi."

"Twatly?" She snorts a laugh.

"His real name is Wattley, but as you can see, he's a total twat, so …"

She nods. "You two didn't get along, then?"

"No." I frown and hope that she leaves it alone. I don't want to get into this now.

"Want to talk about it?"

"Not really."

"Fair enough."

She's curious; anyone can see that, but thankfully, she moves on.

Rather than Steve, the first waitress brings our food, and aside from the occasional flicker in my periphery, Steve is out of the picture. I assume he swapped tables so he wouldn't have to wait on me. I'm glad, and it's a shame the food here is so good because I can't see myself coming back anytime soon now I know who works here. Thoughts cross my mind of what could have happened to Steve that he came to be working here in the first place. Was he fired because of the video he illegally recorded of Tracy and me shagging on the desk in the office, or did management finally realise he was a work-shy layabout? The pay here has to be a massive down-grade from the tech support role at Bio-Digi. Maybe he has other jobs to pay the bills. I don't have sympathy for him, far from it. He deserves to suffer. He inflicted enough suffering on me and others during his life.

I shake away the thoughts. I don't want to waste any more brain cycles on his pathetic life.

Over dinner, which is delicious, despite the staff, Philippa tells me about baby Toby, how she's coping, when she plans on going back to work and countless other things. Mother-hood, it seems, is extremely taxing, stressful and exhausting. I don't know how she does it. More to the point, I don't think I could be a dad, now I've heard all the nitty-gritty details of what parenting is all about.

I've never really thought about the prospect of little

versions of me running around the place. It's both terrifying and amazing at the same time.

I'm happy for Pip, though. She's thriving, even as a single mother. She and little Toby are doing great, bringing a fuzzy warmth to my heart.

When the waitress returns to ask if we want dessert, we skip it, and I ask for the bill. I'll pay with cash that I took from a Brummy scammer. That stash will keep me going for a while if I'm careful. Rent and bills for a good eighteen months at least. Breathing space, or if I want to, escape funds. Either way, it was a nice find. I wonder what Robert Donnelly is doing now. Probably moved his operation to a new scabby office somewhere else, bought new equipment and started all over again. I sigh inwardly at the thought of it, but there are some things I can't fix. At least he isn't dangerous or holding sex slaves as prisoners or something.

"Toby." I look up. Steve looms over our table. He looks nervous.

"Steve, I just want to pay and leave. Not interested in any hassle. Okay?"

"No." He shakes his head. "This is on me." He points to the table. "Please accept it as part of an apology from me for all the … well, shit I gave you at work before."

Well, that was unexpected. I'm genuinely stunned. My mouth drops open, but no words come. I glance at Philippa, but she's looking up at Steve.

"Look, I know I was a knob, and I'm trying to better myself. I lost my job, my wife and, well, everything because of how I was. So," he swallows and takes a deep breath. "I'm trying to make amends."

He offers a weak smile and bends down to clear the table. He's clearly tense, and he clutches the dirty glasses and cutlery.

Suddenly a rage boils up inside me, catalysed by Steve and his stupid words. I had suppressed all thoughts of him, of his incessant bullying, of how he would torment me every single day to the point I dreaded going anywhere near work. He dumped all his daily support tasks into my night shift bucket, and he set up a camera to try to catch me out. He did, in the end, but lucky for him, I didn't care any more. I had changed, I had run the FSMI program, and it gave me the courage I needed to get the hell out of there. Now all these thoughts swirl into chaos in my mind again, and this stupid pitiful twat is the cause of it all again. This time he's apologising, but not for what he did, not really. He's doing it because it will make him feel better. Make amends, my arse. If I hadn't accidentally come to this restaurant, would he ever have contacted me? Of course not. This apology is worthless.

Bastard.

Philippa looks at me, sympathy on her face. She doesn't know the history, doesn't know how shit he made me feel. She doesn't understand that this is all just another act. I keep my poker face and look up at Steve again. His eyes plead forgiveness. Rage sweeps through my body in a wave of adrenaline.

I push back my chair to stand up, and as I do, there's a smashing crash, and Steve jumps back, dropping the glass and cutlery from his hands. Blood pours from a cut on his finger, and he turns white, frozen for a moment before he runs off towards the kitchen, presumably for first aid dressing.

"Come on," I turn to Philippa. "Let's go, and be careful of the glass."

Outside the restaurant, the cool night air is peaceful and fills me with calm as I take a deep lungful of the darkness. The anger subsides, and I manage a smile to Philippa.

"What the bloody hell was all that about?"

"Ah, I'll tell you another time. He's full of shit, don't let him trick you."

"No, but those glasses … they sort of exploded in his hands!"

"He must have been gripping them too hard or something." I wave my hand dismissively.

"I don't think so. He was holding the stems. I saw the glass just, well, yeah. Explode." She opens her fingers out in front of her, eyes wide.

"Weird." I nod back along the street towards the pub. "Fancy a quickie before I take you home?"

"Go on then." She winks with a grin.

CHAPTER
FIVE

A LIGHT MIST swathes the area in a gently meandering cloud of softness. It's early yet, and daylight barely touches the world with pale fingers of light, filtered and dappled through the leaves of trees and the dirty atmosphere.

Silence surrounds me, and a textured, tangible calmness is clammy on my cheeks and fake beard. My hoody and sweatpants are sodden and damp. A mixture of sweat and rain. I'm a soggy lump, fingers almost prune-like as if I've fallen asleep in a bathtub. That happens all too often. It will likely happen later today once I'm home again, with any luck.

I sit waiting on a wooden bench as hundreds of bodies all around me lie dead and cold. An oasis of peace amid the chaos not half a mile in any direction.

The dead don't bother me. It's the living that make all the problems.

If anyone asks on this misty morning in Highgate cemetery, I'm a jogger taking a break. But no one will. That's the beauty of London. No one gives a shit. Head down. Look away. Get on with your own life. Suits me fine.

I'm waiting for Jenny. Our time has come.

We've had no contact at all since the night of the rescue. We both got rid of our burner phones and since the first news report, I haven't looked at the media to see any developments or revelations. I don't want sensational reports. I prefer to get the real truth from Jenny. We agreed to meet here, two weeks after the event, early morning, come rain or shine. It's a mixture of both, and I've been waiting for half an hour with no sign of anyone. She'll be here, though, unless she's somehow got herself locked up in jail. I doubt it. She's a slippery one.

The need to move strikes me, so I take a walk around the graveyard and pay tribute to the grave marked '42' that brought me to this spot. I recite the words of a Vogon poem under my breath in honour of the man buried beneath the ground.

That dinner with Philippa plays on my mind. Not her so much, but that bastard Steve. Why did he have to be there? Why couldn't he have stayed away and not delivered that pathetic apology? Philippa doesn't get it. She doesn't agree that he was saying words without meaning. She doesn't know him or the torment and hatred he administered every day. You can't take that back in one half-hearted speech. Bastard. I don't forgive him. I won't forgive him. I'll definitely avoid him, but that's the best he can hope for. He deserves revenge. He deserves a beating, but I won't stoop to his level. Fuck him and his wretched life. I have better things to worry about.

For example, the smashing glasses.

I know very well that I can make a pane of glass resonate and vibrate so hard that it shatters into thousands of shards at a distance, but that's a conscious effort. A will to direct energy in a particular direction at a specific object. It takes concentration and focus, something I have total control over. Or, so I thought.

The wine glasses that broke in Steve's hands … those were

different. I had no control over that effect, and that fact has rolled around in my head on an infinite loop ever since. It scares me if I'm honest. It implies things that I hadn't considered. It means I can't trust myself. It means my raw emotions are dangerous, chaotic and wild.

I need to talk to Evelyn. Did she know this could happen? She has never mentioned it if she did. A side effect, perhaps? An unknown consequence of the FSMI program living in my brain.

I'll need to be more careful. If only not to accidentally give myself away or destroy my kitchen.

"Hiya."

Back on the bench, tuned out from the world, caught up in my thoughts and saturated with rain, I didn't notice anyone sitting down next to me. I jump and turn to find Jenny not quite as damp as me. She wears a waterproof coat with a hood pulled tight around her face. Garish pink, but that's the camouflage of the modern era. She's quiet as a mouse, gaunt and skinny. Her face is drawn and tired. Her bones are sharp behind the skin that's pulled tight over them. There are skeletons in this very cemetery who'd look fat compared to Jenny and she's so pale she could be a ghost of one of these long demised people. And I thought I had problems.

"Hey. You okay?"

She nods, but I don't believe it. I stand up.

"Let's go find somewhere less wet and grab a bite, yeah?"

"Aye. Cheers."

Aside from a few words about which direction the nearest cafe is and the pitter-patter of rain all around us, we walk in silence. Slowly, not hurrying. Finally, in the Pret A Manger, I motion for

Jenny to find a table at the back out of sight and mind, and then I order two toasties and coffees. The dude behind the counter looks me up and down, undoubtedly because I'm a walking sponge, soaking and dripping. I'll change and dry off later. A bit of water never did anyone any harm.

"When did you last eat?" I drop a coffee cup in front of Jenny, along with a handful of sugar packets and a wooden stick.

"Dunno." She shrugs, and she barely has the energy for that movement.

"Drink that, eat, then we can talk."

She nods.

Despite my growing desire to ask, I wait until Jenny is completely sated. She takes her time, but I can't rush her. She sips at a second cup of coffee, having finished every crumb of her toastie and she's saving the doughnut I grabbed for later, she says.

"Feel better now?"

She nods. "Aye. Thanks, Toby." She offers a weak smile.

"No problem. It's the least I can do." I remember the cash in my pocket and glance around to make sure no one is watching and no cameras are pointed at us before pulling out my wallet. I extract five hundred pounds in small notes and slide them over the table to Jenny. Then, I throw a napkin on top to hide it.

Her eyes widen. "What's that for?" Then she leans forward and whispers. "How much is that?"

"Five." I smile. "It's for you. Food, clothes, place to stay. Whatever you need."

"No!" She shrinks back in horror. "I can't take that much just like that." She shakes her head with a hint of tears in her eyes.

"Don't even think about that crap. Take it. Use it wisely. Be careful and shut it."

She opens her mouth to say something but then scoops up the napkin and cash and hides it about her person.

"Thank you."

"No need, but please, make sure you eat … every day, yeah?"

"Aye." She nods, a nervous smile on her dirty face. I didn't get a hotel this time and feel guilty. She could have come back and cleaned up. We could have done this in a comfortable room. Didn't think it through. Shit.

"Where are you sleeping?"

She shrugs. "Same old, you know …"

I don't know exactly, but I can hazard a guess. I frown but put the thought aside. "So, what happened?"

Jenny sits back, sighs, and gently shakes her head. "No much, really."

"Not much? What happened with your friend, Oleksandra, the other girls?"

"They're still in hospital. Well, not the same one. Some place for rehab, you know?"

"What happened, exactly, after I left you?"

Jenny sips at her coffee, then brushes back hair from her face and begins her story.

After I rescued the girls from the loft brothel and almost killed the bent copper who was running the place, they were picked up by an ambulance and taken to the nearest hospital. There were many conversations with uniformed police and then some plain-clothed varieties, but they finally relented that Jenny didn't know how the girls managed to escape the building. Good girl. She kept to the story.

The three girls were too out of it to make a statement and were cared for in a private, guarded wardroom. The drugs gradually wore off, and they were able to give the police some details about their imprisonment. The guards had all eventually been found and arrested, thanks in no small part to the video footage that the police received anonymously, and the boss cop remains in his coma after his swift rooftop exit from the scene of the crime. Police continue to be interested in talking to a dread-head man spotted at the scene but have no leads on his whereabouts. CCTV camera footage in the whole area was oddly non-existent. Funny, that.

Jenny was allowed to visit Sandy only a few times over the last two weeks, and now they have all been taken to another hospital, and she has no further information. They were recovering from the forced drug use and being treated for trauma. The good news, if there can be any at all from this, is that they weren't physically hurt. Mentally, though, I doubt they will ever recover. Repeatedly raped, chained to beds, drugged to oblivion and punished if they didn't do exactly what they were told. They were all scared and silent. Sandy, having the least English of all of them, was the hardest to engage with. The police found an interpreter, but she couldn't get much more information. The case was fairly clear cut in the end; each girl was able to positively identify Detective Inspector Ryan Turner as the man running the venture, and given his comatose state, he has been in no position to confirm or deny the accusation. He may never wake up from the coma, and his injuries were extensive. Broken legs, arms, ribs and a fracture to the skull would likely be the cause of the coma. He doesn't deserve the intensive care that he's been receiving. Let the fucker rot as he did the girls. One girl, Madalina, said she thought there were two other girls at some point, but she didn't know how long since they were no longer around or what happened to them. Chances are that nothing good happened to them. There could have been many more. We might never find out.

The three girls will remain in care until they are fit enough to leave, but the problem is that none of them have anywhere better to go. What will happen to Oleksandra, Madalina and

Georgiana? All refugees running from war or problems. All found themselves on the streets of London with no family, no one to care for them, and nowhere to call home. No safety. Will they land back under the same bridges as before? Will they end up in another horrific situation?

The system should take care of them, shouldn't it? But it was the 'system' that failed them. The law was not on their side. And all for what? A few extra quid in the pocket of a dodgy copper. No one could blame them for not trusting in the system ever again.

Jenny's eyes are red raw when she finishes her story. I swap sides and sit next to her on the bench seat, and she rests her head on my chest and cries out the pent-up emotion that she's been saving up for weeks. Her tears barely made a difference to my already soaking wet hoody. I wrap my arms around her and hold her close, not wanting to let go until she's ready.

"Sorry." She sniffs, raising her head.

I shake my head. "Shh. Nothing to be sorry about."

"I snotted on your top."

I chuckle. "It'll wash."

She smiles, but there's another wave of tears behind it waiting to drop like a tsunami. I change the subject. "Another cuppa?"

"Nah, I'm fine, thanks."

"What now, then?"

She shrugs. "I dunno. Go back to normal, I suppose?"

"Right, what the hell is normal, anyway?"

"Aye, I don't know." She pauses and bites at her lip with her broken teeth. "Can I ask you something, though?"

"Sure." I smile.

"How did you get in there and get them out like that so quickly? How did you deck that big bastard copper, and there wasn't even a scratch on you?"

"Ah," I start.

"And you got by those bouncers like they weren't even there."

"Yeah, I …"

"One of them had his head nearly burned off, and then he got run over!"

I chuckle at that, remembering the scene. "Yeah, not bad work if I do say so myself."

"How did you do it? Are you bloody Batman or something?"

"No." I resist the urge to say 'Flash Gordon, actually' and smile at the girl. "Just got lucky." I shrug.

She shakes her head. "All the windows were smashed. That bastard polis was thrown out of another window. What happened in there?"

I can't tell her, of course. I know I could trust her to keep my secret, but even so, I can't let on anything about my abilities. It's too dangerous. "The less you know, the better. Believe me."

"Aye, well." She looks me up and down. "I'm glad you're on my side."

"Yeah, same, Jenny." A thought occurs to me. I almost blurt it straight out but pause for a moment to consider the ramifications. I weigh up the pros and cons, then go with the usual method of 'fuck it' and say it anyway. "Why don't you come stay with me for a bit?" Her eyes widen with a look of horror briefly. I raise my hands. "In a spare room, I mean. Nothing funny."

She smiles. "Aye, I know. Thanks, but I want to be around if Sandy gets out. She'll need me."

"It could be a while, though."

Jenny nods. "Aye, but it could be tomorrow."

"We could check up every day."

"Mind we thought about this? What if she recognises you and polis are still sniffing around? Too dangerous."

"Yeah, okay. Still though. I just … worry."

"I'm fine, Toby. But thank you." She takes my hand and squeezes gently. There's some energy flowing through her now since the meal. A bit of colour returns to her face.

I hold her hand for a lingering moment and pulse out some wavelengths of energy. Safety, confidence, trust. Everything will be okay. She'll see. The girls are safe now. The good guys won. Jenny smiles and I can see how she was once pretty despite her malnourished state. What happened to her? I haven't asked. She'll tell me if she wants to.

"Right." I smile. "Oh, almost forgot." I unzip my waterproof backpack and rummage inside pulling out a new burner phone, already charged and topped up with credit. I drop it onto the table in front of Jenny.

"Keep it switched off until you need it. My new number is already in the memory. You know the deal."

"Aye. I do."

"If you change your mind, you know, shout, and I'll come get you."

She nods but waves me away. "You can't save every girl, Toby."

And she's right. I can't.

CHAPTER
SIX

"GRAN!"

"Well, hello, Cassie, my darling." Gran stands in her doorway with her arms wide open. I rush into them, but I'm careful not to slam into her with too much force. She is getting on a bit, not that she'd let you know. "My, how you've grown!" I stand back and feel the grin spread across my face. She looks down at my chest, and I feel a bit self-conscious. "You're all grown up, more or less."

"Not quite." I feel my cheeks burn.

She smiles, and now I come to think of it, where I would have looked up to see her before, now she's more or less on my level. Is that because I have grown, or has she shrunk? Bit of both, perhaps. How long has it been since I saw her? Not since Christmas.

"Well, don't stand on the doorstep all day. Come in, come in!"

I bounce in as Gran moves aside, and the delicious smell of baking cakes pulls me towards what must be the kitchen.

"Cassie!" I hear a yell from outside and turn. Oh, yeah. Mum. I feel my eyes roll. "Aren't you going to say bye?"

Mum stands at the end of the garden path next to the car. Dad is fiddling in the boot.

"Yes, Mum." I drop my bag in the hallway and nudge past again, going out to give my parents a hug.

"We'll miss you, sweetie." Mum turns her head towards Dad. "Won't we, Anthony?"

Dad sticks his head out. "Yes, of course, darling. Have you seen the WD-40?"

Mum ignores him. "You'll be okay, won't you, Cassie?"

"I'll be fine!" I insist. We've already been over this a dozen times.

"She'll be better than fine. We're going to have the best time, aren't we, Cassie?" Gran has wandered down the path now. "Don't worry about her, Sue. You two have a great time. Bring me back a souvenir?"

"Thanks, Evelyn. Yes, definitely. What would you like? A boomerang, Kangaroo pouch, jar of Vegemite?"

"Ewww!" I shudder. "What?"

"Found it." Dad calls. But no one is listening to him. He pops the bonnet of the old car and sets about spraying something with the can he found.

Mum finally releases me from her hug.

Dad gets into the car, turns the key, and the engine splutters back into life. It had stalled when we arrived. It does that.

"There we go!" He yells triumphantly, getting back out of the seat. "Come on, Sue, we better go before it dies again."

Mum leaves me with a sad smile, then goes to the car's passenger side. She opens the door, but she doesn't get in straight away. Now it's Dad's turn for the hugs.

"You be good for your gran, eh, Cassie?" He picks me up and starts to spin me around.

"Dad," I cry out. "I'm not five anymore. Put me down!"

He does so with a jolt.

"You'll always be my baby, Cassie. That's just how it is." He leans down and kisses me on the head. "Right, see you in three months, then. Bye, Mum."

"Bye, Anthony, Sue. Take care of yourselves. Mind the spiders!"

"We'll ring when we get there." Mum calls out.

With that, Mum and Dad get into the car, and then the engine roars. They spin away down the road, leaving peace and calmness in their smokey wake.

"Right." Gran claps her hands. "Now they've gone, we can have some fun!"

I look over at her, and she has a mischievous grin all over her face.

I think Gran has lived here for about three years, yet this is my first time visiting the new house. I suppose it isn't that new anymore. Still new to me, at least. She always comes to ours normally; she says it's easier. She used to live much closer, and I'd see her more often. I've missed her always being nearby. This visit will have to make up for all that lost time.

Dad says I've been rabbiting on about it non-stop for months, which is how he knew I'd be okay while they went off galavanting to Australia on their own. They wanted me to come, but I didn't want to go. Too hot, too dangerous, too upside down and weird for me. If they think I was going on about seeing Gran for months, they were yapping on about Australia for years. In the end, I told them to go without me. They took some persuading, but they saw sense, eventually. Of course, they should go on their own. I'd be absolutely fine. Better than fine. Go for the whole summer, in fact! It will allow me to get some science study done with Gran, the absolute best science teacher in the world. By the time they come back, I'll be discovering gravity and explaining the universe in microscopic detail, as well as baking cakes, going for walks, and — bonus, there's a wildlife park nearby, and Gran says we can go and have our car aerial ripped off by playful monkeys. She told me she used to have a monkey called Kong when she was working for the government and that Kong was probably her best friend ever. Well, until I came along, at least.

Gran and I get on like best friends, and I already know this will be the best summer ever.

My room is at the back of the house upstairs, looking over the garden, which is a mix of lawn, flowering bushes and a little path that leads to a wooden shed at the bottom. There's loads of room, and I even get my own bathroom with a shower over a huge bath. After she gave me the quick tour, she told me to dump my stuff, and we'd get started on the cake. It smells delicious, and there's fresh cream to pour over it. Mum and Dad never make anything fun like that.

This house is much too big for Gran alone, and she only seems to use a few rooms. Kitchen, obviously, and she's got the front bedroom. The living room has a ridiculously huge couch opposite an equally huge television, but she said she barely ever uses the room, let alone the TV. I told her we were going to change all that, and she said we could go to the video rental place, and I could pick out a movie later. I already know what I'm getting, even though I've seen it a dozen times already. The 'Lord of the Rings' trilogy. We're going to have a marathon!

My room also has a small portable TV, but I doubt I'll use that much.

Then, there's the laboratory downstairs at the back of the house. From what I could make of it, it's absolutely chock full of old junk. There's a big desk in the middle of the room which is piled high with papers and broken bits of things, half unscrewed, half taken apart, circuit boards, switches, and cables twisting around in bundles. A jungle of junk with occasional coffee cups and plates planted amidst the chaos.

There's a stack of four small TVs like the one in my room, each one with two huge speakers next to it. Does she watch four channels at once?

And then there's the computers. Good grief. I lost count, but it has to be more than a dozen. Some are on another desk, some on shelves, and some are piled on the floor. They all look ancient, apart from the laptop that was open and running some kind of weird screensaver. Gran said she's working on 'this and that' and that she might have something really fun to show me one day, but for now, I should 'not touch anything' because it could be dangerous. I think I'll take her advice. She's got more computers than my school, and they all look weird and complicated.

I know she used to work for the government, but she retired before I was born. Yet she's always tinkering away with something or other. Dad says she's an old mad professor type, and she even worked on the Enigma machine decoding during the war with Alan Turing. We learned about that in history class last year, and of course, I had the benefit of Gran's first-hand experience for my presentation. I sent in my essay with an Enigma encryption on it and left clues for the teacher to crack the code. I got an A+ … once I helped Mrs McCormack decode the text. Major eye-roll.

"This is the most insane cake I've ever seen!" When mum makes a cake, which is a rare event, I must say, it's usually a cylindrical shape. A layer of cake, a layer of jam, another layer of cake and then a spread of watery pink icing on top. Candles stabbed in, and there you go.

This one is nothing like it.

Gran has covered a big wooden chopping board in rice that's been cooked with bright green dye. It's spread out to look like grass. In the middle of the meadow of rice, there's what can only be described as a henge of cake. Cake Henge!

Twelve standing 'stones' of chocolate cake, monolithic and glorious, standing in a circle, maybe six inches tall, all smothered in chocolate icing and sprinkled with hundreds and thousands on top. In the middle, there's a 'W' shape made out of five silver stars in a very familiar pattern. The constellation of Cassiopeia. "This is amazing!"

"Hope it tastes good. I may have added too much chocolate to the recipe."

"There's no such thing as too much chocolate." I laugh.

"You have a point there, Cassie." She smiles. "Fancy a slice?"

"Try and stop me, but I don't want to destroy the diorama."

"Nonsense. It's made to be eaten. Don't forget the whipped cream. You cut us a chunk each, and I'll put the kettle on. Then we'll see about going to the video rental shop."

I feel a big grin spread across my face and eagerly grab the cake knife and two plates.

After a long day, way too much cake and tea, and three hours of awesome hobbit antics, Gran tucks me into bed.

"You know where everything is if you wake up before me?"

"Yes, don't worry."

"And you've got everything you need?"

"Yes, Gran. I'm absolutely fine." I smile.

"Well, good. Just call out if you need anything. I'll be up for a while."

"You aren't going to bed?"

She taps the side of her head with a grin. "Always do my best work at night. Don't know why."

"Work?"

"Not work, work. I'm just tinkering, as your father would

say." I nod. He certainly would say that. "Now, sleep well, Cassie, my darling."

Gran kisses my forehead and then squeezes my hand.

"Night, Gran."

"Oh. I almost forgot."

She walks over to the small TV and flicks it on, then fiddles with the remote control until there's a sort of wavey screensaver pattern on the screen and a soft white-noise sound coming from its speakers.

"What's that?"

"This will help you sleep and keep you safe, Cassie."

"How?"

"Just something I've been working on." She taps her nose. "Trust me, it's great for those times when you can't get to sleep."

"Okay, thanks."

"Night, night." She waves and quietly closes the door, leaving me with the patterns and sounds. The screen is mesmerising, and I feel my eyes closing and sleep rushing in as I sink into the soft, warm bed.

CHAPTER
SEVEN

MY MIND WANDERS SOMETIMES, well, almost all the time, if I'm honest. There's always something that's cycling around in my noggin, twisting and raging through my neurons, keeping me up when I should be sleeping, distracting me from the world around me.

Something ridiculous most of the time, something that happened to me twenty or more years ago, utterly unimportant and irrelevant, but the brain cells don't care about that. When they decide it's time to think about a stupid thing I once said to a girl I was trying to impress, or when I sharted in my underwear on a date after too much curry and beer, or a song that I always hated that will get stuck on infinite repeat, then no amount of coercion will convince those electrical impulses from torturing me relentlessly for hours. I know this happens to everyone, but you'd think that I, of all people, would have more control over the thoughts in my brain, but no. I'm as scattered and messed up as I always was before the Flash Gordon stuff ever happened. It's an overlay, not a total reprogramming. That's what Evelyn said. I'm not brainwashed. I'm augmented. Tweaked, perhaps. Enhanced. Something like that, anyway.

Today, the distraction is from the distant heavens. From the night sky that's looming clear and pinpricked with tiny lights above me. From a particular pattern that's brighter than the surrounding blur of light that has travelled so far and so long just to burn out in a negligible fizzle on my retinas. Such a long, cold journey, and for what? Seems so pointless.

The constellation of Cassiopeia shines in the sky above me as I make my evening rounds, heading for a quick pint in the same pub where I first met her namesake. Before I knew that Cassie was the granddaughter of my … my what? The person who instigated a change in my head. The person who changed my life, unknowingly, unintentionally, from decades in the past with decades of secret government research into a project that was never meant to see the light of day. I don't know if there's an appropriate word for the relationship between Evelyn and me. My tutor? Mentor? Catalyst? No. None of those fit. My elder, for sure. Evelyn is more than double my age. At last count, she celebrated her one-hundredth birthday and she's fitter than many people thirty or forty years her junior. Certainly more mentally agile than anyone I've ever met. Evelyn was a genius long before she ran the FSMI process on herself. She created it from research and toil over many, many years, testing on rats and monkeys, honing the process, and building a system that could change the world.

Cassie. Cassiopeia Andromeda. Miss Wright.

Perhaps I should give her a call? Make sure all is well. Nothing weird. Just a check-in. Maybe I should pay her a visit and keep an eye on her house every so often. The chances of there being any comeback from the Department now are slim to none, but never say never. As far as I know, the members of the secret government Department for the Prevention of World-Changing Technology all still live. I only wiped out their equipment and home in the middle of nowhere, County

Galway. That ought to be enough, so why do I still worry about Cassie?

Some of it is surely down to the memories planted in my head. I have a deep and unbreakable loyalty to Evelyn. She made sure of that. Cassie is her flesh and blood, so by extension, I have a loyalty to Cassie, as well. Makes sense. But I think there's something else.

Cassie is beautiful, there's no denying that, but she's also intelligent, funny, quick and just a little bit unpredictable. Dangerous, you could say.

She's got something else, too. Something that makes her almost irresistible to me. Something that tortures and torments me whenever I linger on the subject.

What is this thing she's most certainly in possession of? An absolute and total indifference towards me in any kind of romantic way. She's not bloody interested one single bit, and that drives me mad, and I don't even know why. It's not like I've had a huge list of sexual conquests. Before I was transformed, I was a timid chap who wouldn't say boo to a goose, let alone flirt freely in clubs and bars. It took months of effort for me to get a girl interested, and consequently, there were few in my past. Philippa, being the most recent. I'm not looking for a notch on my bedpost. Still, Cassie has an appeal that I can't dismiss. Frustrating, more than anything.

Sure, Cassie and I get along in a business-type way, friends even. I did save her from the clutches of the Department, after all. But ever since I saw her sitting in the bar, just two stools away from where I now sit, I've wanted to get to know her in a more than friendly way.

Evelyn would likely kill me if she knew I had these notions. She and Cassie are close as best friends, and although Evelyn knows I can only have honourable intentions, I think where her beloved Cassie is concerned, all rational logic goes out the window.

I should call. No, I'll send a text. Just a casual 'Hi, how are you doing?' Can't hurt, can it? Maybe another pint first.

I nod to the barman and then down at my empty glass.

And then there's Jenny. A girl who I have no romantic interest in but whom I do care about a lot. A girl who has seen pain and suffering and yet keeps her hopes up. A girl who could use my help but doesn't want it. I worry about her a lot.

Since we met up last week, I haven't heard a peep from her. She knows how to get in touch if she needs me, so I suppose I should leave her alone. Yet there's always a niggle of doubt and stress.

I also wonder about how the three girls are doing in the hospital. Have they recovered? Will they ever recover? Questions I have no answers to. I need to stop worrying about things I have no control over. Jenny told me herself, I can't save every girl.

I glance up at the mirror behind the bar and casually scan the room behind me. A few groups of people chatting, an older bloke on his own reading the paper and nursing a pint, a couple laughing at something on a phone screen. This is a nice pub. Never seen any bother in here. There are a few rooms above to stay in. Cassie stays here whenever she visits her Gran.

I don't want this to turn into a session of booze and misery, so I should think about making a move, carrying on my round of the town, checking for scumbags and arseholes who need to be put out of business. I'm entitled to a night off, though, aren't I? A day when I take care of my own problems instead of other people. Another drink and a bit of a linger here won't hurt, but I switch to water. I don't like to be out of control, just in case.

A man swaggers in behind me, reflected in the mirror. He stands next to me at the bar and drops down a big wooden key fob from one of the rooms upstairs. Room 3. He turns to me with a friendly raise of eyebrows and a nod, then waves over the barman.

"Pint, please, mate, when you're ready." His accent isn't local. Somewhere flat and boring, nasal with a hint of Midlands. He checks his watch and then looks around the bar. He's obviously waiting for someone. He's done up like a dog's dinner and stinks of cheap aftershave, so I'm going to wager he's waiting for a woman. He's probably in his late thirties, tanned as if he's just come back from Spain, male pattern baldness setting in nicely on his shiny head, aggressively clean shaven, chunky gold jewellery around his wrists and neck, rings on three fingers, but not the wedding finger and his white shirt is open by three buttons, revealing a thick, dark rug of chest hair. A smooth boy. A lounge lizard. I already hate him. He's got golfball cufflinks, for fuck's sake. What an absolute bellend.

His pint arrives and he takes a deep gulp, then wipes his lips with the back of his hand. He's nervous, and his eyes dart furtively around the bar. I see all this in the mirror. I'm scrolling around on my phone if anyone casually glances at me.

The front door opens, and a gust of chill wind follows quickly. Then, a woman steps in tentatively, looking around as she smooths back her hair from the wind and checks her reflection in the window. She's a brunette with tight shoulder-length curls, wearing a long red coat and matching heels.

Cufflinks turns and sees the new arrival, raising a hand. She sees him, and there's a moment of recognition. Her face changes to a big smile, and she walks over to him. He makes no move to approach her. I turn back to my phone, leaving them to it.

"Nigel?" The woman asks him. They probably met online. A dating app, no doubt. A shudder runs through me. Those things are terrible. I know from experience. A cesspit of the worst of humankind. I glance up as Cufflinks Nigel gets up off his stool and grins at the woman. She's pretty; now I see her close up. Delicate features, bright red lipstick and dark eyes.

"That's me. Are you Rebecca?"

"That's me, yep." She smiles, and I look away. But I can see them in the mirror. Her body language is stiff. I think she was expecting something other than this suited monkey when she agreed to come out. They embrace, nonetheless, and she sits down on the stool where Cassie sat all those months ago. Nigel flags down the barman again and gets her a white wine.

I don't want to be part of their evening, but I'm not moving just because they decided to sit next to me. I'm far too British for that.

"You found the place, okay, then?" He swivels on his seat and faces away from me and toward his date. Rebecca. Surely they would be better off at one of the myriad empty tables away from me?

"Yeah, I've been here a couple of times." I hear Rebecca answer. I glance up at the mirror and she brushes back her hair from her face. Her cheeks are flushed and I think she's already had a glass or two of wine before she came out.

"Nice place," Nigel observes and makes a show of looking around the bar.

Rebecca stands up again and takes off her coat, revealing a slinky black dress. Low cut and bare shoulders. A push-up bra is just visible at the edge of the fabric. She's petite. Just my type, if anyone is asking. I can't see Nigel's face, but I imagine his eyes bulging at the dessert menu just presented to him. If he plays his cards right.

"Phwoar," he exclaims. Seriously?

In the mirror, I can see her smile as she sits back down on the stool, her coat now draped over the seat. She takes a sip of wine and seems to ease into the evening. I should walk away, this has nothing to do with me, but there's a fascination with people watching that I've always been susceptible to. Cheap entertainment, if nothing else, and as noted, Rebecca has a certain something about her. Early thirties, I'd say. Minimal jewellery and nothing on her ring finger. Her accent is local, but that could mean anything these days. She said she's been here before, though, so that adds credence to her home town being this one.

Nigel Cufflinks starts chatting about himself. No doubt his favourite topic. Something about golf and a course he's just joined. My earlier knob-end assessment of him is justified by that alone. I turn back to my phone screen and tap out a text to Cassie.

> Hiya, I just thought I'd say hello and see how you were doing.

My finger hovers over the send button for a long moment. Then I tap with a resounding fuck it. What harm can that do? I put the phone down on the bar and order another drink. Back on the beer, but I pop to the toilets while the bartender pours the pint.

When I get back, Nigel and Rebecca have moved to a table just behind where I'm sitting. Now, when I look in the mirror, I can see both of them clearly. I should take the opportunity to bugger off somewhere away from them, but now I feel like I'm committed to finding out how things go. I still get the feeling that Nigel isn't going to get lucky tonight. Rebecca came out thinking she would, but she changed her mind when she clocked him at the bar.

Was it the baldness or the cufflinks that did it? I'll never know, but I'd wager on the cufflinks. Neither can help, though.

My phone buzzes, and I glance down at the screen.

> Hey, Toby. I'm doing great, thank you. You?

It's from Cassie. I pick up the phone and tap another message out.

>> Yeah, not bad. Just tipping along, you know. Nothing strange going on with any departments or similar?

She replies straight away.

> LOL, no, thankfully.

>> Good. How's Gran doing?

> She's very well, thanks. I must give her a call tomorrow. Thanks for the reminder.

>> Say hello from me.

> I will. Thanks, Toby.

I don't think Cassie really believed my story about how I knew her grandmother. It was deliberately vague, something about tech support. Cassie knew enough not to poke around too much. We left it at that.

I get the impression that the brief text conversation is over for now. Friendly, but not flirty. I should probably just resign myself to the fact there will be nothing more. I sigh and take a sip of my pint.

Cufflinks comes back to the bar and flags down the bartender. He glances around, deliberately at me, but I'm focused on scrolling aimlessly through junk on my phone. I blend into the furniture, I'm nobody to think about. He turns back and then looks up at the spirits on a shelf.

"You fancy a cocktail?" He shouts back to his date, still sitting at the table.

"Oh, no. I shouldn't." She giggles. "Just wine, for me." She nods towards the glass in front of her.

"Go on. You only live once, eh?"

She shuffles in her seat and checks her phone screen. Then she looks back at Cufflinks and nods. "Okay, then. Just one, though."

He smiles and turns back to the barman. "Two Piña Coladas, please, mate." then he turns back to Rebecca with two thumbs up and sings "If you like Piña Coladas and getting caught in the rain …"

Good grief.

Rebecca chuckles and shakes her head in mock shame. Rupert Holmes has a lot to answer for.

Rebecca gets up, grabs her handbag and points towards the toilets. "Be right back."

Instinctively, my eyes flit to her unguarded glass of wine that's still half full on the table. There are some right bastards out there, and you can't rule anything out, even in a decent place like this. Date rape is far too common.

Next to me, two cocktails are set down in front of Nigel. He glances furtively around the bar and then takes off the golfball cufflinks, rolling up his sleeves. There's a flush of red in his cheeks now, probably from the booze. There's more, though. Something strange. A vibration of danger and excitement from him. I glance up at the mirror, and he catches my eye with a wink.

"Hole in one, eh!"

I look away but watch him as he carries the cocktails to the table and sets both down in front of him. He changes his mind about the sleeves and rolls them back down, reapplying the stupid novelty cufflinks in the process. Then, he purposely moves one glass over to the side where Rebecca was sitting.

He looks around the bar and seems to relax, leaning back into his seat with a grin.

His frequency has changed. His nerves are gone. Now, he's filled with confidence and bravado. I don't like this.

I get up quickly and walk towards the toilets.

There's only one of each, male and female, tucked away at the back of the bar. I wait outside, formulating a plan.

I don't have to wait long. The door of the ladies opens, and Rebecca comes out. She sees me hovering and smiles, then looks away. I make my move.

"Hi. Sorry, can I talk to you for a second?"

She turns, startled, but flashes me the smile again. "Hi, yeah, okay."

"I'll get straight to the point. How well do you know that man you are with?"

Her face turns to a confused scowl. "Err, not very well. What's this about?"

"I don't like him."

She snorts a laugh. A little tipsy. "Well, he's not my first choice, either, but hey, ho." She waves a hand dismissively.

"No, I mean. I think he may have … err, bad intentions."

Her scowl returns. "How do you mean?"

"I'm not sure, but he may have spiked your drink. The cocktail."

"What?" She exclaims. "Are you serious?"

"I didn't see it, but, well, I have a feeling."

She hesitates. "You didn't see it?"

"He was fiddling with his stupid cufflinks. Then his demeanour changed." I blow out a sigh. "It's hard to explain. Look, I don't mean to cause trouble, but I don't think you should drink the cocktail."

"Jesus. Should I call the police?"

I ponder on the question. Probably, yes, she should, but something better occurs to me.

"You can, if you like. I'll back you up. Or, we could try something more interesting."

Her eyes widen as she looks up at me. "Go on …"

I return to my seat at the bar, not paying any attention to Nigel Cufflinks. Rebecca follows thirty seconds later and sits back down in her chair. I watch them reflected in my periphery, waiting for my cue.

Rebecca reaches for her wine glass but then switches to the cocktail glass. She raises it to put the straw in her mouth. I watch Nigel's reaction. He flares up like a beacon. Vibrations pour from him across the spectrum. He bounces around inside his body like a jumping bean, but his face remains fixed in a friendly grin. Rebecca stops before her lips touch the metal straw, and she puts the cocktail back down again. She giggles, feigning a level of tipsy that's a few notches higher than she really is, and then her eyes dart to the jukebox on the opposite wall of the bar.

"Shall we put that song on?" She bats her eyelashes at Nigel, then licks her lips.

"The Piña Colada song?" He asks.

"Yeah, I bet they have it on the jukebox."

"Why not, yeah." He makes no move to stand up.

"Come on then. Get in the mood, yeah?"

"Go for it, if you want." He still makes no move to get up.

"No, come with me and help me choose a few songs. Then, who knows …" She flashes a seductive smile in his direction. That does the job, and he pushes back his chair.

She grabs his arm, leaning on him in a show of needing the support, and then they walk over to the jukebox. This is my cue.

Quickly, I get up, turn around and switch the identical

cocktail glasses around. Nigel now has the one that could be spiked, and Rebecca has the other. If I'm wrong, then no harm done.

The key to not looking suspicious in whatever it is you are doing is not to act strangely. No need to be furtive and weaselly. You do what you need to do openly and confidently. No one will bat an eyelid. No one saw my switch around.

I sit back down and order myself another glass of water. Now I wait.

The opening beats and guitar strums of Escape, by Rupert Holmes, ring out in the pub, and I cringe inside. Presently, the couple returns arm in arm and sits down at their table. I turn and catch Rebecca's eye with the briefest of nods. She flashes a smile, then turns back to Nigel, picking up her cocktail and, this time, taking a long sip through the straw. He copies her and sings along to the lyrics, arm-dancing at the table. She plays along.

The music changes to Kokomo by the Beach Boys, then Margaritaville, Jimmy Buffett. The cringe level kicks up a notch every minute. As it does, the expression on Nigel's face changes from a confident grin to a slack-jawed droop. By the time Don't Stop Believin' by Journey comes on, Nigel is ready for bed. My cue to step in again.

"Well, well, feeling a bit tired, are you, mate?"

I grab his room key from the table and nod to Rebecca. She looks at me, then Nigel, as his eyes roll around in their sockets, seemingly disconnected from each other.

"Come on then, let's get you up to bed, eh?"

"The fucking little prick," Rebecca points at Nigel, slumped in his chair. "You were right!"

"Unfortunately, yeah."

"What do we do now?" She stands up and walks over, prodding him in the chest. He doesn't react.

"Let's get him up to his room."

"Why?"

I shrug. "Teach him a lesson?"

She smirks, but then the alcohol buzz leaves her in a flash of panic. "Jesus Christ, that piece of shit was going to rape me?"

"Yeah."

"Fuck!"

"Exactly. So, we can either call the cops now or have a bit of fun first. What do you reckon?"

Rebecca looks at me with a grin. "Well, I could do with a bit of fun."

It isn't the easiest manoeuvre, but between us, we manage to drag a limp Nigel up to his room. I made a show of calling out that he's got a little too drunk and needed to sleep it off, in case anyone was listening, but the barman didn't seem to care, nor did any of the other patrons. The night is still early, and he's just another drunk twat.

I gladly drop him down on the bed, and Rebecca closes the door, locking it from the inside with the old key on the wooden fob.

"Grab his phone and wallet for a start." I nod towards him, spark out on the bed. Rebecca goes straight for his pockets. I look around the room. There's a laptop closed on a small desk and a small overnight bag with some toiletries and clothes stuffed into it. I empty the bag out onto the bed next to him.

Rebecca, fuelled by anger, booze and mischief, pulls open his wallet and rifles through the contents.

"Couple of cards, about fifty quid in notes and change, driving license." She peers at the license. "Nigel Bailey"

"Got his phone?"

"Yeah," she hands me the device. It's a few years old and has a fingerprint biometric instead of Face ID, perfect. I tap his limp finger on the phone and unlock it, scrolling around in his apps. He's logged into Facebook, Linked In, Instagram and Twitter, and there are a few group text threads in his messages app that look like they are among golfing and football buddies. At least two dozen people between them. Excellent.

"Right. Get his kit off." I nod to Rebecca.

She snorts a laugh. "What!"

"You got any lipstick on you?"

"Yeah." She reaches into her bag and pulls out a tube.

"Great. Get his clothes off." She hesitates. "That's exactly what he would be doing to you right now if we hadn't switched the drinks."

Encouraged by this fact, she sets about stripping the wanker of his dignity. His shoes are lobbed straight out of the window into a yard behind the pub. His clothes follow shortly after, and all the spares that were in the overnight bag. The drizzle and wind should sort those out nicely. We pause when he's down to his Union Jack boxers. Rebecca sniggers a laugh. All through the process, he hasn't even begun to wake up yet.

"Now what?" She looks over at me for guidance.

"You want to do the honours?"

She laughs and whips the boxers off in one swift move-ment revealing his shrivelled prawn of a dick.

"Bloody hell." She puts a hand over her mouth in shock. "A very lucky escape, eh?"

"Indeed. Okay, I don't know how long this will last, so let's hurry." She nods.

"Pass me the lipstick."

She does, and I open the cap and roll up the stick. I write a note on his gut with the bright red lipstick.

'I'M A DATE-RAPING PIECE OF SHIT' in clear, capital

letters. Then I draw arrows pointing in the direction of his nasty little cock.

I stand back to admire my handiwork, then grab his phone and snap a few photos of him naked, sprawled and limp on the bed. I take some more close-ups of the message on his torso and post all of the photos in turn on his Facebook, Instagram, LinkedIn, and Twitter accounts. Then, I send them to the group chat messages with his sports buddies. There's another chat thread called Mum, and I attach the photos, one by one, to that as well.

"Do his Tinder." Rebecca giggles as she peers at the phone in my hand.

"Good idea." I update his profile photo to one of the close-ups of the lipstick message and add the rest of the photos to his album.

Once I'm sure everything has been sent, I take the phone to the bathroom, drop it into the toilet and flush. It doesn't go down, so I grab a toilet brush and push it through the U-bend. Rebecca stares at me in shock, then grabs the brush from me and rushes back into the bedroom. I follow her out and burst into a laugh when I see what she's done. Nigel Bailey is now intimately friendly with the stick end of a toilet brush. Rebecca rushes back into the bathroom and washes her hands.

"Well, that's him royally fucked!" I call back to her. She smirks at me in the mirror.

We take a moment to look around the room, and then I pour out all his shampoo and toothpaste into the toilet, take the cash and cards from his wallet and stash them in my pocket.

I notice the laptop again. Do I have time? We need to wipe as many surfaces free of fingerprints as possible in case he calls the police, but I have a feeling he won't, given the circumstances. Still, I grab a towel and use it to open the laptop, bending the screen backwards until it crunches in a horrible breaking plastic sound. That will have to do.

Then, I remember the cufflinks. I left them on the night-stand before tossing the shirt out of the window. I pick them up and examine the golf balls.

"I think this is where he stored the drugs. They must unscrew or something."

Rebecca looks at me in shock. "The slimy little shite."

"Yep." One of the golf balls is loose, and when I twist it, a drip of liquid falls out. I shake the other one, and it may have more of the drug inside.

"What do you want to do about these?" I show the drug dispensers to Rebecca.

"Flush them."

"Sure? Don't want to give them to the cops as evidence?"

She looks around the room and the damage that we've done. "Well," She points to the unconscious, naked man on the bed with a toilet brush shoved unceremoniously up his arse, and bright red lipstick announcing his intentions on his chest, "Maybe not a good idea?"

I ponder our options and then come to a conclusion. "We'll leave them at the bar. Say he dropped them or something?"

She nods. "Yeah, good idea."

"Finished?"

Rebecca looks around and nods. "Finished."

We exit the room, and I lock the door from the outside, taking the key on its big wooden fob and dropping it into the paper towel bin in the men's bogs on my way out; then, we casually leave the cufflinks on the bar. I call to the barman. "Think your guest dropped these on his way up the stairs."

He nods acknowledgement, and we walk calmly out of the front door into the night.

• • •

"I don't even know your name." Rebecca looks at me outside with a mixture of horror and humour on her face. "You saved me from getting raped and who knows what, and I don't even know who you are."

"I'm Toby," I tell her. "and you are welcome, Rebecca."

She pushes her arm through mine and pulls me close. "Well, Toby. I came out tonight hoping for some fun, and you sure gave me that! Now I think it's my turn to say thank you properly."

"Don't mind if I do."

CHAPTER
EIGHT

Please be here at 11 O'Clock on Monday
morning. Sharp. I have something to tell you.

A MESSAGE from Evelyn popped up on my phone
yesterday. I hadn't heard from her for a while, so it was a
surprise, and all my requests for more information went
unanswered. So what else can I do? I got in the car at 10:35
and drove to the care home.

Now it's 10:55, and I'm waiting in my car parked outside
Cherryoaks Lodge, bracing myself for something strange.
Experience tells me that any interaction with Evelyn is always
out of the ordinary and just a bit surreal.

Rain pelts down on the roof and blurs the windows, my
chest feels tight, and my guts are in turmoil. Anticipation of
what this 'something' is that Evelyn needs me for is churning
me up. She has this power over me.

However, I will wait until the allotted time before going
in. Sharp, she said, which means not early and not late.

My weekend was somewhat different from the usual, too.

After Rebecca and I left the pub on Friday night, she

insisted I come to her house, a short taxi ride away. She wanted to thank me, she said, and I was in no mood to decline. The stupid thing was that she had decided early in the evening that she would sleep with Nigel — the date-raping shithead. There was no need for him to drug her.

He wasn't her first choice, not even her tenth, but she's a busy woman, and all she wanted was a bit of fun every now and then. Nigel's turn came up, and she was willing to give it a go with low expectations.

Not after she discovered his intentions, of course. His cheat-mode plan cost him his chance and a lot more. Still, It could have been much worse. She could have ended up raped and murdered.

I convinced her to report him to the police the day after, because who knows how many other women have already fallen foul of his hollow golfball cufflinks filled with benzodi-azepines. She said she would. Whether the little twat ends up in jail or not is a different story, but at least we served him some justice in our own way. I'm sure his golf buddies and mother will appreciate the photos. Ironically, his reputation, if he had one, will be royally fucked — unlike him anytime soon when women see his Tinder profile photo.

Nigel really shot himself in the foot, because Rebecca turned out to be a feisty little thing. Skilled in the art of the Karma Sutra and very open-minded. We spent the best part of the weekend in her bedroom, and I mean the very best part. A shiver runs down my spine at the memory. Rebecca is a naughty girl, for sure.

She told me she's not interested in a relationship. Fair enough. She's too busy working as a receptionist in an office in town by day and studying for a degree in psychology by night. She doesn't have the time or the energy for a compli-cated thing. Occasional fun, no strings, no stress.

A 'fuck-buddy' is what she was looking for, and as she grabbed me for the fifth time that night, pulling me in for a sultry hot kiss, she said that, unlike Bono, she reckons she's finally found what she was looking for. Me.

I couldn't argue with that. Seemed like a solid plan. She didn't want to know my back story. I didn't ask hers. We swapped numbers and bodily fluids, and on Sunday afternoon, I made my merry way home. It was good to get my mind off things.

On my brisk walk home, I found Nigel's bank cards and cash still in my pocket, so I posted them through random letterboxes and gave the cash to a Big Issue seller.

A car pulls up next to me, startling me back into reality. A woman immediately gets out and pulls a hood up over her head, squinting into the rain towards the care home. My heart jumps in my chest, and adrenaline courses through me. I get out of my car and call after her as she makes her way towards the entrance.

"Cassie?"

She turns and stops.

"Toby?"

"What are you doing here?" We both say at the same time.

There's a hint of a smile on her face, and she turns back to the home and quick-walks out of the rain. I follow.

Inside, Cassie pulls down her hood and shakes off some of the rain from her jacket.

"Should have brought an umbrella." She mutters to herself, then looks back up at me.

"I was summoned," I start, reaching for my phone in case I need to prove myself. "I don't know why."

"Yeah? Me too." Cassie eyes me suspiciously. "Right, well. We better go see what Gran is up to, then."

. . .

We both sign into the visitor book, then I lead the way to the common room. Nurse Rosie on reception told us that Evelyn was waiting there for us, and to go straight through.

The big windows are streaked with rain, like my car's windscreen. The garden is a blur of green and grey with no discernible features. Consequently, the common room is sparse with patrons. They are probably lingering in their rooms, complaining that the weather is doing their legs and backs no good.

"Thank you for being on time." Evelyn doesn't turn when I get to her usual seat. She sits alone, staring out of the window into the garden, seemingly oblivious to the soft-focus version of the vista.

"Hi, Gran," Cassie stops next to me, tentative.

Evelyn turns with a broad grin aimed at her granddaughter. "Cassie, darling."

They embrace while I stand awkwardly waiting, and then Cassie sits down opposite Evelyn. The chair all but swallows her up into its sumptuous cushions.

"I would say we should go for a walk around the garden, but the weather is hardly conducive." Evelyn scoffs. "Anyway, thank you both for coming." She turns to me. "How are you, Toby? Keeping well?"

I nod, nervous for some reason. "Yeah, you know. Not bad."

"Busy with work?"

"Err, well, I've been doing this and that."

Cassie side-eyes me, but I don't acknowledge her. Evelyn nods knowingly.

"Staying out of trouble?"

"For the most part, yes."

"Good, good."

Evelyn isn't cold towards me, but when she turns to Cassie and smiles, it's like I am standing in a freezer and Cassie in an oven. Evelyn lights up as she looks at her granddaughter, and a smile cracks over her old face. "Cassie, my darling. And you, how are you?"

"I'm doing great, Gran. Thank you."

"Lovely to hear." Evelyn reaches forward and holds Cassie's hand. "Work treating you well?"

"Yeah, not bad. Usual, you know."

"And your other projects?"

Evelyn is probably referring to the computer model that Cassie had made of a system for heating water with minuscule amounts of power. An energy creation device. Something that the world needs but hasn't been able to invent just yet. Cassie may have, though. That's the model that got her into trouble with the Department. They tried to destroy her research, including the knowledge inside her head, but Cassie had hidden a backup in a locket still around Evelyn's neck on a silver necklace. I had wondered if Cassie was still pursuing that myself. The Department wasn't able to hack into Cassie's brain, despite them claiming to have wiped the memories of various other people over the years using an adapted version of Evelyn's FSMI process. They took the power and used it for evil instead of good, naturally.

"Bit stuck, but I'll get back to it."

Evelyn nods. "Excellent." She claps her hands together, but the sound is so weak it barely registers. "Well, I suppose you will both be wondering why I asked you to come?"

"Yes, a bit," I admit.

Cassie nods. "It's lovely to see you, either way, Gran."

"We'll have to go to my room to talk. Toby, if you will, please help me up. My poor legs aren't what they used to be, you know?"

Cassie perches on the edge of the bed, Evelyn in her comfy chair, and I bring over the hard wooden seat. I sense that Cassie is equally eager to know what is going on. The atmosphere is thick with tension. This summoning doesn't bode well.

"So …" Evelyn starts but immediately pauses. She takes a sip of water, then puffs out a sigh. "I wanted you both to know at the same time, to hear it from the horse's mouth, as it were." She chuckles. "So there's no confusion."

"Hear what, Gran?" Cassie is looking worried.

"My solicitor visited yesterday." She shudders. "Annoying chap, but that's beside the point. I updated my will, and I've included both of you." She looks at both of us in turn with a smile.

Cassie's eyes widen and she glances at me. I feel my mouth drop open. This isn't what I was expecting at all.

"What? Your will?"

"Yes. There's quite a bit of money, and it needs to go to a good home. You'll both be taken care of."

"But …" I begin, but I'm waved down by a bony hand from Evelyn.

"No. There will be no buts or whats or ifs. The deal is done. I made my decision and the papers are signed, witnessed and sealed. I won't hear any arguments."

A thick silence fills the room with energy. No one dares to break it for fear of electrocution.

Finally, I look up. "Well, thank you, Evelyn."

Cassie sniffs. "Gran …" her voice breaking. "Why now?"

"Yes, well, that's the other thing, isn't it?" Evelyn flusters.

"Other thing?" I ask, trying not to put two and two together.

Evelyn looks at us both in turn, then down at her lap. "I'm dying." She says, matter of factly. "There's no point in sugar-coating it."

Cassie jumps up from the bed and flops down on her knees in front of Evelyn. "Gran, no!"

Evelyn puts a hand on Cassie's head. "It's all right, Cassie, my love. It's natural. I'm very old. I had an amazing life and I got to spend a good part of it with you, and, well, now it's over."

Cassie's sobs are muffled as she buries her head in the blanket covering Evelyn's lap. I feel a burning in my chest, my mind racing. I'm *programmed* to be eternally loyal to Evelyn, to protect her, to make everything good. In this situation, though, I have no experience to call on. I don't know what to do.

"What happened, what's wrong? Is there something I can help with?" Gears grind in my brain. Perhaps there is something?

Cassie raises her head and looks around at me, hopeful. Her face is red with emotion.

"They found some kind of lump in my stomach."

Another tense silence falls around us.

"Can't they operate? Do something?"

Evelyn shakes her head. "I'm not going through that now. What for? No, I refused any treatment. Bloody doctors are a bunch of fools, anyway."

I open my mouth to speak, but words don't come.

"Gran!" Cassie wails.

"I'm one hundred years old, Cassie. Think about that for a moment." Evelyn pauses. "Either way, I'm going sooner or later. Treatment only works if the body is young and healthy, and I am neither."

"Shit. I'm so sorry, Evelyn."

"Hardly your fault, Toby." Evelyn smiles. "I'm sure you will soldier on."

Cassie excuses herself from the room to freshen up. I think she just needs some air and space. I know the feeling. My emotions are in turmoil, and I've only known Evelyn for a short time. There's the added complication of Evelyn being inside my head, though. Cassie doesn't know that, of course.

In fact, she must be wondering why I'm here at all at such an emotional family time.

"What do you need me to do?" I ask Evelyn once Cassie is out of earshot.

"Look after her, Toby. Keep her safe."

I nod. "I will."

"Good. I know you will."

"How long have you got?"

Evelyn shrugs. "They can't say for sure. Weeks, months if I'm lucky. Days if I'm not."

"Shit."

"Quite so."

"What about Cassie's parents?"

Evelyn waves her hand. "Useless fools. I've written them a letter, not that they'll notice."

I raise an eyebrow.

"Don't worry, Anthony and Susan will also be taken care of in the will."

"Fair enough." I focus on Evelyn and try to pick up on her frequencies and energy. I can't read her. "How are you, Evelyn?"

"Oh, I'm right as rain, Toby. No complaints." She smiles.

"You aren't suffering?"

"No more than usual." She chuckles. "I'm on so many pills every day that I rattle. I'm bored out of my skull in this bloody place, and you know what?"

"What?"

"I'm ready to say goodbye. Hard as it is, especially for Cassie. I've done what I can for this world, said my bit, and changed things for the better, I hope. That's me done."

"You certainly changed me for the better, Evelyn. Thank you."

She smiles again. "Are you really keeping out of trouble?"

I look away, but I can't hide the smirk. "Let's put it this way, I haven't been caught, yet."

Evelyn shakes her head, but there's a grin with it. "I suppose that was inevitable. All for good, I trust?"

"Oh, yeah. I'm slowly doing my bit to incapacitate the scumbags of the world."

"Speaking of which … the Department. Has there been any more activity?"

"No, not that I am aware of, at least."

"Good. But don't become complacent. They could appear again. I don't trust any of them as far as I could spit a coconut."

"Noted."

"Be subtle, but you must protect Cassie from them. She has great potential and … well, you know what to do."

I nod. "I know. Don't worry."

Evelyn flashes me a look of suspicion. "Do you have a woman in your life, Toby?"

I shift in my seat. "Well, sort of. Yes."

"How many?" The hint of a grin comes back to Evelyn's face.

"I mean, depends on how you count …"

She shakes her head with a chuckle. "Stands to reason. I did add a good dollop of womaniser into your code. It was the way of the world, back then."

"I don't think much has changed in that regard over the decades."

"Just you watch it with Cassie, understand?"

I nod. "I know. Cassie is off limits." I shoot a look at the door in case she comes back in.

"I wouldn't go as far as that, but … well, make sure you get all the playboy out of your system before you go near Cassie." Evelyn points at me with a stern finger.

I'm shocked. She isn't banning me completely. "Understood."

"Protecting her means her emotions as well as her safety."

"Agreed. Don't worry, though. I don't think she's interested in me that way."

"Hmm. Well, we'll see about that."

I tilt my head. "How do you mean?"

There's a knock on the door before Evelyn can reply, then it opens and Cassie comes back in. Her face is less red than when she left and she's got a resigned smile on her face.

"I've rung work. Taken tomorrow off as well so I can spend the day here with you, Gran. I'll drive back and I'll come back here at the weekend."

"Lovely, thank you, Cassie. I don't want you to be upset, though."

"I know. It's okay."

"I'll leave you to it, then." I stand up.

"Thank you for coming, Toby."

"Not at all. I'll see you soon." I turn to Cassie. "Let me know if there's anything at all you need, yeah?"

"Thanks. I'll get a room at the pub. Should be fine."

"Pub?" She means the place where I apprehended Nigel Rohypnol-Cufflinks the other day. I hope she doesn't get room three. An idea hits me, and I blurt it out before I can ponder too much. "You could stay at my place if you like?" I sense an awkward pause. "In my spare room, I mean. I don't live far from here."

Cassie hesitates, then looks to Evelyn for approval. Evelyn nods.

"Thanks. Yeah, actually, I'll take you up on that. Save me a few quid."

"Cool. I'll text you the address. Catch you later, then."

CHAPTER
NINE

THURSDAY, MARCH 14, 2013. 2:30
PM. WOBURN, BEDFORDSHIRE.

DOES anyone enjoy going to the dentist? Maybe there are some weird perverts out there who get a thrill from having someone mess around inside their mouths with drills and weird-shaped metal instruments, but they have to be few and far between. Conversely, I count myself as one of the many who absolutely dread the dentist and all the associated procedures. Don't get me wrong, I brush my teeth twice a day like a good girl, every single day for as long as I can remember, but aside from that, occasionally flossing and random spurts of using mouthwash, I avoid any medical intervention of my oral cavity where possible.

Sadly, this is one such time when I can't avoid it any longer. I have a toothache, and Gran insisted I go to a dentist. I tried chewing a clove, taking ibuprofen, and rinsing my mouth with whiskey, but none of those were long-term cures. So here I am, waiting in the waiting room. They call it a waiting room, but it could equally be called the dying room. I can't remember a time when I wasn't here, waiting. In pain, I might add. Waiting while other people come and go. Lingering with an appointment that must have been made in some other time dimension, because the numbers on my wrist bear no relation to the number on my appointment card.

I avoid eye contact with the old bloke who sits opposite, clutching a bloody handkerchief to his mouth, desperate to strike up a conversation and share his grief with someone. I cancel out the sound of the snotty toddler who whines in an incessant tone towards his utterly oblivious mother. I uncross and re-cross my legs once more to keep the blood flowing. I tune out the radio that blares a never-ending stream of local carpet and car sales adverts into my ears.

Time stands still in the waiting room of doom.

I pick up a magazine. One from the bottom of the messy stack that sits in front of me on a low coffee table. One I hadn't already picked up, glanced through and thrown back down in disgust. I flick through the pages of disinterested models posing for perfume adverts, watches that cost more than my annual salary, and full-page spreads for life insurance and holidays. Australia, one of them boasts from the page in garish colour. 'Come and say G'Day' it blurts. I scoff. Over my dead body.

Mum and Dad went to Australia ten years ago for a three-month trip. Not a holiday, but an adventure, Dad was keen to point out. They had been planning it for as long as I could remember, and it was me who was stopping them from going. Too complicated with a child, they said, and once I got to be old enough to understand what it all meant, I absolutely didn't want to go, anyway. Everything in Australia is out to kill you. It's upside down, weird, too hot and too far away. I wanted nothing to do with it, and after a lot of discussions with Mum and Dad, I convinced them to go without me. I would stay with Gran for the summer. It would be fine. More than fine.

And it was. I had a great summer. Every day was a new experience, and I loved it. I learned about some of the science that Gran used in her career, such as how to use resonating frequencies to change states and how to program computers—real computers, she said, not the new-fangled toys we have now. I must admit that Cobol still gives me nightmares.

We watched films, baked cakes, went for long walks, and generally had the best time together. Gran is skilled at everything, no matter how weird and wonderful.

When the date approached for Mum and Dad to come back and collect me, I dreaded the thought of it. Returning to my normal life would be a dreary experience. I wanted that summer to last a lifetime.

What I didn't expect was that Mum and Dad would never come back.

They left me here with Gran.

I'm not bitter. I think I'm all the better for it, and yet I can't help but feel that things didn't quite go how they should have. I haven't seen my parents for years. They have visited exactly twice since they left all those years ago. Once to say they weren't coming back, which was odd in itself, and once for my eighteenth birthday. I barely recognised them. They picked up the local accent within minutes of getting off the plane, apparently.

They seem happy, I'll give them that, but realistically, they abandoned me and left me with an octogenarian.

Gran said she wasn't surprised. Her son, my dad, was always a bit wayward, she said. I've heard the stories many times. He's a carpenter now. I sometimes get an email from him with a photo of one of his latest creations—a sideboard or a table. They look good. I had no idea he was interested in wood.

Mum, even more surprisingly, became an avid gardener. Now, they grow a lot of their own vegetables. It's what they always wanted, probably. Gran says they are total hippies, and she cites my name as evidence of the fact. Cassiopeia Andromeda. Conceived under the stars, so they say. I shudder at the thought.

The thing is, Mum and Dad are happy, and Gran and I are

happy. So I suppose it turned out okay in the end, if slightly odd.

Now, Gran is ninety-one years old, and I fear for her health. I try to visit as much as I can, but it can be hard to find the time. I don't have a social life to speak of, but nevertheless, the drive is a pain.

I worry that she will need to go into a care home soon. That will be a tough decision. She isn't senile or anything. Far from it. She's sharper than a box full of razor blades, but her body is frail and weak. She avoids cooking because she can't open jars or cans anymore.

She says she's fine and that I mustn't worry, but I do. Every day. I can't imagine life without her, and she's all I've got.

"Cassie Wright?" The receptionist calls out. Good grief, I've waited here so long that, for a moment, I forgot that was my name. It takes a long few seconds for my brain to come back to reality and realise that I've finally been summoned to the dentist. I stand up, and blood rushes to my arse, which has been numbed on the hard waiting room chair.

"Yes. That's me."

"You can go through now."

'Thank fuck for that.' I mutter under my breath. Pardon my French.

Gurgle, whizz, gurgle, slurp, poke, poke, gurgle.

The delightful sounds of the dentist's chair. I'm trying to disassociate myself from the hellish reality of the industrial-grade demolition work going on inside my mouth right now. The noise alone is enough to make someone puke their guts up. That, and whatever drugs they pumped into me, are making things quite strange.

Something Gran always tells me flickers into my mind. 'Tune out the sounds. Cancel them with equal opposites. Your mind is capable of incredible things.' So I try. I take control of the situation and turn the volume down on life. It doesn't work, of course, but I keep trying for something to focus on instead of the drilling into my gums that's happening in full-colour, three-dimensional, shit-the-pants-vision here and now. I tune it all out, phase away reality, blur the edges of the universe and exist only inside my head.

Calm

Peace

Ocean waves gently lapping at my toes

I imagine myself on a yellow sandy beach with crystal clear water slowly tickling my toes as I stroll along the edge of the water. Hot sunshine glows all over my body, and fresh, salty air fills my lungs.

Calm

Each step I take into the water makes a ripple, and each ripple flows out into the ocean, extending my reach. Growing and multiplying until they are as wide as the ocean itself. My footsteps change the world for someone on the other side of the planet. Mum and Dad, perhaps.

I have the power to change the world in ways I have never imagined. I resonate, and my frequency is unique. Gran always tells me this, and she has shown me this many times with diagrams and computer models. Brainwave patterns and ocean waves aren't so far removed from each other.

Energy. That's the key to everything. Without energy, there would be nothing.

What if you could contain the energy instead of it dissipating away through the waves? What if the waves had nowhere to go, and more of them just kept coming? You might end up with friction, which leads to heat, which leads to something useful … what if you could agitate the water so much that it boiled, and all you had put in was the splash of a footstep? What if this actually worked?

I might be off my tits on laughing gas, but this is making some sense now. If I could write this down so I don't forget, that would be great.

"You'll feel a little prick, now." The dentist leans in close, shining a light into my face.

'Said the Bishop to the Nun.'

I snigger, but it comes out as a cough through a mouth stuffed with cotton wool.

CHAPTER
TEN

THE SHOCK of it persists and lingers in my thoughts.

Evelyn is going to die.

I mean, it shouldn't. She is undeniably very old. But she's become such a fundamental part of my life that if she were gone, I know I would feel the loss on many levels. It's not even that we keep in touch frequently, but the part of me that cares always knew she was there if I needed her. It doesn't seem real. None of it does, but this especially.

Not long ago, she was a total stranger. I didn't even know about her involvement in cracking Enigma until I went digging for it, but that was before her Flash Gordon brain programming was embedded in my memory. Before she gave me fantastic skills beyond imagination, before her memories were implanted over the top of mine. She's a part of me, and when she's gone, a part of me will go with her. Having said that, a part of her will also stay alive with me. Much more than a memory of her. I have some of *her* memories. That's something, I suppose.

Evelyn is taking it well, and I should have expected that. Pragmatic to the last. I can't see impending death being more than a mild annoyance to her. A silly thing that can be brushed away and dealt with later. No need to spoil the day with something so minor as that.

Cassie also seemed to find peace with it, at least as far as I could tell. More implied than outright spoken. She had to go back to work, but she'll be visiting every weekend until … well — until she doesn't need to anymore. If things seem to get bad, she'll stay with her grandmother until the end.

Given that I no longer have a day job, my house was adequately clean and tidy, which is why I felt confident in offering Cassie a place to stay. In my previous life, the place was never anything like woman-friendly, even on the rare occasions when women came to stay. Things are different now. I'm bordering on house proud. I reckon that is in no small part due to the influence of Evelyn.

We didn't talk much. I ordered pizza and flicked on a movie, but Cassie retired to bed before it was even halfway through. I nodded a good night and fizzled out soon after myself. The emotion was raw. There was a lot to process. The silence spoke more than perfunctory words ever could.

Cassie had perked up a little in the morning. I made eggs and toast and a pot of coffee. Cassie complimented me on the spare bedroom being comfortable, we made small talk about the drive from here to her house being easier just before the evening traffic started, and we avoided with a mile-wide berth anything to do with why we were both summoned to Cherryoaks Lodge.

Until it came out.

When I asked if she wanted another mug of coffee, the words just exploded from Cassie's mouth without warning or context. Her mouth formed the words without her brain filtering the meaning.

"Why did Gran include you in her will?"

It wasn't unkind. Not jealous, not accusing. Just a question. I suppose she had every right to ask it, given the situation. Who the bloody hell am I, after all? Cassie has known her grandmother every day of her life, and here I come in from nowhere and inherit a chunk of cash. It must have been on her mind ever since Evelyn mentioned it.

To be honest, I didn't know the answer. Perhaps Evelyn still feels a little guilty for what happened to me, even though it wasn't her fault whatsoever. It was an accident that the Project Flash Gordon code even survived the decades, let alone ran when I was in the vicinity. Evelyn couldn't have known, couldn't have predicted, couldn't have stopped it.

Nevertheless, it happened, and my life changed.

Then it dawned on me why she was leaving me money.

She knows that with my very specific set of skills, I wouldn't be able to work in any normal day job. I can't exactly walk into a government spy job, either, if they even exist in the same way as back in the sixties. Yet, my urges keep me going out and battling the scumbags of the world. Evelyn wants me to be able to keep doing what I do, and she knows that requires an income. A sponsor.

I couldn't tell Cassie any of that, though.

"Err. Well, you know that your gran worked for the government?"

"Yes, super secret stuff." She nodded, and her eyes narrowed.

"It's to do with that."

Cassie stared at me with suspicion and then looked me up and down. "Are you about thirty years older than you look?"

I burst out a laugh. "Jesus. No … it's complicated." I flashed a 'sorry, I can't say anything else' smile and got up to get more coffee.

"Of course it is." Cassie pouted. "Right. Okay." And that was that.

She's coming back this evening to stay the weekend so she can visit Evelyn first thing in the morning.

I should get some food in.

. . .

If. No, when Evelyn passes, perhaps I should move to be closer to Cassie. Just in case. Not next door, not too close, but at least in the same town. A quick drive away, so I can keep an eye on her. That will be a tough sell. Perhaps Evelyn can suggest the idea to Cassie so it doesn't look like I'm a stalker. Cassie might not want to talk to me at all after Evelyn is gone. I'm sworn to protect her. Evelyn was very clear about that.

Maybe the money from Evelyn is specifically so I can keep Cassie safe from the Department or anyone else who comes knocking at her door to cause her harm. How long can I be her personal bodyguard, realistically? If Cassie gets married one day, is that me off the hook, or is this my life now until one of us dies?

Speaking of knocking, a text message buzzes into my phone.

> Hiya. I'll be there about 7. Thanks for the room again. Cheers, Cassie.

I tap to start a reply, but another message vibrates in my hand.

> Hey Toby. I'm making lasagna, your favourite.
> :) If you're hungry, it will be ready at about 7.
> You can meet baby Toby if you like? Pip x

Oh, that's awkward. Philippa is a great cook, but I can't dump Cassie, can I? I mean, she's not coming to see me. I'm just providing a spare room. Would she be upset if I left her to it and went to Philippa's for dinner?

My phone buzzes again before I can decide what to do.

> Hi Toby, fancy coming over. About 7? Bring
> wine and a smile ;) x

The last one is from Rebecca.

Well, that's an avalanche of women in a short space of time, all wanting a slice of Toby pie. I daren't touch the phone in case another one pops out at me. Jenny, Evelyn, Nurse Rosie?

I stare at the screen for a long moment, but no further female attention comes my way. I need to make a choice; which one of these beautiful women do I spend the evening with?

Do I want to feed my stomach, my mind or my sexual urges?

I'm only human, after all. The choice was made the second I saw the text, if I'm honest. I replied to Rebecca with a smile emoji. Then I organised with Cassie that I'd hand her a key and make sure she was okay. Then, 'something' came up that required my attention, and I would be away for the night. She didn't seem to mind. She may even have been relieved not to have to endure my company all evening. The silence becomes awkward, and I know she wants to press me for more information on how I came to be such a good friend of her grandmother. I can't tell her any more. Evelyn made me promise. It's for her good and all that. But since when did that ever stop someone, especially as headstrong as Cassie, from being curious?

I also replied to Philippa, saying I couldn't make it this evening, but I left my options open by mentioning that lasagna is always better the day after. No sense in waste.

"Hiya," Rebecca opens her front door with a mischievous grin. She's wearing only a large towel wrapped around her and another wrapped around her head, presumably fresh out of the shower. I'm punctual, and clearly, she is not, despite my postponing by half an hour. Still, I admire the view as she wiggles into her house in front of me, beckoning me on.

She grabs my arm, pulls me down and pecks me on the cheek. I feel the heat of her body rising along with a subtle lavender scent from her shower soap. I'm in for a fun night and there's an icy tingle through my body.

"Make yourself at home. I'll only be a second."

I sit down in the living room, easing into the sumptuous couch. Her house is cosy and dimly lit. Easy on the eyes. Everything is soft and feminine. There are no sharp angles or bright lights. No primary colours, only faded pastels and muted shades. No expanses of clear surface or straight lines. There's a plant pot where a windowsill allows it, a cushion or three to complicate the seats, dark shades on lamps, scented candles and dishes of potpourri.

The seating in the living room is not focused on a television, which I find refreshing. There isn't one at all. Instead, she told me last time, she usually watches YouTube on her iPad if she feels like it, but mostly, she reads books. There are plenty of those. In this room, there are three stuffed bookshelves, and in her bedroom, there is another large shelf unit, equally full. A good few of them are psychology textbooks, but there's a significant helping of romance and general fiction. I know she has a Kindle by her bed, too.

The place is nice, easy, comfortable, and warm—romantic in the old sense, homely. I like it.

I left Cassie at my house with a key and an expectation that I wouldn't be home tonight. "Don't wait up." She smirked and rolled her eyes but otherwise didn't seem to care. The fridge is stocked, the WiFi password on a Post-it note stuck on the front, beer, wine, crisps, and bubble bath. I tried to think of everything she might want, even various local takeaway menus neatly laid out on the kitchen counter. And I'm just a call away in case she needs me.

She waved me off after I had asked how was her drive

down, how was work, and how she was feeling generally? I'm genuinely concerned, but I was pushed for time. I asked Cassie to pass on best wishes to Evelyn in the morning, and as before, we tried not to talk about why these frequent visits are important.

Music starts to play from hidden speakers somewhere in the room. I'm startled for a second, but I assume Rebecca triggered it from her phone. There's distant creaking from upstairs floorboards as she presumably gets dressed. She needn't bother. I doubt the clothes will stay on for long if last time is anything to go by. Still, if it makes her feel comfortable. The tease is part of the fun, after all.

Rebecca appears in a clingy, slinky, short black dress, dark eyeliner drawing me in, bare legs teasing me as much as the low-cut cleavage. I resist the urge to shout out 'phwoar.' She sees me looking and twirls around.

"Like what you see?" She smirks.

I stand up and walk towards her.

"Not half."

I move to sweep her into a passionate embrace, but she bats me off after a quick kiss.

"Hold your horses, mate." She walks away towards the kitchen. "I need a drink."

I follow her, an eye lingering on her behind as she enjoys teasing me. I'm sure she adds extra wiggle for my benefit. I can't complain.

"Beer or wine?" She opens the fridge and motions towards a stool at a small island counter. I sit down.

"Beer, cheers."

"I'll stick to wine." She smirks. "Unless you want a Piña Colada?"

"No. Thanks!" I'm reminded of how I met Rebecca and the slimy prick who was trying to date-rape her with a cuff-link full of Rohypnol. "By the way, what happened with Nigel Rapey-Fuck?"

"Not much." Rebecca pulls a stool up on the opposite side of the counter to me and pours a glass of wine from a bottle that was already open in the fridge. White in a screw-top.

"Did you tell the police?"

She hesitates. "I was going to … but in the end, I decided it wasn't worth the hassle."

"Rebecca!" I start, but she waves me down.

"It's me who'd get the bloody hassle. If they even believe me, I don't have evidence."

"Yes, you do!"

"No," She shakes her head. "I escaped, thanks to you. I wasn't drugged and raped. We humiliated the bastard and left him naked in a hotel room with nothing. They would all take his side. He'd make up some story about how I drugged him and stole his wallet and phone. Blah, blah. It's not worth it." She takes a sip of wine with a scowl at the thought.

I open my mouth to object but say nothing. She's right. The only evidence is the cufflinks and we handed them to the barman. There's nothing to say that he definitely tried to drug and rape Rebecca, so there's no case against him.

"Shit. I suppose so."

"Fuck him. We got him back." She waves a hand, dismissing the thought.

"Not enough." Now, I wish we had served some more appropriate justice. I could have inflicted some damage or cut his balls off and shoved them up his arse or something. That's what he deserves. However, it isn't exactly my style to slice up a guy when he's unconscious.

"His profile is deleted off Tinder now, but I checked it the day after and that photo was there. You know, of the lipstick writing. He's fucked. You sent it to his mother!" She bursts out a laugh.

"Yeah." I chuckle. "Smooth move, that, if I do say so myself."

"Not too shabby!" She rests a hand on my arm. Her warmth taking the edge off the anger rising in me.

"Still, I don't feel like it was enough. Have you got his address or something?"

"No, Toby. Leave it." I look her in the eyes, pleading, and she flashes a hopeful smile. "Leave it. Okay?"

"Okay." If my path ever crosses with Nigel Rapey-Cuff-link-Fuck's again, I can't promise I'll be so relaxed.

"Enough about that prick. I didn't ask you to come over to talk about that." Her mischievous grin returns.

"Oh? What did you ask me here for, then?"

"Get that beer down you, and we'll go find out, won't we?"

She raises a suggestive eyebrow and squeezes my hand in hers.

"Right, then," I look down and grab the glass, lifting it for a toast. "I'll drink to that." Something catches my eye, though, and I look back down at the counter. There's a newspaper folded over. The headline is just visible. A word registers, and a subconscious subroutine starts somewhere deep in my head.

DEATH KNELL FOR COMA KARMA COP

A pulse of adrenaline throbs around my body. I grab the paper and open it up, revealing the rest of the headline and a photo of Detective Inspector Ryan Turner hooked up to various hospital machines, eyes closed.

Corrupt Officer's Demise Seals the Fate of a Sinister Empire!

Oh, shit.

CHAPTER
ELEVEN

I KILLED A MAN.

Not on purpose, not by choice or malice aforethought, but nonetheless, I caused it. I ended his existence.

Yes, he was a sack of shit, and he deserved to die, but no matter how I try and justify it, the guilt is a heavy burden that has tormented me since I read that headline. I had imagined that he would be punished for his crimes after the rescue and the truth came out. Imprisoned for a long slice of the rest of his days, if not all of them. I didn't plan for him to die so suddenly at my hand.

I wasn't prepared for this. I should be, shouldn't I? It was inevitable, given the things I've been getting up to. There's a difference between breaking a few bones, burning a few phones, pilfering a few quid from a scam artist, and ending someone's life. Did Evelyn miss something in my programming? I have military knowledge. Shouldn't something in the code cover this situation? Some subroutine that bypasses the guilt mode, a switch I can flick in my brain to cut the constant swirling of thoughts and be fine with it.

Will the cops come looking for me now?

What if I get caught?

There's no evidence tying that attic struggle to me. I made sure of it … didn't I?

Did he have a family?

Did they know he was running a brothel with underage refugee girls to make himself a few extra quid?

How many others had he already tortured and forced into slavery?

Perhaps he murdered plenty of girls in his brothel with his daily drug injections. He had no value for life, so why should I value his?

Have the cops gone back to Jenny?

Has she said anything about me to anyone?

No. Fuck him. It was his fault. His momentum. If I hadn't moved, it would have been me through the window and dead. He wouldn't have shed a tear in that case. He would have danced on my broken bones and carried on his illicit ways. He was in far too deep to just walk away.

Fuck him and his karma coma. He got his just dessert. Fuck him all the way to hell.

Another scumbag permanently off the streets. There's no bad in this.

And yet … the tightness in my throat disagrees.

Why do I care?

The spurious chaos in my brain churns out acid that flows around my guts. My legs ache from the pacing. Am I anxious about getting caught, or do I feel genuine guilt at taking a life? Will it get easier? Who will be next? In this new life I inhabit, there's bound to be more casualties. My head is full of questions and very little in the way of answers.

I made an excuse and left Rebecca bemused and disappointed. I can't even remember what I said. Maybe nothing? There was no way I could focus on her, sexy as she was. The shock left me numb. I couldn't enjoy the evening after that news. Have I ruined our 'fuck buddy' relationship? Possibly. I'll cross that bridge another time. If need be, I can call on my skills to swap any lingering anger in Rebecca for lust. Those emotions are closely related.

I walked the streets most of the night in random directions, letting the streetlights guide me, each step shaking loose another thought, each foot thud on the pavement causing an avalanche of anxiety. I tried a million times to brush the guilt away, but it lingers like the stench of death. Rotting and decomposing.

No. Enough. I don't care. It happens. People fall off roofs, people die, people are scumbags. It wasn't my fault. I saved the innocent girls, and if that meant the sacrifice of one piece of shit, then so be it. The bastard can rot in hell. I did nothing wrong.

The cycle continues, and the chaos in my mind whirls around again. I need a distraction.

"You're up early."

I'm startled from my pondering by a voice behind me. I look around, and Cassie comes into the kitchen with a fluffy pink dressing gown wrapped around her and worn-looking slippers with bunny ears that may have once been white dragging across the tiles of the floor. She smiles thinly and shuffles towards the coffee machine.

"I've made a pot. Help yourself."

"Thought I could smell it." She yawns and looks up at the clock. "Bloody hell, you are up early. It's barely six."

"Yeah. I'm used to the night shift." I shrug, but the movement is lost on Cassie as she turns around to pour herself a mug of coffee. She takes it black, no sugar. But sometimes she likes a cappuccino. I don't have a frothy thing, so she makes do.

I won't mention that I haven't been to bed yet, so technically, I'm not up early at all.

"Date didn't work out then?" She flops down at the

kitchen table opposite me and I can't tell if she's smirking behind the big mug she sips from. Steam rises into her face, and she breathes it in, feeding on the vapour.

"Something came up." I wave a hand noncommittally. I can't easily explain that I just found out I murdered a cop who was running a brothel in London, from which I rescued three teenage girls from a life of sex slavery. Too early for that.

Cassie scrunches up her nose and pouts but doesn't press me for details.

"Sleep okay?" I change the subject.

"Yeah, fine. Thank you."

I nod. "Good." I glance at the clock. "You are up pretty early, yourself."

"Had a bad dream. Woke up, needed to pee, then … wasn't worth going back to bed."

"Fair enough. You hungry?"

She shakes her head. "Not yet. I will be in a bit, though. I'll make a fry up if you like?"

"Nah, you are my guest. I'll make something."

"It's fine, Toby. I don't mind. Keep me busy. Take my mind off things."

I know that feeling. "Okay, if you insist." A thought occurs to me. "Oh, but I forgot to get eggs. I'll nip out to Tesco if you cook, deal?"

She grins. "Deal."

Eggs, eggs, eggs. Why do they insist on moving things all the time? No, I know why; to piss me off, that's why. Probably watching on the CCTV now, laughing, cackling to themselves. Another fool can't find what he's looking for and is going around in circles, getting increasingly angry. Sure, that's how to sell more products. If I wanted to hunt and gather for my food, I would be out in the woods, not in bloody Tesco!

I'm not going to ask one of the acne-ridden specimens that

roam the aisles in their blue uniforms. I won't give them the smug satisfaction. How hard can it be to find a box of bloody eggs?

I go back to the start and perform a methodical, aisle-by-aisle search pattern, turning my head from left to right as I go. This is ridiculous. Do they not sell eggs anymore?

Other shoppers are scant in numbers, but the ones that are here are the slow-moving, utterly oblivious types. Trolleys block my way as they spend a solid fifteen minutes contemplating a box of cereal. Make a choice, Albert, and bugger off. I scowl ahead, hoping that through staring alone, I can clear the path. Shelves that insist on not containing eggs fly past me, up and down, left and right. I even remember to look at the end-of-aisle displays where they hide batteries and odds and ends like scissors and sewing kits. Toothpaste, mouthwash and, on the other side, baby food. The eggs wouldn't be here, would they? I press on regardless. If they have hidden them then I'm not going to be caught out. But they aren't here, and I exit out into the row of tills, all unmanned, just as a fully laden trolley spins out of control from around the corner. I pull back to avoid it, but the listing wheel sends it directly back into my path, and I slam into the bloody thing, sending it careening into the chewing gum display by checkout number seven.

"Shit!"

"Oh, sorry!" A female voice calls out. I find my balance and try not to stamp all over the fallen gum packets.

"Bloody thing won't go in a straight line." The voice continues. "Are you okay?"

I turn to face the voice, which has a familiar tone. As I do, the reason becomes obvious: "Hi, Tracy."

She pauses for a moment, still in shock and embarrassment, but then her face twists into a smile of recognition. "Toby!"

I smile, then bend down to pick up the debris, stuffing it

randomly onto a shelf. I'm sure one of the staff can fix the messy display.

"What are you doing here?" Tracy pulls her trolley back and comes towards me.

"Shopping." I flash a grin.

"Ah, yeah. Of course. Sorry." Tracy flusters.

"And yourself?" I nod towards the trolley. "Hang on. You've got eggs!"

"Err, yeah."

"Where did you get them from?"

Tracy looks at me like I've got two heads. "Just round the corner, up at the end of the row." She tilts her head at me.

"Show me!" I demand.

Tracy squints at me in confusion but then leads the way to the mythical egg shelf.

A box of eggs finally acquired, I follow Tracy to the till.

"You go first, Toby. You've only got one thing."

"Thanks, Tracy." I smile.

She seems nervous, then she takes a breath. "Don't suppose you fancy getting a coffee?" She nods towards the bland cafe area of the supermarket.

"Yeah, okay then."

"I've been wanting to talk to you for a while now." Tracy flashes a sad smile towards me as I sit down with two cups of what might be coffee. At least it was cheap.

I helped her unload her trolley of groceries into her car. Then we came back to the cafeteria.

"Really?" I wonder why, but then I remember the circumstances that separated us. We had random awkward sex on the desk at work, which led me to get fired from Bio-digi. Worth it, I reckon. Perhaps she still feels guilty about it. She shouldn't. It gave me a bargaining chip to get a payoff from them instead of just leaving empty-handed.

Now that I stop to look, her hair looks different. It is shorter, with roots showing through the dye. Dark bags are under her eyes, telling of many a late night. Maybe they have her on the night shift at Bio-Digi?

"How are you doing?" She looks at me, hopeful.

"Not bad." I shrug. "You know?"

"Did you find a new job?"

"Ah, well, sort of." I won't tell her the details of how I made my last payday by scamming a scammer out of sixty grand. Still quite proud of that one. "Pays the bills."

"That's good." She smiles. "I was worried about you."

I raise an eyebrow. "No need, Tracy. I'm right as rain."

"Good." She repeats, then she pauses. After a moment I realise she's waiting for me to ask her how she's doing.

"And yourself? How's things?"

"Been better." She grimaces.

"Oh?" Here it comes.

"Yeah." She pauses. "Me and Ant, well, Ant and I … ugh. He dumped me."

"Dumped you?"

"Kicked me out. Wants a divorce."

"Oh, shit. I'm sorry, Tracy. What happened?" I don't think I want to know, but the wetness in her eyes all of a sudden is hard to ignore. She needs a shoulder. I have a spare one for a while. Never could resist a damsel in distress. A thought occurs to me. "It wasn't about us, was it?"

"No! No, not at all. He never found out about that."

"Right, good." I wait for an explanation, but nothing comes. "What happened, then, if you don't mind me asking?"

Tracy hesitates and bites her lip. "I fucked up, Toby. I really fucked up bad." The tears that had been welling in her eyes now break free and run down her cheeks as she silently sobs.

"Hey, it's okay." I grab a napkin and hand it to her. She takes it and dabs at her face.

"God, you must think I'm a wreck and regret bumping into me." She gushes, tense and red-faced.

"Hush. Not at all. What's up?"

"Well, if you are sure you want to know? There was a new guy at work …"

Through strained sobs and cathartic release, Tracy tells me the story of how a new chap, Brendan, took my old job as the night shift IT guy, and she was assigned to train him. They got on very well straight away. So well, in fact, that they ended up repeating our one-night stand, or more accurately, one-night desk event. Tracy had checked for hidden cameras this time, but what she didn't account for was that she'd fall for Brendan big time and one evening, after a few too many glasses of paper-cup wine, blurt out her desire to leave her poor neglected husband, Ant, to be with Brendan.

She had already packed a bag and left a note on the fridge explaining her departure for Ant to find. She was in deep.

This was a mere three weeks after Brendan had started at the job. His interest in Tracy quickly faded afterwards, and with the demise of the short-lived relationship came a nagging feeling that she had made a huge mistake. The situation escalated. Ant, understandably, decided he wasn't going to take Tracy back after the humiliation of being dumped by a fridge magnet for some prick at work, threw her out and started divorce proceedings.

Tracy has been living with her mother. Brendan left the company and hasn't been heard from since.

"The whole thing is utterly ridiculous. I can see that now." Tracy stammers over her now-cold coffee cup. "But I got caught up in the moment. I don't know what came over me. I was acting like a stupid teenager."

I reach over and clasp my hand over hers. I notice that the ring has gone from her ring finger. "Well, things happen. It'll be okay." I sympathise.

She smiles a sad smile. "Thanks, Toby. I knew you would understand."

"I mean, who hasn't had a silly fling at work?" I give her a wink.

She laughs, then sniffs back tears. "You were different."

"Oh?"

"Yeah, you are at least attractive. When I think back now, I can't imagine what I ever saw in Brendan. He's absolutely not my type. I didn't even fancy him, so God knows how it happened."

CHAPTER
TWELVE

AS TRACY SAID THE WORDS, 'I didn't even fancy him', a bolt of adrenaline coursed through my veins, and my fight-or-flight response bristled. I tensed up. That was a familiar situation. I had seen it before. Heard those very words before.

A woman caught off guard and unwittingly led into something she didn't want. No Rohypnol this time, but something that tricked and persuaded her, distracted and deceived her into a romance that was never meant to be. A trick of the mind. A frequency of lust.

Alarm bells rang.

"I need to get back and get breakfast." I motioned to the eggs I had bought. "But can we meet for a drink later?"

Tracy nodded and smiled through her embarrassment. "Can't imagine why you would want to have a drink with me, looking like Miss Piggy after a mascara explosion, but yes, that would be lovely. Thanks, Toby."

We arranged to meet at a pub. I would have invited her to my house, but the complication of Cassie would be hard to explain.

It is Cassie that I'm worried about. If my gut feeling is correct, then we could have a problem.

. . .

When Cassie asked why I was so long buying eggs, I played it cool and said I bumped into an old friend. Someone I'm meeting for a casual drink later. She didn't flinch. Wished me better luck this time, and after we ate, she went to see Evelyn at the care home. I lay down in a hot bath for a while, pondering on things, but then woke up much later in a cold bath, my skin similar in texture to a box of raisins.

Cassie came back early afternoon. She was quiet and introspective. I asked her how Evelyn was, and she said she was as good as I'd imagined. She didn't want to talk about it, so I didn't prod. Evelyn is strong but also fragile. I try not to think about her impending passing. My brain doesn't know how to process those thoughts.

There is nothing I can do, and the feeling of helplessness is unpleasant, to say the least.

Cassie settled down with a Chinese menu and Netflix as I left the house this evening, and part of me wanted to stay and keep her company, but I think she prefers space and peace. She'll ask if she needs my help.

Early by a few minutes, I'm shocked to find Tracy already waiting for me at the bar. She's made an effort. A tight black dress with a swooping cleavage-enhancing neckline, black stockings, heels, deep red lipstick and rims around her eyes. The dark bags under them that I noticed earlier are now hidden with deft strokes of foundation, and with a heady scent of Dior wafting from her, she presents quite an intoxicating visage. She looks good and she orders me a beer, bringing it to me at a table in the back corner, away from the rabble.

"Thanks, Tracy."

"Welcome." She takes a sip from her drink — some kind of gin cocktail with a straw and olives on sticks.

I get a niggling feeling that she hopes this drink will turn into something more, and a stab of guilt hits me in the gut. I didn't want to lead her on. I'm not looking for a repeat of our midnight liaison in the office. I knew she always had a crush on me, and I should have made it clear.

"I can't stay too long."

"Oh." She sags in her seat, deflating.

"Early start tomorrow." I lie. I make a 'sorry, but what can you do' face. She flashes a weary smile.

"No problem." Her body language tells me it is a problem. Maybe I can save this, somehow.

"You look amazing, by the way."

"Thank you." She blushes. "Thought I'd make an effort, after embarrassing myself earlier."

"Not at all, Tracy. Hey, things happen. What are friends for, eh?"

She reaches over and squeezes my hand but then retreats and picks up her drink.

"Do you want to tell me what happened? Who is this chap, Brendan? Want me to beat him up for you?"

She snorts a laugh. "Will you?"

"Yeah, no problem." I grin. "It would be my pleasure."

She shakes her head. "Nah, you're all right. It was all my fault, anyway. I suppose I got the wrong end of the stick."

"Or maybe he was giving off the wrong signals. Leading you on?"

She shrugs. "Maybe."

"It's all over with Ant, then?"

Tracy rolls her eyes. "Afraid so. I royally fucked that up, didn't I?"

"What are you going to do, then?"

She looks me in the eyes. "I have absolutely no idea, Toby. Maybe I should become a nun and move to a mission in Albania or something." She chuckles.

"Do nuns need much in the way of IT support?"

"Probably not, no." She shakes her head with a grin.

"That'll never work, then." I smile. "You still work at Bio-Digi I take it?"

"Yeah, for my sins." She rolls her eyes again and slurps the last of her drink. "Where else am I going to go?"

I ignore her question. "Does Raymond still work there on security?"

"Oh, yeah. He'll never leave. Not until they cart him off in a box, anyway." She snorts. "Or a body bag. That bitch from HR had a go at him the other day about falling asleep during his shift. It's all got much worse since you left."

"My round. Want another?" I change the subject.

"Go on then."

I go to the bar, order her cocktail and get myself a zero-alcohol beer as I want to stay in control of my actions. I watch Tracy sitting at the table. She takes out her phone, swipes around, and then puts it back in her purse. I feel sorry for her. Her life turned upside down like this, and I have a horrible feeling I know the source of her downfall.

"What did he look like?" I drop Tracy's drink down in front of her and slump into my seat opposite.

"Who?"

"This Brendan. You know, the one who isn't your type." I grin.

"Don't make fun of me, Toby."

"I'm not. Just curious."

She shrugs. "Dunno, really. Just sort of average, you know?"

"Do you have any photos of him on your phone?"

"No," she shakes her head. "Deleted all trace of him."

"Where did he come from? Do you know his history?"

"Not really. Something to do with IT, I suppose. He knew his stuff, especially with the servers. Think he said something about working with various hi-tech systems in his previous roles."

"Did he live around here?"

"Err, I suppose so. Not sure." She looks confused.

"You never went to his house?"

"No, only met him at work."

"Did he have a car?"

"Toby, why are you so interested in Brendan?" She flinches back, suddenly nervous and tense.

"Just curious" I lean back. "You know — about what an average bloke could do to grab your attention so much when you'd ignored me all those years."

"I did not!" She exclaims, offended. "I was just married, and I didn't think you were interested."

I leave a pregnant pause and look her in the eyes, staring until she looks away, picking up her drink as a shield.

"Were you really going to leave Ant for Brendan?"

Tracy screws up her face but then nods. "That's what I wrote, yeah."

"Can I ask why?"

"You can ask, yes. But I don't have an answer for you, I'm afraid. I've thought about it a lot since then — believe me, and all I can think is that I must have completely lost my mind. God alone knows what I was thinking."

I nod. "So you definitely wouldn't do it now, let's say, if he turned up and asked you?"

"Fuck no. I'd slap his face and knee him in the nuts." Tracy snorts a laugh.

"I'll hold him down for you." I grin.

Tracy pouts and I change the subject again.

"You mentioned the servers a minute ago. Was that Brendan's speciality?"

"I don't know, Toby." She seems touchy, so I flash a warm smile. It will take more than that, though, so I focus on a feeling of trust, peace, calm, and harmony. I pulse a burst of wavelengths toward Tracy and then slowly reach for her hand, boosting the signal. She eases, relaxing again.

"Sorry."

"No, I'm sorry. You are only being nice. No need for me to be a cow. Yeah, He was always up in that server room, doing some database optimisation or something, he said."

I nod.

"Vickie was okay with that?"

"Yeah, she thought he was great. She was a bit annoyed when he left all of a sudden. I didn't tell her what happened between us."

"So you are a man down again?"

She nods. "Night shift is cancelled for the time being. Spokane is complaining again that they should move the data centre to the States." She blows out a sigh. "Anyway, enough shop talk. Why don't you tell me about what you've been up to?"

Tracy smiles and curls a strand of hair in her fingers, subtly licking her lips.

The least I could do was see Tracy home after the pub. After I told her the absolute minimum about my life I could get away with, and we downed another couple of drinks, I walked her to her mother's house, kissed her on the doorstep and waited until she went inside. It wouldn't have been a stretch to say I'd have been welcome inside, and into her bed, but I don't have time for that now. Tracy doesn't need me messing with her head. She'll be okay once everything settles down. Maybe I can have a word with Ant and explain that she was having a moment of madness. I've never met the chap, and I'm guilty of shagging his Mrs myself, but I can be very persuasive when I put my mind to it.

That's a problem for another day, though, and I walk back towards my house and get in the car, then head off towards the office of Bio-Digital Pharmaceutical.

. . .

"Thought I'd find you here." I sneak up behind Raymond, the night security guard in his usual retreat in the smoking bunker. He jumps out of his skin and almost, but not quite, drops his fag.

"Bloody hell, you scared the shit out of me!" He clutches at his chest.

"Sorry," I smirk. "All right, mate?"

Raymond takes a deep drag on his ciggy then blows out a fug of smoke. "Well, not now. I need a bloody heart bypass." He looks me up and down. "What are you doing here, anyway? Thought you'd left?"

"Just passing, thought I'd come say hello. No harm in that, is there?"

He eyes me suspiciously. "Fair enough."

"How are things, then?"

"Shit. Same as usual."

"Right."

"Worse, actually."

"Worse?"

"That bitch has put in a camera pointing right over my desk. Caught me having a sly forty-winks and reported me for negligence."

"Who?"

"Sharon O'Neil in HR, horrible old cow. I'm hardly saving the bloody planet here, am I? What difference is it going to make if I have a quick nap? Never done any harm before." He grumbles.

"Oh, yeah. I am familiar with her. I take your point. What do you do now, then?"

Raymond glances around to make sure no one is listening in the dark, empty car park, then leans down and quietly speaks into my ear. "I've got a little secret nest out of reach from prying eyes." He taps the side of his nose. "Bastards aren't going to get me that easy."

"Yeah?"

"Yes. Nice and warm, it is, too. Back of the boiler room. Only problem is I have to swipe my card every thirty minutes on one of the sensors to prove I'm awake. Haven't figured out a workaround for that yet. Bloody knackered, I am."

"Well, Raymond, me old mate, tonight is your lucky night. I think I can do you a favour."

He sucks down the last of his fag to the butt, then flicks the glowing embers into the bushes. "Oh, yeah?"

Reluctant at first, Raymond wasn't sure if he could trust me, but a quick blast of the old reassuring frequencies in his direction and a promise that I'd take care of the regular swiping on sensors, plus his desire to have a good long kip did the trick. I borrowed his jacket, hat and swipe badge and told him to go get a few hours of shut-eye. As long as I kept my head down around the many cameras, no one would know any different.

Just what the doctor ordered. And, coincidentally, just what I need to do a bit of covert research.

The camera above Raymond's desk is having some technical problems tonight, it seems. Somehow the signal on that monitor is showing only static. Odd, that. I'm sure they'll replace it in time, but for tonight it suits my needs.

I do a quick circuit of the empty building, bringing back horrible memories of the many thousands of hours I've spent in this ugly building alone at night. I wander past my old desk and run my fingers over the same old printers, plant pots and cubicle dividers that haven't changed or moved an inch since I left. Not surprising, I suppose. But I have changed so much that to find this place stoic like a time capsule is jarring.

With Raymond's badge, I have complete access to every door. I swipe it over the readers to log his presence, and then I find a vending machine cranking out a cup of nasty coffee.

I go back to my old desk, then look around for Tracy's and

next to it where I imagine Brendan must have sat. There's nothing obvious that tells me what I need to know.

I finish the revolting coffee and walk towards the server room.

When I get to the door, I'm reminded of the transformation that I went through in that small room not so long ago. I went in as a caterpillar and came out as an ornate butterfly, metamorphosed from a normal human into whatever the bloody hell I am now. A Flash Gordon type, with extra powers. Superman but without the flying or the laser eyes. Mind control, speed, languages and skills. It all happened in this room, and this room is where Brendan had been focusing his attention. That, and the tales of what he did to Tracy, make me very suspicious.

I tap the entry badge on the door, and it unlocks without argument. I go in.

Inside is exactly how I remember it. A clean room, kept cool by powerful air conditioning with a lingering smell of hot electronics. Thousands of tiny blinking lights and the constant drone of fans as they blow over smouldering silicon.

Data powering the world of medical research is all locked up in these memory banks.

I drag one of the screens-on-wheels to a server rack, fumble with the cables, and plug them in. The screen lights up with a blank terminal and a flashing cursor. So far, nothing strange has happened, but all my login credentials have long since been deleted.

Raymond has physical access to the whole building, but he doesn't have a network login to this machine. He is limited to the real world. I'll need to improvise.

Tracy would have access.

I type in her email address at the login prompt. Then I'm asked for a password.

I tap my fingers on the edge of the keyboard, pondering. What would Tracy use as a password?

I try 'GameOfThrones' as I know she loved that show.

Incorrect. Access denied.

I try a few variations on the spelling, with zeros instead of o's. No go.

I try 'Brendan' and again, I'm denied access.

Then I try 'TobySteele' With just a little blush of arrogance. Surely not?

Denied.

I add an exclamation point at the end and try again.

It works.

Well, I'll be …

I'm presented with the simple terminal menu. I should probably call Tracy soon and help her through these tough times.

I shake my head to get rid of the dirty thoughts and get back to the task at hand. I log into the admin panel and find the list of usernames. I search for the name Brendan and find a few dozen people working globally in the company. I didn't get his surname, so I'll have to improvise. I sort by date created and scroll to the bottom of the list. Brendan Blackwater. There he is—a fake name if ever I heard one.

Created about ten weeks ago and deactivated just over a month ago. He didn't stick around long, did he?

I pull up the profile and scan through the info.

His home address is in town. A flat by the looks of things. I pull it up on my phone and 'Street View' the area. I know the place. There's a kebab shop at street level and his flat seems to be above it. Handy for a night out.

I note the address and phone number and carry on reading.

Brendan had the same user access rights as I did when I worked here. Not surprising if he did the same job. That means he would have had access to the same databases I did. What was he looking for when he was here? If he's who I think he is, then I have a pretty good idea of what he was trying to find. His history log file has been deleted, so I can't check. Damn.

I go back to Brendan's public profile and tap the link to view his avatar photo. After a moment, it opens on the screen.

"Shit."

My fears are confirmed, and all the blood drains from my body in a sickening shiver. A cold wave of air blows over me, chilling me to the core followed quickly by a film of sweat that covers my body. I feel nauseous but with rage and confusion mixed in.

It's Brian Sullivan from the Department.

Yes, he's changed his hair and grown a pervert moustache, but it's him. The same weasel that dragged Cassie to the middle of nowhere in Ireland and tried to fry her brain. The same little shit who must have run a variation of Evelyn's FSMI process on himself, giving him a similar set of powers as I have. He can put people to sleep, and not just with his boring conversation. And he can make women think they love him, while he tricks them into following him and giving him what he needs. I grab a photo of the screen with my phone.

The slimy little shit was here, at the very site of my transformation, digging into the server. What did he get?

I need to talk to Evelyn.

CHAPTER
THIRTEEN

FOR THE SAKE of peace and stress levels, I decided not to mention the Department activities to Cassie just yet. I waited until Monday, when she was safely back at work, miles away, before going to visit Evelyn in the home with the news. There's no need to cause her worry just yet.

I don't like to burden Evelyn, either, but she would want to know. My brain won't allow me to hide anything from her. Cassie is potentially in danger, as is the entire world, if Brendan, or Brian, or whatever his real name is, has managed to extract the Flash Gordon code from the Bio-Digi servers. My understanding is that the Department managed to cobble together a variation of Evelyn's original code from the broken basics they had stolen from her on the old Cray system. They had decades to hone and develop it, but their code is very much branched from Evelyn's, and a thin, withering branch at that. Still, I can't let myself underestimate them. I know Brian has skills, and he's fine with using them for nefarious purposes. If he got hold of the real FSMI codebase, there's no telling what they could do with it.

I knew I shouldn't have become complacent when it came to the Department. They were knocked back but not out. Still in the game, still very much playing.

Shit.

Yesterday, I walked by the address I got for Brendan above a kebab shop in town. It looked empty, but I didn't get close. I walked by again late in the evening, and there were no lights on. I may have to pay a more inquisitive visit at some point.

The rest of Sunday, I spent messaging Tracy while she caught me up on various other details of her life that weren't of particular interest. I did ask her casually if Brendan had ever asked about me while he was at work. He had, apparently. Questions about what I was working on, mostly. A line of enquiry that could be interpreted as harmless, claiming that he wanted to carry on with the work I had been doing.

Definitely a cover story.

How did the Department know to look here? If they are tracing my history, they must have a reason to do so. Do they know I have the Flash Gordon code? Did they manage to read something in the brief period I was hooked up to their contraption in County Galway? Or did my exploding wheelie bins give away their incendiary secrets? How did they know the old code was stored on the servers at Bio-Digi?

I haven't told anyone except Evelyn about what happened to me.

So many questions, no answers.

I wonder if Evelyn will be able to shed any light.

They must know where I live, maybe even what I am doing now. This is not good.

I also got a message from Rebecca asking what happened to me the other day. I had forgotten about her with all the drama. I replied that I had some family emergency and needed some time. She seemed okay with that, but the messages trailed off. She hadn't heard anything from Nigel Cufflinks, so I think we're at least safe on that front.

The lingering guilt about the death of D.I. Turner still rides around in my guts, rent-free, but there's sod all I can do about that now. I don't think the cops are onto me, and I've heard nothing more from Jenny, so I suppose I'll continue to ignore it for as long as I can.

I should check in with Jenny soon. Make sure she's okay.

"Toby, how lovely to see you." Evelyn flashes a weak smile in my direction. She doesn't like to leave her room anymore, but at least it is comfortable and warm. She motions for me to sit, and I pull up the usual chair.

"How are you feeling?"

She waves a hand. "Like death, Toby." She delivers the words with the slightest hint of a grin. "I'm old, tired, and mostly bloody bored."

"Sorry." I feel the need to apologise.

"Not your fault, dear boy. I'm just waiting, now." She pulls a blanket closer over her shoulders and waits for me to speak.

"I'll get straight to the point. I don't want to alarm you or cause panic, but I have reason to believe that the Department are back in the picture."

Evelyn holds her poker face for a tense moment, then relents and nods. "It was inevitable. How do you know?"

"I bumped into an old … friend when I was buying eggs, and she told me something that triggered a suspicion. I followed it up, did some research and, long story short, Brian — remember he was Cassie's 'boyfriend' who dragged her to Ireland? Well, he has been working in my old company, doing my old job. He was digging around in the server room."

Evelyn's eyes are wide. "Go on."

"The server room where I went through your FSMI process. The exact site of the Flash Gordon transformation."

"I see." Evelyn nods. "Where is he now, this Brian?"

"Don't know. He left the company only a few weeks after

he started. He got what he needed, I assume. He was also seducing my friend. He made her fall madly in love with him, to the point where she left her husband for him. Then he left. Bit of a dick move, that was."

Evelyn's eyes now focus on something distant. She stares through the window for a long time, silent.

"Evelyn?"

She shudders back into focus. "This is not good, Toby."

"No."

"Not good at all."

"Could he have somehow recovered the FSMI code?"

Evelyn pauses for a while again before speaking. "I don't know. Let me think for a moment." She waves me away with a tone of annoyance. I shut my mouth.

Evelyn flickers back into reality. "They knew your name, they saw you in action, they put two and two together and researched your history. It wasn't a stretch to figure out the company history that they acquired Massachusetts Chemical Industries, where I hid the code all those years ago. They wouldn't have known about that, but they did know the code survived and was run, on you. With enough research and data mining, it was bound to come out. Brian then weaselled his way into the company with the hope of stealing the full FSMI codebase. But he won't have it." She smiles and points a finger at me. "The code was set to delete itself after being run."

"Sometimes it is possible to get data back, even if it has been deleted."

Evelyn shakes her head. "No, I took care of that, too. A random dump of data would be overwritten a dozen times over the disk. It should be utter gobbledegook. A self-destruct protocol."

I scratch my head, pondering. "Technology has progressed quite a lot since you set that system up, Evelyn. I'm not sure that would be enough."

"Really?"

I nod.

"Ah. Fuck." She steeples her fingers in front of her. "Pardon my French."

"Let's assume for the time being that the Department were able to extract the code." Evelyn continued after I explained the basics of SSD storage and the tape-backup system that I know Bio-Digi use. "Or at least a chunk of it."

"Okay."

"What does that mean, realistically?"

"Well, they seem to act with evil intentions. Preventing progress, deleting anything they deem to be too disruptive to the world. They'd probably create an army of evil versions of me. Something like that?"

Evelyn shakes her head. "Possibly, but they were after Cassie and her invention."

"Yes. Right."

"So it stands to reason they will start there. You need to protect her, Toby. After I am gone." She looks at me sternly.

"I will."

"This is no joke. You are her only hope against the Department. If they have the full Flash Gordon now, there's no telling what they'll do with it."

"I understand."

"Does Cassie know about this Brian chap being around again?"

"No. I haven't mentioned it."

"Good. But you need to make contingency plans. Preparations, take precautions."

"Okay." I pause. "Any ideas on what, exactly?"

Evelyn raises her eyebrows at me. "You are the hero, Toby. I'm sure you'll figure something out."

"Yeah, right. No worries." I feel like a schoolboy given

detention. "It will be fine. Maybe I should track him down and … deal with him?"

"He's dangerous, Toby. What do we know about him?"

"Well, I know he can induce sleep in someone more or less immediately, and he can make women attracted to him. Other than that, I don't know. He's a pain in the arse, I do know that much."

"Delta waves … interesting." Evelyn ponders, and she taps a finger on her lips.

I wait for an explanation that doesn't come.

"Delta waves? Can I do that?"

"Hmm? The sleeping thing? No, no. I didn't include that function in the code. They must have developed it themselves. Very interesting."

"I wonder what else they have done."

"Indeed. Take care, Toby. You are going into the unknown."

I nod and stand to leave.

"Err, Evelyn, one more thing."

"Yes?"

"Are you sure I can't tell Cassie about … you know, all this?" I wave my hands around and point at my chest. "It would make it easier to explain to her that I need to protect her."

"No, Toby." Evelyn sternly announces. "It would put her in more danger. There's already too many people running around with that information."

"Okay. Fair enough. How about Brian? Do you think I should tell her he's around again?"

Evelyn taps a bony finger on her lips in thought. "I'll leave that to your discretion. If you think it will help the situation, then do as you feel necessary."

I nod. "Right. I'll do my best. Thank you, Evelyn."

"I know you will, Toby."

Dear Miss Wright,

RE: Regretful Decline of Prototype System Development Proposal

Thank you for considering EcoPower Dynamics, Inc. as a potential partner for the development of your innovative prototype system. We appreciate the effort and thought you have invested in your proposal. After careful evaluation, it is with regret that we must decline your offer at this time.

Whilst we recognise the merit and creativity of your invention, our current project portfolio and resource allocation do not align with the specific requirements of your prototype system. Our decision is not a reflection of the quality or potential of your project but is solely based on our strategic focus and existing commitments.

We genuinely appreciate your interest in EcoPower Dynamics, Inc., and we wish you success in finding the right partner to bring your innovative ideas to fruition. Please do not hesitate to reach out in the future should you have projects that align more closely with our capabilities and objectives.

Sincerely,

Douglas Snodgrass,

Director of Product Development.

BLAH, blah, blah. This must be the tenth rejection letter I've received in the last month, all boilerplate text, lies and deceit. They probably didn't even read the proposal; they just passed it on to the rejection bot.

It's exasperating. I know I have something wonderful and world-changing, a fact confirmed by my being kidnapped and some government department trying to wipe any record of it, including my brain, from the face of the Earth.

Well, sod them. I won't be put off. I know my invention is solid and eventually, someone will see sense and help me to build a prototype unit. Once that is up and running in the real world, they can't hide the truth anymore.

A system half the size of a normal hot water boiler could power every home and business, providing heat and electricity without pollution or mess. The only output is steam, and with a closed system, there isn't even that.

I know it seems unreal, but I've lost count of the number of computer simulations I've run on this now, and they all indicate success.

It has to work.

It will work.

But this latest rejection comes with a price I was hoping not to pay. Gran won't live to see my work completed, and that is the hardest pill to swallow.

I'm not stupid. I know she can't live forever, and she is already pushing the limits, but she's always been there, as far as I can remember. Solid, dependable, always had an answer and knew what to do. Gran is my anchor and my mentor. I would be nothing without her. My parents abandoned me, but they weren't much use when they were around, if I'm honest. Gran taught me everything I know, raised me, and pushed me to change the world. I hoped I could show her I had succeeded, but now she will be gone soon, and I can't process the emotions, let alone the gap it will leave in my universe.

Gran has always been old for as long as I can remember, but she seemed immortal. She is not constricted by the normal rules of life. She is something higher, something amazing. She should live forever.

There's no point pretending, though. She's dying, and the bottom has fallen out of my world. I don't know where to turn.

And then there's that Toby chap.

Where did he come from, how does he have such a strong relationship with Gran? Enough that she would write him into her will? He was nowhere, and suddenly he's everywhere. He rescued me from the wilds of Ireland in a Department prison. How, I don't know. He doesn't have a job anymore, and yet he seems to have money, and there's something a bit odd about him. Gran seems to like him, though. She trusts him absolutely. She told me so. Said I should listen to him. If he says there's danger, then I should take heed. He is a bit of a mystery, that's for sure. Confident, brave, strong, and a little bit demented, I reckon. Yet he's gentle with it— polite, generous, kind, resourceful.

He's also gotten to be a bit of a hunk, of late. I think he's always at the gym or out walking and swimming. I won't tell him it, of course, but in the right circumstances, the right light, the right amount of wine, he's a bit of a hottie.

I'm cautious. The last relationship I was in turned out to be a fake, just to lure me to have my brain scrambled. Not something I want to repeat. Not to mention, he's always off meeting some woman or another. I think he's got his hands full.

Yet, if Gran trusts Toby, then there must be a good reason. She is a good judge of character. There's no need to rush into things, though. I should get to know him better if he's going to be around.

He's also the only other person who knows the details of my invention, and it would be nice to discuss my plans with someone. Maybe he has some ideas, or he might even know people who could help to get my prototype built. He did work in a big global pharmaceutical company. They surely have resources.

I pick up my phone and dial Toby's number.

"Hi, Toby. It's Cassie."

"Hey, Cassie." He pauses. "Is everything okay?" He says with a hint of urgency and panic.

"Oh, yes. All good,"

"Right, okay. Good." He seems relieved. "Did you forget something?"

"No, nothing like that. I was just wondering if we could have a chat about … things."

"Err, okay. What things?"

"Be easier to talk in person. Would you like to come to mine for dinner?"

There's a pause. "Oh, yeah. Sure. Okay."

"I know I was just at your house, but something came up today, and, well, I'd just like to get it off my chest. I don't know who else to talk to." A thought suddenly occurs to me. "Not a romantic type thing, just a chat and some food." I feel myself blushing.

"Yeah, I understand. No worries. I wanted to talk to you, anyway."

"Oh? Okay, well, when are you free?"

I hear Toby blow out his cheeks. "Anytime, for you, Cassie."

God, he's so annoyingly smooth. I ignore the flirt. "Tomorrow evening, then?"

"Sure thing. I'll see you about seven?"

"Perfect. See you then."

I hang up, wondering if I've done the right thing. Did I give him the wrong impression? Surely not. I was very specific in saying it wasn't a romantic thing. You never know with men, though. You only have to smile once, and suddenly, they are in love with you.

I roll my eyes. Christ, who the bloody hell do I think I am? This isn't a Hugh Grant movie.

It will be fine. I need to get to know him better. I can talk about my invention, and Gran says he's a perfect gentleman. What could go wrong?

I wonder what he wants to talk to me about.

CHAPTER
FIFTEEN

SERENDIPITY, luck, or just coincidence? I needed to talk to Cassie about protocols and plans, and she invited me to dinner just as I was about to text her asking if we could get together.

Curious. Perhaps Evelyn prompted her to get in touch?

In case of an emergency, I need a better way to be able to contact her or find her if she's been kidnapped again. I know the chances of that are low, but there's no denying that the Department are back on the scene, sniffing around where they shouldn't, and they could easily be planning another heist where they try again to rid the world of Cassie's invention. Maybe this time using the full power of the Flash Gordon skills if they were able to recover the code from the Bio-Digi servers.

There's no harm in having a plan. Failing to plan is planning to fail, as my old Dad would say. So, I spent last evening coming up with some ideas: code words, regular check-ins, and maybe even a tracking device, if she'll allow it. It wouldn't be hard to put a tiny tracker in the sole of a shoe or sewn into a pair of jeans, for example.

She'll probably think I'm being ridiculous, intrusive, and

even voyeuristic, but I hope Evelyn will ease Cassie's concerns about these procedures.

I don't particularly want to know where Cassie is every hour of day and night; that's her business, but I do want to know if she's been removed from her normal life unwillingly, and there's a lot of that about lately.

Short of sticking to her like glue, these plans will have to do.

I arrive at Cassie's house just before seven, as planned. A bit of a drive, but I don't mind. It gave me time to think and ponder and come up with a set of daily codewords for her to post on social media. I've made a special fake account that looks like a band page for a fictional musical group called 'The Heavenly Bodies.' I poached a few photos from a stock photo site of gigs, made up some song titles and lyrics, and threw together a plausible fan page. Cassie will post on this page every day using one of our pre-arranged daily words. If she does, then I'll know all is well. If she doesn't, then I will start to worry. From there, we move up a notch.

I park and sit in the car for a moment, checking that my hair is neat and my breath is fresh. Silly. I saw her only a day ago, but that was at my house, and she was my guest. Now, it's the other way around, and she invited me for dinner. I feel that requires a bit more effort.

I knock on her door precisely at seven and step backwards, looking up at the house. The door opens, and a waft of hot air blasts out, bringing with it the delicious scent of cooking. Cassie appears as beautiful as ever. I realise only now that I turned up without a bottle of wine or anything as a gift. Shit.

"Hiya, you're bang on time." She's casual in tight blue jeans and a long dark-pink knitted jumper. Hair loose, minimal makeup.

"Of course."

"Come in. Food isn't ready yet. Grab a beer and sit down somewhere."

"Thanks," I shuffle in past Cassie and she closes the door behind me. I head for the fridge, but then guilt hits me, and I turn around. "Sorry, I forgot to get a bottle of wine or something. Would you mind if I pop out and grab something?"

She laughs. "There's no need, Toby, I've got loads in."

"Still. I feel bad now. Sorry, I didn't think."

She waves a hand. "Seriously, no problem. You've already saved me loads in hotel costs staying at your house, not to mention food and stuff."

"Okay, but …"

"Shush. Get a beer, sit, chill. That's an order." She smiles.

"Fair enough." I do as I'm told and sit down on a dining chair just outside the kitchen.

"Won't be long now." Cassie joins me, and cracks open a beer for herself. "Cheers." She taps her can on mine.

"Cheers."

"So …" Cassie grins at me. "How was your date the other night, we didn't get a chance to chat since."

"Date?" I tilt my head. "Oh! Tracy? Nah, we're just friends. I worked with her at Bio-Digi. Just a catch-up drink."

"Right, okay." Cassie very subtly raises an eyebrow. I don't think she believes me.

"That's sort of why I wanted to see you, as it happens."

"Yeah?"

"Yeah, but no rush. I'll let you go first, whatever it is you wanted to talk about."

She nods. "Be right back. Need to stir things." She dashes into the kitchen to tend to a pot on the stove. "You can lay the table if you want?" She yells through.

"Will do." I look around for equipment and find crockery and cutlery stashed in a dresser next to the table. This is the same table where Cassie had her big desktop computer before, or rather, where it was before the Department stole it. Now, there is no computer present, but I know she has a new one upstairs. More hidden from casual passers-by, she said. I helped her choose a fast model that was a significant boost to her previous one that got destroyed in the fire in Galway.

I set the table for two, including placemats and mats in the middle for whatever Cassie is making. The food smells like chilli, and my tummy rumbles in anticipation.

"Good man." Cassie gives a thumbs up in appreciation of my efforts. "Two minutes, and it will be ready."

"I'm starving. Smells delicious."

"My famous chilli con carne." She grins. "Hope you like spice?"

"I bloody love spice!"

"You'll bloody love me then once you taste this!" She blurts out, then realises what she's said and blushes. "Sorry, you know what I mean."

She flits back into the kitchen. I chuckle to myself and wonder where this evening will end up.

Over dinner, which is indeed delicious, we make the usual awkward small talk that accompanies all the meals at my house. Mostly about Evelyn and how she's doing. Cassie seems to warm a little as we drink our way through one and then two bottles of wine. I'm still assuming I'm on the couch tonight. No need to be presumptuous.

Cassie pours herself another glass of wine, then catches herself and pauses halfway. "Ah, fuck it." She makes a decision and continues pouring. "Gran says you are a gentleman, so I know you won't take advantage of me." She flashes a grin.

"Certainly not." I raise my palms. "The thought hadn't even crossed my mind." I chuckle.

She squints at me, then shakes her head with a grin. This

is curious. Cassie has never shown any hint of flirting with me before, even after I rescued her from her Department prison in Galway. Strictly business, friendly and casual, but staid and held back. She's a proper lady, after all.

I don't know what to make of this turn of events.

"We need to talk, anyway. I mean about things, not chit-chat. And we'd better do it before I get too drunk."

"Yes, agreed." I wait for her to speak. She doesn't, so I present a palm for her to continue.

"Right. Yeah." She clears her throat. "You are one of the few people who knows about my invention thingy."

"Your water frequency heater thingy?"

She points at me. "That's the one." She may not be **drunk** drunk yet, but she's certainly tipsy.

Another pause.

"What about it?"

"What about what?"

I raise an eyebrow. "The water thingy?"

"Oh. Yes. I've been trying to get a prototype made, but every company I approached has more or less told me to piss off."

"Oh, that's a shame. Did you tell them what it does, exactly?"

"Well, no. I can't give too much away. I just use very vague descriptions of clean energy production." She flutters her fingers up in the air to simulate the energy being generated; at least, I think that's what she's doing. "To get the full monty, they would need to sign a non-disclosure agreement."

"Wise. But they aren't interested?"

She shakes her head. "Not at all." She leans back, picks up a letter from a sideboard, and thrusts it towards me.

I read the rejection and look back at Cassie. "Yeah, that's a pretty conclusive piss-off, isn't it? Looks like they asked an AI bot to write it."

"I was thinking that."

"Sorry."

Cassie deflates. "I was hoping you'd have some ideas of what I could do?"

"Me?"

"Yes, you! Aren't you Gran's fixer or something? You make things happen, don't you? And you worked at that pharmaceutical place ... well, I was hoping you might have something up your sleeve."

"Oh, err, right." I pause. "I'll give it some thought. I mean, I can't promise anything, but sure, I'll help." I have no idea where to start, but if Cassie asked me to get her a mile-thick chunk of the Moon, I'd make it happen somehow. She's connected to Evelyn, and I am bonded to her. My brain won't take no for an answer.

"Thank you. It means a lot to me." She sniffs, and I notice a wetness in her eyes. "I really wanted Gran to see it finished." She takes a breath. "It's important."

"I understand." I reach over and gently squeeze her hand. She doesn't resist.

"Right, well, that's me. Now, what did you want to talk about?"

I sit back, hesitate for a moment, take a deep breath and exhale. "You remember Brian from the Department?"

She scoffs. "Oh, yes. How could I forget?"

"He's back on the scene." I leave that statement hanging.

Cassie starts forward in her seat, suddenly alert. "How? Where?"

"I mentioned I met my friend from work, Tracy. She told me someone had taken my old job, and he was," I realise I can't tell her what he was doing, digging around in the servers for the Flash Gordon code. Cassie isn't allowed to know what that is. I'll need to come up with something plausible instead. "... He was asking about me, digging around in the databases trying to find my files and things."

"Okay, and it was Brian?"

"He was calling himself Brendan, but I did some, err, investigating, and I found a photo of him." I pull out my phone and scroll to find the photo. "He tried to grow a moustache, and now he looks like a pervert, but it's him, isn't it?"

Cassie looks at the photo and shudders in disgust. "Yeah, that's him."

"He's left now. He got a job, dug around in the files, seduced Tracy, and then he left. Seems a bit shady, doesn't it?"

"When was this?"

"A few weeks ago."

"And there's no sign of him since?"

"No. But I don't know exactly what information he managed to get from the servers."

Cassie looks confused. "But that wouldn't be anything about me or my invention, would it? I mean, what info could there possibly be on your old work servers?"

Shit. "No, you are right. It wasn't information about you, but what I'm saying is that the Department is sniffing around again. I thought I'd taken care of them with that big fire, but it turns out they aren't finished, and they are still playing the game."

"I sort of expected it, to be honest. But I don't see what harm they can do just by getting your old emails or whatever. So what?"

I shuffle in my seat. "It wasn't old emails he was looking for."

"What then?" Cassie looks at me expectantly.

"It's to do with Evelyn. I can't say anymore."

"Gran?" Cassie stands up. "Is she in danger? Toby!"

"No, no. She's not. Don't worry." I motion for her to sit down again. "Do you think I would be here if Evelyn was in danger? Christ, no."

"Right, well, what the bloody hell is going on, then, Toby?"

I sigh and take a sip of wine. "Can we just leave it at the

Department are around again, and I'd like to suggest some precautions and protocols in case of emergency?" I don't like to use my skills on Cassie, but in this case, I need some help to get my point across. I pulse out a gentle flow of wavelengths in her direction that will smooth over any doubts she has about what I'm saying. A bit of trust and calm. I focus and boost the signal. Cassie doesn't react.

"Okay. What's the plan?"

"You are still working on your invention, and you are actively going out to companies to try and get a prototype made." I raise my eyebrows.

"Yeah, fuck their stupid Department of stopping progress, or whatever they call themselves. I know my invention will change the world for the better. So, yes, I'm still doing it. They can kiss my arse." She mutters indignantly, gulping wine.

"No, fair enough. I agree with you. But what I'm saying is that we need to be careful. If something happens, I want to be able to help you. I can't be with you twenty-four-seven, so I'd like to propose a system where we covertly stay in touch every day. If you don't make the connection, I'll know there's a problem, and I'll investigate further."

I explain my plan to Cassie, which involves using a fake social media page that she should post on every day. She objects at first, saying she hasn't got time to play spy. I point out that she probably spends a good amount of time on social media every day anyway, and all she has to do is post a single sentence while sitting on the toilet. She laughs but sees my logic.

"Can't I just text you?"

"I suppose you could, but if someone was controlling your phone or making you do things under duress, I wouldn't know the difference. The system I have would be hard for someone to fake or trace."

"Yeah, okay."

I find a notepad on her coffee table and write down the words.

Monday: Marvel
    Tuesday: Tranquil
    Wednesday: Whimsical
    Thursday: Twilight
    Friday: Flare
    Saturday: Serene
    Sunday: Sparkle

"All you have to do is memorise these words, and each day, use them in a sentence you post on the fan page I made."

"Twilight and sparkle?" She laughs.

I shrug. "We can change them if you like, but I tried to think of words that wouldn't seem too out of place but aren't commonly used otherwise."

"No, fair enough. That's fine."

"So you'll do it?"

She sighs. "If you think it is necessary, then yes, I suppose I have to." She sniffs. "Gran told me to listen to you. I hope you know what you are doing."

"Thank you." I hope I do, too.

"So, what happens if I don't post every day?"

"I'll know something is wrong, and I'll try to contact you other ways. I'll ring for a start. But if I can't get hold of you in a reasonable time, then I'll assume something bad has happened, and I will find you." I look down at Cassie's shoes. She's wearing worn-looking trainers. A decent thickness of rubber sole. "Would you object to a tracker in your shoe?"

"What?"

"Sorry, I know this seems intrusive, and trust me, I don't want to be nosing into your life like this. We can get rid of all this once the threat is over."

"When will that be?"

I shrug. "I have no idea."

"Great," She sighs again. "God. Well, right, okay. Put a bloody tracker in my shoe." She slips her shoes off and kicks them over to me. "Fuck's sake. What next?"

"I'll do it tomorrow." I smile. "Sorry."

She shrugs. "Can't a girl just change the world without the fear of being kidnapped and brainwashed?"

"Apparently not in this world." I flash a sympathetic smile. "Now, we need a danger word as well. If you use this word or phrase in any post, text, phone call, postcard, or any means of communication at all, then I'll know you are definitely in danger."

"Oh, right."

I glance at Cassie's hair. She keeps it long and over her ears, but I know that she has at least three piercing holes in each ear. Sometimes, she populates all of them, other times just a tiny stud. "How about 'Lost earring.' If you were to post. 'Damn, I lost my earring walking in the park today.' Something like that, then I'd know you were kidnapped, or in danger, or needed help but couldn't say so."

"Yeah, that works."

"Good. Are you planning to go anywhere soon?"

She shakes her head. "Nope. No holidays or trips planned for the time being."

"If you do, please let me know, yeah?"

"Sure." Cassie picks up the wine bottle to top up her glass, but it's empty. "I need more wine. You want another?"

"Go on then." Already in this deep, I may as well go for it.

She stumbles ungracefully to the kitchen and returns with another bottle. "This all seems utterly ridiculous, Toby. You know that, don't you?"

"Yes, I know, but tell you what, better to be ridiculous and nothing bad happens than you vanish, and I don't know about it for a week or something."

"Yeah, I suppose." She slumps down in her seat and twists open the wine bottle. "Let me see that photo of him again," I show her my phone. "Jesus. That genuinely is a horrific moustache, isn't it."

CHAPTER
SIXTEEN

I LIKE a good kebab now and then. Today is one of those days. Whether this place makes a good one is yet to be discovered.

I got back from Cassie's house earlier today, and hanging around makes no sense. No time to waste, as they say. I need to find Brian and figure out what he's up to.

His flat seems like a good starting point.

I slept on the couch at Cassie's as I reckoned I would, but there's no rush. If things are meant to be, then they will be. I'm fine with it.

I tell myself that, at least. Cassie is beautiful, but she's also Evelyn's pride and joy and only granddaughter. I must tread with utmost care in these territories for fear of stepping on a land mine and blowing myself to pieces.

Cassie agreed to all the ridiculous protocols we have in place now, and she's already started posting her updates. Today, her message read:

> Lost in the twilight whispers, where shadows dance with echoes of forgotten dreams.
> #TwilightMagic #SerenadeOfShadows

Perfect. It means absolutely nothing, but it seems like she's trying to sound spiritual or poignant. "Serenade of Shadows" is one of the fake song titles that I made up for the band page she's posting on.

Today, at least, I know Cassie is safe. All we have to do is keep this up until the Department threat is over, then we can go back to being standoffish and very British and not talking about emotions or desires or any of that messy stuff.

The night once more coddles me in her soft caress; I blend into the darkness and meander, languid and carefree, in the direction of the Kebab Palace.

A grand name for a filthy-looking alcohol soak-up, post-pub-munchies venue in the arse end of town. I saunter in and squint up at the menu, glaring bright above the counter. There's one chap idly staring at a fuzzy picture on a TV in one corner, and another older guy behind in a kitchen area tending to the equipment. Fans blow stale, greasy, hot air, and the whole place is tinged yellow with a varnish coating of decades-old kebab effluent. There's nothing strange about this place. It resembles a million other late-night fast-food venues. At this time, I'm the only patron.

"Yes, boss. What can I get you?" The counter-bloke decides I've had enough time to ponder on the delicacies his restaurant has to offer and beams a smile in my direction.

"Doner, please, mate." I lean slightly to one side. I'm not drunk, but he expects me to be. I'd wager ninety per cent of his normal patrons are shit-faced after a pub session.

"That it?"

I shrug. "Chips and a can of coke. Cheers."

He sighs. "Large or small?"

"I dunno, large, I suppose."

"Curry sauce, cheese, chilli, or ketchup?"

"Bloody hell, just salt and vinegar will be fine."

"Eating in or takeaway?"

I glance around the small waiting area. There's a single cheap white plastic garden table with three chairs around it, empty. I don't want to touch it, but needs must.

"I'll sit down, thanks."

He punches buttons at a till. "Fourteen ninety-seven." He doesn't look up at me.

"Yikes." I shake my head and hand over fifteen quid in cash. "Keep the change." I chuckle. He doesn't seem to find it amusing and slams the till shut, then goes back to watching the TV.

From my previous reconnaissance, I know that the flat above is accessed from a door immediately adjacent to this wonderful eatery. A door marked 'Staff Only' at one side of the restaurant must lead into the same entrance hallway. There's a camera pointing vaguely in the direction of the door, one covering the whole 'seating' area and another over the till. Standard stuff.

I decide to start some shit.

"Do you live here?" I slur, leaning on the counter and nodding towards the door. The dude glances up at me, then at the door. He shakes his head, then looks away.

"Does anyone live there?"

He doesn't take the bait and ignores me.

"Must be bloody handy, living above a kebab shop." I grin.

The dude flashes me a look, then vaguely shrugs.

"That place available for rent? I might be looking for somewhere."

The guy finally tears himself away from the TV and looks at me properly. He yells something in a language I can't even recognise back towards the older man in the kitchen, who is busy preparing my meal.

The other man comes forward and glowers at me.

"You starting trouble? I will call the police." He folds his arms.

I raise my palms. "No, mate. I'm genuinely interested in a flat. Was wondering if the one above here is available, that's all."

He relaxes slightly and wipes his hands on a filthy-looking tea towel that's tucked into his sweatpants.

"Available in February next year. Come back then."

"Oh, so it's occupied now?"

"Rent is paid until the end of January."

I suspect the place is empty, but I would appreciate a confirmation. "Oh, right. Thanks. Is this your place?"

"Yes."

"Could I maybe have a look at the flat?"

He shakes his head. "Come back in February."

"Would they mind if I had a quick peek, do you think?"

"The tenant is not here at the moment, but you cannot enter until the contract is over."

There we go, that's what I needed. "But, if the tenants aren't here, what does it matter?"

"Sir, please come back in February if you want to look. Rent is paid until then. No looking now." He shakes his head violently back and forth.

I back off. "Yeah, yeah. Okay. I might come back in February, then."

He says something to the front desk chap in his language, then goes back to the kitchen and continues making my kebab. I sit down on the plastic chair.

I'll need an alternative means of ingress.

The food is adequate. Nothing spectacular, but what could I expect? It was greasy, salty and vaguely meaty, so I'm sated for now. I will probably regret it in the morning, but these are the sacrifices we make.

I nod thanks to the staff, but they don't look up. A few more customers passed through while I was eating, but not many. Maybe business doesn't pick up until the wee small hours.

I head back out into the cool night. The fresh air cleans my soul and my lungs, and I stride away to an alleyway that should lead behind the building. I glance around, checking for cameras. There are some, but they are pointing away from where I'm going. There's not many folk around. I time my entrance to the alley to coincide with a gap in traffic, and I slip unnoticed into the gloom.

At the back of the Kebab Palace, there's a royal wheelie bin corral chained to a fence and a huge drum of oil or fat or something disgusting next to the bins. It reeks of rotting flesh and I jog on fairly lively. There's a gate in the fence, and I peer through the slats. There's a backdoor to the kebabery, but as I had hoped, there's also a rickety metal stairway that leads up to the flat above the restaurant. I can't see much in the gloom, but there's a door and a couple of windows. All dark. I need to get up there.

The extractor fans in the kitchen should mask any noise I might make creeping around. I just need to sneak up, unlock the door and have a little rummage around.

I go home, change into the obligatory hoodie and black jeans then grab my spy bag, which is an ongoing project I've had fun putting together. Currently, it consists of lock-picking equipment, my trusty big torch plus a few smaller wearable lights, rubber gloves, alcohol wipes, a small but sharp knife, a thermal imaging camera plugin for my phone, a mini pair of binoculars, my wireless cameras and recorder, and an ultraviolet lamp. I also pick up a can of energy drink. Old habits die hard, and my bedtime is all over the place lately. I sleep when I need to, not by any regular schedule, and tonight is going to be a late one, for sure.

I know that the hours of two until five in the morning are

the quietest around here, so I aim to get to the flat around half two. I've got a few hours to kill until then, so I try the usual online searches for the name 'Brendan Blackwater'. Socials and Google come up with nothing relevant. Does that mean the Department is getting sloppy, or wasn't this assignment worth the effort of curating a backstory for the guy? I wonder why he bothered seducing Tracy because as far as I can tell, there was no need for that to get the data he wanted. I reason that he did it for his pleasure rather than any part of the charade. Dirty bastard. He went too far with it, and that was his mistake. If he had kept his dick in his pants, I may never have found out he was here.

My phone buzzes, and I slide it from my pocket. A message.

> I was thinking, and I reckon that if I have to post stupid messages every day to let you know that I'm okay, then you should have to do the same. :P

It's from Cassie. I chuckle to myself and read the message a second time. I pause, consider my response then send a reply.

> LOL. Well, I suppose that is only fair. Okay. Same protocol?

Cassie is typing … I can almost see the smirk on her screen-lit face as she taps at her phone, miles away.

> Yep, KISS.

For a split second, I get excited by that last word, but then I realise what she means. The maxim: 'Keep it simple, stupid.'

She used that same abbreviation in the messages she hid on postcards to Evelyn when she was held in Ireland by the

Department before. She's right. No need to reinvent the wheel. We have a system, so I'll use that as well. If it makes her happy, or at least more inclined to play along, then I'll do as she asks.

I ponder on what I should write.

In twilight's embrace, fleeting shadows weave tales of ethereal whispers.

Good grief. How trite is that? I can do better.

Another message pops onto my screen.

> Hurry up, you've only got a few minutes
> before the day is over.

I check the time. She's right. It's almost midnight, and then the codeword changes.

> Hold on, all right. Give me a second.

I close my eyes and ponder.

> Beneath the willow, where twilight softly grips,
>   a wisp of mystery in the shadows lightly
>   skips.

It will have to do as the clock ticks past 11:59. I quickly type it onto my fake band page and hit submit.

> There. Done!

I cringe as I read it back. There's a pause and then another buzz in my hand.

> Nicely done. :) Now I know you are safe.
> Night. x

I know Cassie enjoys all the cloak-and-dagger espionage stuff. She told me she would often play games with Evelyn as a child where they would leave each other encrypted messages and have to work out how to read them. To Cassie, this sort of thing is normal and fun, and as I have Evelyn's program in my head, it is second nature to me now.

Night, Cassie. x

———

Now dressed in my uniform of matt black, the night truly engulfs me and invites me to her sultry parlour for what nefarious deeds we'll only find out when we get there. But isn't that where the fun lies?

Darkness insinuates something devilish, playful and rule-breaking. Darkness is not a thing in itself but the lack of a thing. The baseline and the default state. If you had a big red reset button for the universe and you whacked it with the almighty godly force it would undoubtedly take to trigger, then presumably, what you would end up with is a lack of anything. Total darkness. Peace at last.

Merely existing on the quiet streets at this hour is dangerous enough, but to relish it and feel the twinges of excitement as I head in the direction of the Kebab Palace from my convoluted maze-like path is decadence itself. Why not indulge my fantasies and take some enjoyment from the jaunt?

I have to admit that I rather enjoy bringing justice to the scumbags of the world, and by justice, I mean the harsh type of justice inflicted by the slamming of their heads against something hard like the ground or a wall. Brick or stone, I don't mind.

The satisfying wet thud. Sometimes a crack, sometimes a gush. Meat slaps, cries of pain, hurled insults, then silence as they inevitably shut the fuck up, ceasing the activities that grabbed my attention in the first place. They are so slow and lumbering that it's almost unfair sometimes. Their game is over, and they've barely grabbed the joystick. Not all of them, of course. There's the odd wily one, the ones with the psycho-eyes that emit a dangerous glare. No empathy, no love for anything, no reason to care. They have the fighter instinct, and they strike back. I have the scars to prove it.

Brian, Brendan, whatever his name is, he has something more. He's got the psycho-eyes, no doubt, but he's augmented and so more dangerous by a factor of a hundred. I'm confident that he won't be in the flat tonight, but there's no need to be complacent. Be prepared, be on guard, and be vigilant.

Once again, at the back of the Kebab Palace, trying not to linger in the festering rubbish that has grown since I was here a few hours ago. Now, all the lights are off, as they are in most places. Only the sickening yellow glare of distant streetlights creeps through gaps and over walls, barely glinting on windows. There's a camera that points down at the back door of the restaurant. I can't see any others, and that one is well away from where I'm going. Safe. I grab the mini binoculars from my bag and focus on the door at the top of the stairs. The lock should be no issue. No light from inside.

I slip through into the yard and to the base of the stairs, then test the first step. Some rust, some creaks. It will hold. I silently pad up the stairs and kneel at the door, my picks already in my hand.

Sure enough, thirty seconds later, the door opens, and I slide through, closing the door behind me with barely a sound. I've been practising.

I hold my breath, pause, listen, and then turn and face into a dark room. There are no noises, no stirring, and no people.

A tiny keyring light on my lock pick set shines around a clean and empty kitchen. It is musty, as an empty house always is, but with a vague greasy kebab taint. Delightful.

A loud buzzing starts, and I drop to the ground, light off.

The fridge. Just the bloody fridge.

I shake my head and stand up again, walking out of the kitchen into a hallway, through to the front of the building. A living room that overlooks the street below. Venetian blinds on the windows let a zebra pattern through onto the floor and up the side of a plain grey couch. Still no people. I glance around. A flat-screen TV that's way too small for the stand it's on, a wilting rubber plant, an ashtray that was obviously nicked from a pub back before the smoking ban, empty on a coffee table next to the TV remote. Not much else.

Two more doors lead from the hallway and stairs that go down to the front door. I step down carefully in case they creak. The stairway is empty save for a front door, the door into the kebab area, and a few hooks on the wall. I go back up.

The bathroom, small with no window, stinks of mould and a taint of sewage. No towels, but a dried-up bar of soap that could be from the 1960s on the sink. The grout around the sink is black with mould and scum. I shudder.

The other room, a bedroom, is equally empty. A double bed, stripped of sheets, a wardrobe that stands like an obelisk looming next to a window that overlooks the kebab yard below. Another Venetian blind closed tight this time.

Next to the bed, there's a small nightstand. I try the drawer. Stiff, of course. They always are. It opens with more noise than I'd have liked, but oh well. I pause and listen, but I'm still alone and unnoticed, it seems.

Like the rest of the flat, the drawer is empty. This may have been a big waste of time. Brian has cleared out and gone, leaving no trace of him or his intentions. I suppose it was a long shot, but I had to try.

I open the wardrobe and peer in with the keyring light piercing the gloom. Empty and stale.

Why did he pay upfront for months of tenancy and then leave with no trace? Did they expect it to take longer for Brian to get what he needed, or was he disturbed by something, taken away for some other task?

I glance around the room again, even shining a light under the bed. Nothing but dust lingers. I move to the window and crack one of the blind slats open a little, glancing down at the yard, which is still empty.

A glint of metal catches my eye on the windowsill. Coins. A little pile of them. They are different sizes and shapes than I'd expect; they are unfamiliar and jarring. I pick one up and shine my light on it. American. A quarter. There's also a nickel, a one-cent 'penny' and some other more exotic coins. A Polish zloty and I think a few Czech Koruna. Then there's a little coin like a polo mint with a hole in the middle. Norwegian, I think. Some Euro coins and some British, all mixed up in an international pile of strange currencies worth less than five quid altogether, I'd guess.

If nothing else, I can probably assume that Brian is well-travelled. Or maybe they aren't even Brian's. Maybe they have been on the windowsill for years.

I put the coins back roughly where they were and take another methodical walk around the whole flat, looking for anything else I may have missed, sweeping every inch with my thermal imaging camera and UV torch, I must admit, for the fun of it rather than any forensic or scientific reason. I bought the gadgets, so may as well use them. Nothing of note, not even anything in the buzzing fridge aside from a bag of frozen peas in the top compartment. I suppose he didn't have far to go if he wanted takeaway. As I said to the lads downstairs. Handy.

I slip out and back down the metal stairs, away into the shadows of the night once more, thinking that this was a bit of a waste of time. Oh, well.

CHAPTER
SEVENTEEN

CASSIE SPENT the weekend in my spare room again, visiting Evelyn for most of Saturday. We had a quiet dinner together after she got back. As usual, she was subdued and didn't want to talk about Evelyn or the situation we both know is impending any minute but don't want to acknowledge.

She asked if she needed to post a message on our fake social page even though she was in the room with me, and I knew she was safe and sound. I pondered on that.

"Patterns, predictions, algorithms and cadence, Cassie."

"Sorry?" She tilted her head at me and sipped a glass of white wine, legs up under her on the other end of my couch while we both ignored some awful rom-com movie about life after divorce.

"Well, the idea is to create a believable narrative that wouldn't raise any suspicion if glanced at. If there's a post every day except Saturday, for example, then that immediately raises the question, what did Cassie do on Saturday that meant she couldn't post?"

"I suppose, but no one posts stupid messages every single day, do they?"

"I bet some people do, but that's not the point. If you do

post every single day, which is what we need for the system to work, then that's a regularity that a 'bot, for example, would likely ignore."

"A 'bot?"

"Yeah. A human, or even a boatload of humans, can't monitor all of the internet for daily activity. I reckon the Department have software robots that trawl the world constantly, looking for things they have marked as weird or interesting. Only when the robot flags something do they look at it closer and then act on it as they think necessary."

"Right, by kidnapping people and brainwashing them, you mean?"

I pointed a finger across the couch at Cassie. "Like that, yeah."

"Bastards."

I nod in agreement. "Bastards. More wine?"

"Go on then."

I grabbed another bottle and poured us both a glass.

"Sorry, so are you saying I do or don't need to post a message today?"

"Err, you know, I can't remember what my point was now." I giggled and took another gulp of Chablis. "Best to do it anyway, to be safe. Yeah?"

"Okay, okay." Cassie fumbled in her jeans and pulled out her phone, then looked up at the ceiling for a minute before tapping a message on her screen.

"What did you put?"

"Nosey! You'll have to read it yourself."

I chuckled and pulled out my phone, navigating to the fake page and scrolling down.

> Lost in the whispers of a serene reverie, where echoes of meaning dance with the elusive shadows of profundity. Serenity, a fragile veil, cloaks the ephemeral essence of existence in a symphony of meaningless beauty.

"Ooh, fancy. Look at you, all ephemeral and poignant!" I laughed.

"Thanks." She stuck her tongue out at me. "Your turn."

"Hmm." I pondered and sank the rest of my glass of wine, then let the alcohol seep into my thoughts, guiding me to a message of utterly pointless drivel.

> In the quietude of existence, serene murmurs a tale, robust in its ambiguity, a whisper in the enigmatic narrative of life.

"There, go look."

Cassie grinned and tapped at her screen.

"Wow. So poignant. Much vagueness."

I laughed. "Well, that's that bollocks done, now we know we're both safe. You watching this?" I pointed at the TV that was asking us if we were still watching.

"Nah, but leave it on for the background."

I nodded and tapped at the remote.

"No dates this weekend?"

I looked up at Cassie with a barely hidden smirk on her face. "No."

She nodded, "Bummer, eh?"

"There's more to life than ... well, you know."

"Never thought I'd hear a man say that!" She raised her glass in my direction. "I don't know if I should cheer or mourn that sentiment, but I'll drink to it nonetheless."

I stuck out my tongue but then held up my glass. "I mean, if I'm honest, I'm tired and bored of it all."

"Bloody hell, Toby. Are you okay? Should I call an ambulance?"

I sighed. "No, I'm maybe just getting old and tired. Chasing tail seems like so much work now." I shifted in my seat to face her better. "Perhaps I want to settle down or something. I dunno."

Those words came as much as a surprise to me as they did to Cassie who looked at me open-mouthed for a moment, then nodded. "Well, Toby, you could be onto something there. Give it some thought."

"Yeah."

And I did think about it most of the night, but I still don't know where those thoughts came from. My mind is not my own anymore. I have imprints of memories from other brains. Evelyn programmed skills and talents into her Flash Gordon code, but what if you can't isolate those things completely? What if, with the skill to pick a lock, you also gain the donor brain's feelings about love, family, pickled onions and chicken soup? Am I still Toby Steele, or am I a legion of unknown people fighting to make themselves known? Those who know me well say I have changed, and for the better, but part of me wonders if Toby Steele of old died that night on 22/2/22.

Cassie has gone back to her house, and I'm left alone to dwell on the nature of self and humanity. It all feels so bleak and pointless. May as well go to bed.

———

I awake with a jump, and immediately, a headache pounces on me, taking hold and wrenching the back of my head off, jackhammering a pain into my spine just for the hell of it. Great, thanks.

A buzzing sounded somewhere and woke me. What was

it? I instinctively go for my phone on the nightstand, but after fumbling with the screen and shielding my eyes from the bright light, there are no notifications. Three fifteen in the morning, according to the clock.

Another buzz, and this time, I can pinpoint the direction. It comes from a table on the other side of my bedroom.

The burner phone.

Shit.

I roll out of bed and stumble over to the cheap phone that's always plugged in when I'm at home. Only one person has this number — Jenny.

I tap on the screen and find the messages. Both are the same.

CODE BLUE

CODE BLUE

"Fuck!"

I scramble to pull on clothes, grab my kit bag, phones, and keys, and I'm out of the house within five minutes. In the car, I punch in a location into my GPS and set off driving. I'll be there in just over an hour. No traffic at this time of night.

I thumb a message back to Jenny.

ROGER WILCO

It seems so long ago now. Jenny and I discussed emergency protocols in case things went wrong with the brothel rescue and subsequent events. I made her remember the codes, practise, repeat, and recite. She knows the importance of sticking to the protocol and that it is not to be used lightly or incorrectly. CODE BLUE is the worst-case scenario. The police are after her for some reason, and she's gone to ground. She'll be heading to a safe location we planned, and I'll pick her up there. She should have put on a disguise of some kind, too.

This is not good.

I drive at exactly the speed limit. I can't afford to be pulled over or attract any attention. The minutes and miles pass torturously as thoughts flood my brain about what could have happened. The last time I saw Jenny, she wasn't in great shape, but things seemed to be going okay. The rescued girls were in hospital being treated, and Jenny was doing what she could, which was not much, admittedly.

Of course, the cop has since died from the injuries, and Jenny was a potential lead in the case. She had given statements already, but that wouldn't stop the police chasing her up again. She's homeless and invisible, but they have ways to find people, hence the CODE BLUE. I need to get her out of there and find out what is going on.

By the time I arrive at the pick-up location my furious brain has calculated dozens of potential scenarios and plotted out a course of action for each path. Multiple three-dimensional chess games all playing at once, moves planned ten steps in advance. I need to be prepared and ready for anything.

I park in the twenty-four-hour supermarket car park, grab a shopping bag from my boot, and then amble into the shop. Casual, no worries. Just a bloke with the munchies.

As I go in through the automatic doors I pull out the burner phone and tap a message to Jenny.

ON LOCATION

I find the milk section and grab a litre carton, then over to the bakery and a pack of doughnuts. I pay at the self-checkout, using cash, knowing I'll still be on a million cameras, but there's not much you can do about that these days.

I walk towards the customer toilets and tap three times on the disabled restroom door, then wait a second and tap four more times.

The door tentatively opens, and I slip in.

"Hey." Jenny, with a black hoodie over her head, backs away as I go in. I close the door behind me and lock it.

"Toby, thank fuck you came."

"Of course, I came. That was the plan, right?"

"Aye, but. You know." I look at her face now and her eyes are red and her face streaked with tear stains.

"What happened? Are you okay?"

A tsunami wave of emotion seems to flood over her, and she launches herself at me, clinging on for dear life. "No, am no okay at all." Tears once again pour from the girl, and I wrap my arms around her and hold her gently, all the while pumping out frequencies of soothing calmness and sympathy.

I let her burn off her emotions before asking again what had happened. Finally, she releases her grip and backs away, grabbing a wad of toilet paper, wiping her eyes, and blowing her nose.

She looks up at me. "Sandy is dead." She croaks out the words, barely able to say them.

"Oh, no. Oh, my god, Jenny. I'm so sorry."

I drive us back to my house in silence. Jenny stares at the road ahead and I leave her be. She needs time to get her thoughts together, and some food, shower, change of clothes by the looks of things. Eventually, she falls asleep and I slow down, letting her have time to rest before we get back. She's safe now, and if her friend is dead, there's nothing I can do for her.

———

"When you feel ready, you can tell me what happened. No pressure, no panic. Yeah?"

"Aye." Jenny nods.

When we got back, I carried her into the house. She weighed nothing and stayed asleep as I bumped into doorways and gently laid her down on the couch. She slept so soundly that I checked her pulse, just in case. Maybe I went a bit overboard with the calming frequencies, but she was so agitated that I had to do something.

I found a blanket and covered her, left a bottle of water next to her, turned the light down low, and went to the kitchen to make myself a pot of coffee.

She slept for a while, and then I heard shuffling. She appeared in the doorway, looking for a toilet.

I found some clothes for her: sweatpants big enough for three of her to wear at the same time, tied up with a rope, and an old T-shirt. She seems comfortable now, wrapped in a fluffy dressing gown. I'll get her some proper clothes later when the shops open.

She had a long shower, a light breakfast of cereal and I made another pot of coffee. Life flows back into her slowly. At least she smells better.

Now, Jenny sits on the couch, and the first few strands of daylight begin their daily climb, burning through the night. Pale glimmers in the sky, but none of them are as pale as Jenny. She's clutching a cup of coffee and staring at the black screen of the switched-off TV.

"I thought she was doing good, you know?" She begins, but she doesn't look at me. "I visited her in the hospital, and she seemed okay. Happy to see me. Aye, she was plugged into machines and pipes and stuff, but she was there again. No like when you got her out of that fucking place. Then she was a ghost. That wasn't Sandy, just a girl who looked like her. Ken what I mean?" Jenny turns to me. I nod. "But she wisnae okay at all. It was fake." She shakes her head and screws up her eyes like she's going to cry again, but she sniffs the tears back. "She wisnae okay."

"Was she released from the hospital? I mean, was she discharged?"

Jenny shakes her head. "No really."

"No?"

"She wanted me to get her out, so I did."

I resist the urge to raise my voice at the girl, "Why did you do that?"

Jenny bites her lip. "I had to." The tears prick at her eyes again, and this time, she can't hold them back. I grab a tissue from a box on the table I preemptively planted and hand it to her.

"How come?"

"It was the same as in that bloody place … different bed, aye, different chains holding her down, pipes and wires, no handcuffs, no being raped every five minutes, but it was the same. She was tied to a bed, and people were poking and prodding at her. She couldn't cope with it. She had to leave. So I got some things together, and we made a plan. I brought a change of clothes for her, a head scarf like them Muslims wear, and I nabbed a wheelchair and I wheeled her out. Plain as day. No one even stopped us."

"What about the other girls?"

"I don't know what happened to them. They weren't there one day. Mebbe they moved to a different hospital or ward or something, no one would tell me, and Sandy didn't know either."

"Wow," I say, somewhat stumped for words. "Where did you go?"

"There's a squat near Mornington Crescent where I've got a few friends. We stayed there for a bit."

I nod. "Okay, you could have called me, you know?"

Jenny looks down at the coffee, probably cold by now. "Aye, well. I thought you'd make her go back to hospital."

She's right. I probably would have. I say nothing.

"Anyway, she was doing okay, I thought. Getting better, eating proper food and all." Jenny bites at her fingernails with the few teeth she has left. "But then the fucking drugs did their thing."

"Drugs?"

"Aye, she was drugged in that place, and then in the hospital, they gave her different drugs. Meant to wean her off, I suppose, but still drugs being forced into her. She reckoned she was good, and she didn't need them." Jenny looks at me with pleading eyes. "She didn't take anything for three days. Totally clean." Jenny pauses and fights back tears. "Then it kicked in — the cold turkey or whatever it's called. She was shivering, sweating, and puking up any food she ate. I said she needed a doctor, but she wouldn't go. Said she'd be fine once it passed. But it wisnae fine. She was having nightmares all the time, horrible stuff. She'd wake up screaming, and she'd push me away when I tried to comfort her." Jenny's face screws up into pure rage. "It was that fucking place, the men who were raping her, the drugs they forced into her, it was all stuck in her head on repeat, and no hospital could fix that."

I have a horrible feeling I know where this is going, but I say nothing and let Jenny talk.

"She begged me to get her something that would help, so I went and found some gear. I know a guy who knows a guy, and he said this stuff would help."

"What stuff?"

"Methadone."

I nod. "Okay." I choose not to ask who the guy was who provided it, or to mention that she was likely on Methadone in the hospital if she was being treated for withdrawal. There's no point in making her feel any worse than she already does.

"I know it was wrong, but she was so sick, I had to do something." Jenny pleads, and I know she was doing what she thought was right. "Anyway, she never got it." She looks down at her hands in her lap, holding the balled-up tissue I handed to her.

"How come?"

"Because when I got back, she was gone."

"Gone? From the squat?"

"Aye. She'd left, and none of my so-called fucking friends had any idea where she'd gone."

"When was this?"

"Yesterday. I found a note she left for me in my sleeping bag, but I can't read it." Jenny pulls a crumpled sheet of note paper from the pocket of the sweatpants I gave her. She unfolds it and shows me.

Я не можу так жити. Я люблю тебе, Дженні.

I look at the Cyrillic handwriting on the page in shaky blue ink, and by means of the Flash Gordon code living in my head, I can read it easily.

"You don't know what it says?"

Jenny shakes her head. "No, I can't read Ukrainian!" She exclaims.

"I suppose not. What happened then? Did you find Sandy?"

"Aye, well, I didn't have to look very far." Jenny's eyes flood with tears once again, and I hand her another tissue and focus calming frequencies in her direction. "The squat is on the third floor of a block of flats, but there's two more floors up."

I feel a wrench in my guts as Jenny speaks. I think I know where this is going.

"She got up on the roof somehow." Jenny explodes into tears once again. I move over and wrap my arms around her and let the emotion tsunami burst from her until she has spent all her tears and has nothing more to give.

Jenny stutters out the rest of the story. She heard a siren close by and went outside to investigate, by which time there was a crowd of people forming. Jenny couldn't see what was going on, but eventually, she was able to poke through the crowd to see the prone and broken form of her friend lying on the cold ground in a pool of blood. Ambulance paramedics and police were all over the scene quickly, and after a while, they took the body away on a stretcher, face covered with a sheet. Police started asking questions, and she grabbed her stuff and scarpered to the safe location we had established. That's when she sent the message to my phone.

"Do you want to know what the note says?"

"Aye, but how?"

"I can read it."

"You can speak Ukrainian?"

"It's very similar to Russian, and I can speak that." I take a deep breath and force down the emotion rising in my throat. "It says: I can't live like this. I love you, Jenny."

CHAPTER
EIGHTEEN

"THIS IS A NICE PLACE." Jenny turns to me with the faint hint of a smile, more sad than happy, but a smile nonetheless. "Sandy will be okay here."

Not knowing when or where the official funeral would be, and even if we did know, being unable to attend for fear of being detained by police to help with their enquiries, we decided to have a private service for Oleksandra at a venue and time of our choosing. We decided on the same location where we had our secret liaison before — Highgate Cemetery, two days after I picked Jenny up from the code blue signal. Jenny is still raw and emotional, and I hope this ritual brings her some peace.

There's no rain today, but the sky looms cold and grey, fitting for the mood. We got here very early to avoid bumping into anyone and them questioning our reasons for being here. The gates aren't officially open for a while yet, but the fence is no barrier.

There'll be no coffin, body or grave at this funeral, but Jenny says that doesn't matter. It's the thought that counts.

I nod and return the smile. "Where do you think she'd be happiest?"

Jenny looks around the old graves, then trudges off in a seemingly random direction. I follow.

After a few minutes of walking, stopping, looking and pondering, Jenny chooses a spot between graves and under the shade of a huge tree.

"Here is good."

"Yes, this is lovely."

Jenny sits down cross-legged on the ground, back up against the tree trunk. I sit opposite on the edge of a low grave surround.

I wait for her to be ready. After all, this is for her. I barely knew the girl, so I can't miss her. There's no denying the senselessness of the situation, however. The whole thing is awful, and the poor girl had a hard life. Maybe now she can finally be at peace.

"I don't want to think about the bad things anymore. What happened can't be changed, and I don't want Sandy's memory to be a bad thing." Jenny croaks out the words quietly and with reverence. I don't know if she's religious at all, but she respects the holiness of this place today, at least. "I know you didn't know Sandy, but you cared enough to rescue her from evil, so I'm going to tell you some of the things I loved about her so you can remember her, too." I nod. Jenny takes a breath and a sip of water from a bottle. "She did'nae have any family left or any friends apart from me. She came here when her home was destroyed by war, hoping for refuge, but instead, London killed her … slowly and painfully. Not with bombs or bullets, but with torture, slavery and drugs." I nod in sympathy, but I say nothing.

Jenny takes out the note that Oleksandra left her, written in Cyrillic handwriting, incomprehensible to the typical westerner. She picked up some small pebbles from an old grave as we made our way here, and now she uses four of them to weigh down the corners of the note. She adjusts them to her liking, and when satisfied they are where they should be, she continues. "Sandy was starving when I first met her. She hadn't eaten in two days. She couldn't speak much English, and she was frightened and nervous. Still, she was so kind and generous that when she managed to steal a bread roll, she threw some of it to the pigeons that had landed near her." Jenny laughs. "I knew then that she would be my friend, and I took her with me and tried to understand what she was saying. It was hard, but we managed." Jenny drops another pebble in the middle of the note. "If we met a dog or a cat anywhere, she would always drop down low and call them over to pet them, and they would always come. She had a way with animals. Once, when we were sleeping rough, I woke up, and two cats were asleep next to Sandy. She had no idea they were there when she woke up later."

Jenny lays another pebble in the middle of the note. "Sandy would sometimes sing absentmindedly, and I had no idea what the songs were. I couldn't understand the words, and I did'nae recognise the tunes. Her voice was sweet and innocent, and when she realised I was watching, she'd stop and blush like a red apple." Jenny smiles and lays down another pebble. "Sandy would hold my hand every night when we went to sleep. I think it made her feel safe — like someone was watching out for her, and I was ..." Jenny tails off, her face wrinkling and holding back the tears that are pressing up against her eyes. "and every morning she said that this was a new day and we should be happy and that I was beautiful." Jenny sniffs and lays down her last pebble on the note. "I know I'm no beautiful, but to Sandy, I was, and she gave my life meaning."

Jenny looks down at the note covered in pebbles in front of her, and tears drip from her face onto the paper. She doesn't wipe them away or use a tissue, letting them fall like fat raindrops, each with a splash. Suddenly, she looks up at me. "Can you play music on your phone?"

I nod. "Yep."

"Can you play 'The Unforgettable Fire' by U2? It was Sandy's favourite song. We heard it in a cafe once, and she loved it."

"Yeah, of course."

I tap on my phone, find the song, press play, and let the tiny speaker sing out into the cold morning.

Jenny and I sit in silence while Bono sings, and the breeze chills the tears on Jenny's face.

"How come you can read Russian?"

After our private funeral ceremony, we stopped for breakfast in the same cafe we had eaten at before. Then, I drove back to my house. Jenny said nothing on the drive and I let her be in her thoughts.

"Oh, it's just something I picked up here and there, you know?" I shrug.

Jenny tilts her head. "How do you just pick up Russian?"

"Work thing," I shrug again and hope she doesn't push for more information.

She eyes me from her place on the couch, legs tucked up under her, clutching at a cup of hot chocolate. "There's something special about you, Toby."

"Oh, yeah?"

"Aye. When you are on the streets, you learn that you can't trust anyone; there's danger everywhere. But I've never felt that around you. I don't know what it is, but you make me feel safe like I made Sandy feel safe. Calm, too. Even when we were on the street that night about to do the rescue, it was weird, but I think it was from being near you."

I smile. "Thank you, Jenny. That's lovely to hear."

"Aye, but how?"

"Dunno, maybe it's because you are a nice person, and it rubs off on me?"

"Thank you, Toby." Jenny smiles. "But that's no it."

"I just have a feel-good vibe, I suppose." I flash a disarming smile and project a burst of trusting frequencies in Jenny's direction for good measure.

"Aye, well, that's for sure."

I open my mouth to change the subject, but Jenny speaks before I can get a word out.

"I'm gonnae go back to Scotland. I know you want your spare room back."

"Oh, hey, what? No."

"I can smell her perfume on the pillow, Toby. I won't ask what the story is, but it's fine, I already made up my mind. I'm done with London."

"Right. But have you got somewhere to go?"

"No really. Well, maybe. I'm going to see if I can stay with my aunt Morag. She's got a farm near Inverness. I bet she wouldn't say no to a wee bit of help around the place."

I never asked Jenny her story, how she came to be homeless so far from her origins. She'd tell me if she wanted to.

"Okay, that sounds like it could be good for both of you."

"Aye, I haven't seen her for years, but." Jenny lets out a sigh. "Mebbe it's a good time to mend old bridges, or whatever."

"You can stay a bit longer if you want. I'll get you a train ticket, pack some clothes, food, whatever you need."

"That would be great. Thank you again, Toby." She takes a sip of her chocolate and then looks up at me with moist eyes. "Mind I said you can't save every girl?"

"Ha, yeah."

"Aye, well, you saved this one." She points to her chest. "I don't know what magic there is in you, but I hope it never runs out, Toby Steele."

CHAPTER
NINETEEN

FRIDAY, 14TH OCTOBER, 2022,
10:15 PM. KINGS LYNN, NORFOLK.

IT WAS FUN FOR A WHILE, curious and almost sweet, but now, the daily task of proving my existence and safety to Toby Steele, my unlikely guardian angel, has become a tedious pain. The word for today is 'Flare', and I'm too tired, too annoyed and too bloody lacking in shits to give to think of something poignant to post on Toby's fake fan page.

He's already done his post.

> In the darkness of night, a single flare explodes the sky, dancing shadows in its wake.

Which is in his usual style. Nicely done.

I forgot to post the other day, and my phone consequently was buzzing off the table at midnight. I could feel the panic even before I answered it, half asleep. "Sorry, forgot. I know, I know … I'll try to remember next time."

I suppose I can't fault him for his dedication. It all seems a bit over the top if you ask me. Yes, I was kidnapped before and almost had my brain fried or wiped or whatever, but I'm fine, and the Department couldn't seem to get their equipment to work on me. Yes, that was partly due to being rescued by Toby, but he only found me because I sent my location hidden in a fake postcard that they made me send to Gran to tell her I was safe. I was as much a part of my rescue as Toby was in the grand scheme of things. He never did tell me how he set off the explosions outside the house that led to our escape.

Come to think of it, I still don't know why their weird helmet thing didn't do anything to me, that chap Ian was getting quite frustrated with it, and that awful woman Cynthia was on the verge of a rage-induced stress heart attack after a few days of it not working. It was quite amusing by the end as those three bumbling fools farted around with all that ancient technology. The whole thing was ridiculous, now I think about it. Brian with his stupid gun. God, I try not to think of Brian.

I won, in the end. That's the point I'm trying to make. And since then, there's been no sign of trouble. Toby thinks they are back in business and up to no good again, which is why he's so concerned. I should be flattered, I suppose. Gran assures me that Toby knows what he's doing. I wish I had her faith.

I do think he enjoys the subterfuge just a tiny bit more than he should, but that's men for you.

> After months of remission, that nasty rash has flared up again and is getting quite itchy.

I snigger. Good grief. No, I can't write that. He'll be showing up at my door with a tube of hydrocortisone lotion. I delete the text and try again.

> Captured a stunning sunset today, its vibrant hues spreading across the sky like a painter's brush. The sun's final flare before dipping below the horizon always leaves me in awe.

That will have to do. I have better things to focus on, like how I can get my prototype built. It's a catch-22 situation; no company will build it without knowing what it is capable of, and I can't tell anyone what it is capable of because I'd probably end up kidnapped again or worse.

I would build it myself if I had the technical knowledge and equipment. Alas, I have neither. Theoretical science is one thing. Knowing how to precision mill aerospace-grade titanium is quite another.

My other option is to make the idea public knowledge. Put it out there for the world to use. A gift to humanity.

I've seriously thought about this, but the problem with this plan is that it will either fade into obscurity, a pebble dropping into the ocean never to be seen again, or I'll become one of the perpetual motion nut-jobs, ridiculed and derided at every opportunity. My private life ripped from me and plastered all over the press. 'Boffins' will be called in from oil companies to shit all over my idea, telling the world why there's not a chance in hell that such a thing could ever possibly work and that they just need to keep on buying coal, petrol and kerosene as they always have. I'll become a joke, and instead of solving the energy problems, my life will be ruined. I'm not going to allow that to happen.

There's no good solution here. I'm at a loss for what to do, and on more than one occasion, I've considered doing what the Department for the Prevention of World-changing Technology wants: delete the whole thing and forget it. Some days, the battle is too much, and there's only so much energy left in me.

It's a shame, but I think I'll put it on hold for now, at least until some miracle should fall into my lap. I don't know what else to do.

CHAPTER
TWENTY

JENNY ARRIVED SAFELY in Scotland and was met with open arms by her aunt. I made sure she let me know she was okay when she arrived. A tearful reunion, by all accounts. They have much catching up to do, and I feel like a weight has been lifted from me. I no longer need to worry about her welfare while she's sleeping rough and trying to avoid police and general trouble. I don't know what family rifts there are that need mending, but this has to be a good start down the road.

Jenny will never forget her friend Oleksandra, nor should she, but I hope her wounds heal with time.

The only solace I can take from the experience is that justice was served on the ring leader of the sex trafficking brothel, and Detective Inspector Turner will never enslave any more girls from his miserable grave.

I shake the thoughts away because in the dark corners of my mind lie emotions I can't weigh myself down with. Anger and bile rise in me, and woe betide any scumbags that get in my way tonight.

Cassie isn't down this weekend as there's a green energy conference at the Myatt Hotel here in town next week, so she's coming for that with work and staying in the hotel instead. I said she could still stay at mine, but she said something about me running out of hospitality if she used it all up too quickly. I said don't be silly, but maybe she wants a bit of luxury and to be at the venue. She's presenting their company for the first time, and I think she's a bit nervous. When she told me, I remembered the scam I pulled on her boss, Rachel Hazlewood, where I said I'd met her at some other conference and then got her into bed with my frequency harmonising skills. It brought a grin to my face, but I haven't let on to Cassie how I came to know her boss. Rachel thinks my name is Paul or something and I promptly disappeared from her radar soon after I woke up the day after.

I didn't want to hump and dump, but Evelyn made me do it!

Okay, I have to admit, it was quite fun, but normally, I'm not that kinda guy. I hope that Rachel isn't coming to the conference with Cassie. I don't want to ask in case it opens a can of worms.

Tonight, I'm back on my regular patrols around the town. I have been lax of late, keeping an eye on local scumbags with all the other things going on, but it's good to keep watch close to home, just in case the vermin start to build up.

The night wraps around me, and a light breeze flares the end of my long black coat behind me as I walk with purpose ahead along my route. Hands stuffed into pockets, eyes open, I take in the dimly lit world and observe, soaking up the frequency of the town. I smell fear, taste danger, and listen for suffering.

I pass the closed shops, open takeaways, noisy pubs and quiet residential streets that have become my pattern. I walk, and the world behaves itself. I keep walking.

Part of me yearns for a toe rag to show himself and start trouble so I can vent my pent-up anger in an explosion of deserved violence. Another part wonders why I'm still doing these patrols in this town. Why haven't I ditched the place and moved away? No, I know why — I'm tethered by the responsibilities of the Flash Gordon project code in my brain. I can't leave Evelyn when she's close to her end, and I can't leave Cassie when the threat of the Department is still warm and lingering. So here I am, doing my bit for the good of humanity. Not that many of them deserve it. I do it because I have no other choice. Scumbags do their part, so I have to do mine.

I duck into a busy pub where the bar is four-deep, trying to get served. A sea of young pricks with trendy hair and bright-coloured clothes trying to impress girls with thick makeup and skimpy outfits, congregating in groups all vying for dominance in their mating ritual. Music, if you can call it that, blasting so loud the bass is throbbing in my chest.

I did it in my time, I suppose, but now the thought of it makes me retch. So many people, so loud and drunk, so much danger all compressed into a small area, like a landmine ready to explode, blowing off limbs in all directions.

In my day, I would have been the lad who escaped outside at the earliest opportunity, avoiding the throng and yet still trying to soak up some of the ambience. Gigs are different. You are there for a good reason. This feels like mindlessness and fake excitement. All these kids are desperate for a memorable 'good night' that they can brag to their mates about later.

My social tolerance is low at best, and in this place, I've already used up my daily allowance within a few seconds. My body wants to escape, but I force myself to do a round of the place, making sure nothing nefarious is going down. I get to the doorway to the stinking toilets and try not to breathe as

I take the opportunity for a slash, listening for any bad guys or dodgy goings on.

There's nothing, though, apart from a couple of lads who reckon they are in with two girls. One look at their floppy hair makes me doubt their chances, or maybe I'm wrong, and the teen girls of today desire this sort of lewd stick-boy waster?

Gladly, I exit the pub and do the same tour in another one further down the street. Less busy with an older crowd. Sport on the multitude of TVs on every wall instead of loud pop music.

Dry and thirsty, I stop at the bar and order a Coke, then neck it in two gulps. I crunch an ice cube, glance around the lounge, decide these folks are safe enough, and move on, nodding a goodbye to the barmaid and returning to the street, where the night has chilled another degree and a fine drizzle wets the air.

Next is a back street that's painted dark grey by the night and moisture. Colour would be sparse during the day, but now it is utterly absent. Desaturated and bleak. Behind the thin veneer of high street glamour, the access roads and stinking bins are desolate of life. Hidden in plain sight from the public who choose to ignore these roads. These are always good places to hunt for scumbags and ne'er-do-wells who would gladly take money from anyone looking for a chemically induced good time. Occasionally, you'll find a couple standing up against a cold wall engaging in oral pleasures, but none tonight. No dealers, no drunks lost their way, no tramps crouching behind a scrub of bush, excreting their discarded burger meal. I walk on, glad of the cool night to soak away the fever of my anger.

This grey street leads to a grey multi-storey car park that spirals out of the ground, ugly and towering, but I know from previous visits that the top floor, open to the elements, affords a view over a chunk of town. I've stood and observed many times, taking in the frequencies of the tiny people passing by at street level below.

The car park backs onto the Myatt Hotel, where Cassie will be staying soon for her conference. She'll probably park her car in here. I climb the flights, avoiding the lift, bouncing silently up the concrete steps until I reach clean air and another degree taken off the ambient temperature. Not a soul exists within the cold walls. I'm alone in the vast echo chamber, and the silence reverberates around me. Cameras are only on the ground floor and I have a feeling they are broken; I get no vibrations from them.

Out on the roof, there are barely any cars — five in total, probably left over from when the place was busier, as they are haphazard, spread over the lot. I walk to the far edge corner where I usually stand, leering over the streets below.

From here I can see the effluent spilling out from pubs and clubs, restaurants and taxis. People, doing their thing, enjoying their weekend night out. A distant siren and flashing blues pass one way, and a plane passes overhead, invisible in the night but audible up here on the roof away from the crowds. I pause for maybe five minutes, watching and waiting, feeling and listening, allowing my mind to drift and swirl on the wind to thoughts I'd rather not harbour. I shake my head to be rid of them, but they itch and fidget, competing for attention. I focus on the evening and the people below who run like ants after a nest disturbance.

After too long, there's no suffering in the portion of the world under my gaze that I can discern, so I turn to go, onwards on my route, back the way I came now towards home. Another night passes without incident, and I can relax a little, knowing I've at least tried.

I walk the long edge scenic route of the lot back to the stairs and down the concrete steps.

On the landing of floor three, I freeze instinctively. A sound, a feeling of something wrong, goosebumps on my neck. I listen. The sound, again, muffled through the doorway into the parking lot on this floor. A cry? I move to the door and risk a glance through the meshed glass pane. Can't see anything interesting. I pause behind the door, pushing it open a crack with my steel-toe boot. I wait.

There. A voice now. Male, harsh, and a female cry. I push open the door and glide through, crouching behind a car near the doorway. The conversation is distant, but now the echoes carry it to me and I make out the phrase *'have a bit of fun'* in a coarse accent, then a whimper. I glance up over the car roof towards the sounds. Far on the other side of the car park. Three cars between me and them. But I can't yet see who they are, only a shadow creeping around a corner. I dart to the next vantage point — a large SUV, keeping low, staying off the painted walkway in case my shoes squeak. I pause in the shadow of the bulky vehicle and plan my next run. There's another cry and then a scuffle, I bolt to the next car, crouch and now I can see figures reflected in another car window. Dark shadows only, but there's no mistaking the danger. I risk a peek over the bonnet and note two men taunting a woman, held down by a third thug bent down over an open car boot. All this in a split second, now adrenaline pulses through me, rage and panic rising, but I breathe, pause, and plan my attack.

Thug One has his back to me, and he is busy keeping the woman; blonde, heels, long coat, held down. Arms pulled up her back.

Thug Two holds what must be the woman's handbag, and he's rifling through it.

Thug Three leers at the protruding rear of the woman and approaches it with obscene gestures.

I'm close now, but I remain invisible. I plot.

Seven cars are in the area, including the one the woman is being forced into; all are fairly modern. The escape route is behind me, but there may be an exit close by, only on this floor, to this corner of the car park, an entry to the hotel.

Three lumpen thugs and me, Flash Gordon enhanced Toby Steele.

Piece of piss.

I could do with a distraction, though.

I focus as another whimper comes from the car and a snarling, debauched wolf whistle from Thug Three as he lifts the coat and skirt of the woman, revealing her stockinged legs. I focus again, feeling the energy and wavelengths, prodding and poking, adjusting and tweaking until it all knits together, and chaos pours from me in an exploding torrent of invisible frequencies.

The result is immediate as the alarms of six of the seven cars suddenly blast out their manic screeches. Even I'm shocked by the violence of the attack on my ears, crouching behind one of the cars that's angrily flashing and yelling for attention.

I shuffle back and risk another peek. The group are now spooked, ducked down as if expecting weapons fire. Thug One is no longer pulling the woman's arms up her back. Instead, he grips her legs from his crouch on the floor.

Thug Two has dropped the bag and has already started to edge away towards my direction, low on all fours. Thug Three is with Thug One, hiding.

Two pokes his head around the edge of my hiding place and receives my waiting boot to the side of it for his trouble. He falls with a wet slap to the concrete, blood immediately pooling around him. I back away, and his thug brothers move towards him, leaving the woman now they have a bigger problem. The alarms screech all the while, and I sneak around the car in the afforded noise cover. Shadows flickering from the flashing headlights. Thugs One and Three reach their downed compadre and bend down, attempting to lift him, but then wince and pull back when they see the blood. Their first aid will have to wait, though, as I apply the same vigorous boot to the back of one knee, toppling the owner with a wretched tearing sound, and then as the other thug turns to finally see his silent assailant, I bring up my knee into his chin, clattering teeth and tongue with a hollow chomp sound that echoes around the concrete chamber even over the blaring alarms. Head lolled back with a yowl, he recovers and spits blood and possibly a tooth or three, then moves to stand up, hands clutching at his face. I back up a pace, take a breath, spin and thrust the same trusty boot once more with a three-sixty pirouette and perfectly timed kick, this time at the unprotected forehead of leery Thug Three. He goes down on top of writhing Thug One and bleeding Thug Two, making a nice tidy pile of scumbags. I stand back, admiring my handi-work, waiting for signs of revenge. For a few peaceful seconds, assuming you don't count the still blaring alarms — for all this has taken less than a minute, the trio lounge in their reclining positions, seemingly happy to linger. I take the opportunity to pull out my hefty, powerful metal torch and shine it at the pitiful pile. They stir. I risk a turn to check the woman. She stands staring like a rabbit in headlights, but she seems unharmed. I turn back, and the thugs begin a shuffle.

"He's fucking killed him!" Thug One cries, presumably meaning the chap on the ground with blood leaking from his head. I doubt it, but there's always the possibility, I suppose. Oops.

Thug Three reaches for a slack wrist, "Nah, he's got a pulse." He retorts somewhat clumsily and slurred through his bloodied mouth, lacking a few teeth that now litter the car park.

I keep watch and stay silent, shining my light of justice, and focusing on sending out frequency waves of terror towards the twats. Do not fuck around with Toby Steele.

They carefully get to their feet, briefly looking towards me but flinching away from the extremely bright light.

Awkwardly and with a cry of pain from the lad with the torn ligaments in his knee, they pull the unconscious chap up and limp, not very far, to the car that I was hiding behind. The alarm of that car silences with a blip and they open the doors, shoving the guy into the back seat. I back away, still keeping my light focused on them. They could have a gun in the car. I find the woman, still open-mouthed and staring, and in one fluid motion, I grab the bag from the floor, take her hand and lead her to the hotel entrance that is indeed only feet away around a corner from where she's standing. The screaming alarms still ring but are dulled now in the plush welcome arms of the hotel lift lobby. The roar of an engine and screech of tyres signal the three stooges have departed, stage left.

I turn to the woman.

"What just happened?" She blurts out in a Nordic accent. Swedish or Norwegian. "Who are you?"

"Name's Toby. Are you okay?"

"Err, yes, I … I think so. Oh, my god. You saved me. Thank you!"

"All part of the service." I flash a smile and take in for the first time the intense, smouldering beauty of the woman I've just helped. Long blonde hair with salon-finished ringlets cascading from her perfect face, golden brown, finer temptress, with flushed cheeks. She's shaking from the fear and adrenaline, clutching at her bag that I hand her. "I think you could do with a drink."

"Yes, drink." She nods.

"What's your name?"

She's still staring at the car park doorway and suddenly jolts from her torpor and looks at me. "What? Oh, sorry. Yes, my name is Lorelei."

"I thought this was a good hotel!" Lorelei exclaims as we sit down at the back of the luxurious bar in seats that threaten to consume us. I got us both a shot of bourbon, it seemed appropriate, and her a glass of white wine, me a Belgian ale. She realised at the lobby the reason she was out in the car park at this late hour; she was fetching a bag from her rental car. The thugs appeared out of nowhere, she said, then all of a sudden, she was surrounded, and they snatched her bag and had her head shoved into the open boot where she had been pulling out a suitcase. That case now sits at the side of the low table between us, retrieved by yours truly as I shut her rental car boot and made sure the thugs had gone, leaving behind only some bodily fluids and the odd tooth. "I should call the police?" She looks at me inquiring.

I scoff, "If you think it will do any good." In my haste, I didn't pay any attention to the license plate of the car. "Did they take anything from your handbag?"

Dazed, she seems to only now remember the bag. "Oh, shit. My phone." She delves into the depths of her bag and then pulls out the phone. "No, thank god." Then she pulls out a small purse and opens it up. Cash, credit cards. It seems all is well. "They took nothing." She shrugs. "You stopped them in time." She smiles beautifully in my direction, and a warmth rushes over me.

"It was my pleasure." It was a bit of excitement, now I think about it. A relief of tension and anger. I feel calmer now. Warm and fuzzy. The woman opposite me takes a sip of her bourbon and screws up her face but then knocks it back.

"Skål!" She raises the glass at me.

I pick mine up and repeat her action. "Skål, indeed."

A puzzled look flashes over her pretty face. "How did the car alarms all trigger like that?" We had left them ringing out their tortured shrieks. Two had stopped on their own by the time I collected the suitcase, leaving only the stragglers singing their shrill tones. I assumed someone would attend to them presently.

I shrug. "Don't know, maybe an earthquake?"

Her eyes widen. "What? Are those common here?"

I shake my head with a grin. "Not really."

"And how did you do that to all those men so quickly?" Her English is excellent, but that melodic tone of Nordic origin is strangely appealing. Mixed with her striking looks and blonde locks that could have come from a shampoo commercial standing under a waterfall, she's quite intoxicating, or is it the warmth of the bourbon?

"I just got lucky, I suppose." I shrug. "Another drink?"

Lorelei Johannessen
GrønnEnergi Bærekraft Løsninger AS
Spesialist innen grønne energiløsninger
Specialist in Green Energy Solutions
Felleveien 42, 0191 Oslo, Norge
ljohannassen@gebl.no
+47 815 14 525

LORELEI GAVE me her business card and said, in her gentle, melodic Nordic tone, that perhaps I could meet her for dinner the following evening as a token of her thanks for my help with the thugs — her treat. Of course, I agreed. Why wouldn't I? I'd have to be a madman to turn down an offer like that. A Norse goddess wishing to shower me with appreciation. Possibly even in a shower? No, let's not get ahead of ourselves.

Goddess Freyja, now Lorelei in human form, radiating beauty like a lighthouse shining into a misty night.

She's here for the same conference that Cassie is attending. How coincidental, how convenient, how complicated.

She had only just arrived in town hours before and checked into the hotel, only to be met with such danger and trauma. I hoped the attack didn't ruin her experience. She assured me she was tough enough to take it in her stride but grateful that I saved her from who knows what disaster. They caught her off guard. Normally, she would have stood her ground. Three burly — if somewhat useless — blokes against one delicate Norse beauty. I had my doubts about how effective she could have been.

Norwegian, not Swedish.

Coincidentally, it is one of my languages, but I haven't admitted to that just yet. There is no need to give the game away immediately; I prefer to be mysterious.

I'm intrigued.

I left her safely at her room door; she was nervous about walking alone so soon after the events of the evening, and unexpectedly, she embraced me in a tight hug before scanning her room card and coyly waving good night, leaving me with her dissipating warmth and perfume in the carpet-padded corridor.

I went back up to the scene of the attack after that, checked her rental car, the blood stain on the cold concrete, the skid marks of the escaping tyres, presumably in the direction of a hospital as the trio of would-be rapists fled the scene. No doubt they wouldn't have been satisfied with cash and phone alone. Not three of them, dressed as they were in camouflage of black. It happened very quickly, and they were as generic a thug as you might expect. Shaven heads, thick necks, ugly faces. They could be cloned from the thug-making machine, and no one would think it strange. It seems more like a planned attack, not a casual opportunistic bag theft. That seems worrying.

It didn't go unnoticed that Lorelei works in the same area, possibly even the same job role as Cassie. Her Norwegian counterpart. I suppose that isn't much of a coincidence, given the conference here is all about green energy. There must be dozens, if not hundreds, of delegates here, all in the same field. That's the point, after all. Still, it makes me ponder: is she another target of nefarious Departments?

I glance at my reflection in the mirror behind the hotel bar, swipe a hand through my locks, adjust my shirt, scan the room behind me and order a beer to smooth the way. I'm a bit early, waiting to meet the lovely Lorelei for our dinner date. Date or just a thank you dinner? We'll see. I cleaned up for this. She feels like a posh date, elegant and professional but dripping with coquettishness and sultry glances. I couldn't stop thinking about her all day. The thugs, too, but with a different emotion. For a moment, I wondered if I had killed the first chap to go down. It seems my booted kick is more powerful than I realised. Must be all the swimming. The thing that troubles me, though, is that I absolutely didn't care if he was killed. It was justice served, as far as I knew, and if people are going to start shit near me, then they should expect to receive my violent wrath. It would have been an inconvenient mess, but I had no remorse. I've become cold and detached, and I'm unsure if I like that about the person I have become.

In the heat of action, when they surely wouldn't have spared me, I acted in the best way I could. Maybe he will still die from the injury like the brothel cop did. Maybe it serves him right, and another scumbag is taken out of action. Still, I'm not a killer, not even a violent man, but I have become one.

The programming that lives in my head has changed 'me' for better in many ways, but perhaps also for worse.

My beer arrives, and I sip slowly, pondering and nursing, tracing the beads of condensation down the ice-cold glass with my finger.

· · ·

"Hi!" I turn on my barstool to the smiling and delicately beautiful face of Lorelei Johannessen. Her perfume immediately surrounds me in pheromones, and the dangling necklace on her low-cut chest sparkles in the dim bar light, drawing me to her bosom. Her hair flows like golden honey and conjures up daydreams of slow motion running along the edge of a white sanded beach, culminating in rampant passionate entanglement under an overhanging cliff, as the azure waves crash around us. Her dress is dark red and both loose and clingy in all the right places. She's slender and petite, and matching red heels bring her to easy kissing height. She dazzles with simple allure, and I'm genuinely stunned for a moment. I stand and approach, not knowing the etiquette in these situations, but she saves me with a triple-cheek kiss and a gentle embrace. I sway in the heady stupor of her beauty and lose myself again in daydreams of wild passion. She's only said one word. Pull yourself together, Toby.

"Hello," I manage, about as smooth as sandpaper. What is wrong with me? I'm usually Bond-like in my demeanour around women. This gorgeous creature has knocked me off kilter. "Would you like a drink?"

"Yes, please. White wine." She puts down a tiny purse — different from the one she had last evening — and a phone on the bar, then sits on the stool next to mine. I flop back down and wave to the barman.

"So, my knight in, err, shining black armour," she tinkles a laugh, "it's lovely to see you again, Toby. Hopefully under better circumstances tonight, yes?"

"The pleasure is mine, Lorelei, and yes, I agree, better circumstances."

"You know, I almost went home this morning after thinking all night about what happened. It isn't worth being killed for a business conference. But then I remembered our dinner, so I couldn't leave you after what you did. I'm so grateful."

"Well, thank you. I'm glad you did. I would understand if you didn't want to stay here, though."

She waves a hand. "I'm over it now. And I have you to protect me, don't I?" A coy smile over the top of a sip of wine, naughty eyes, a twist of those golden locks with her free hand.

"You do." I admit, "No one will hurt you while I am around."

She reaches over and runs a hand down my arm. "Thank you. I can't believe how you dealt with those guys so quickly."

I shrug. "No problem. They were stupid, slow bullies."

"Well, I am impressed." She smiles again, and butterflies flutter in my stomach. "It is lucky you were there. Are you staying here for the conference, too?"

"Oh, no. Not at all. I live nearby. I'm not staying in the hotel or attending the conference."

"Really? But I thought the car park was just for the hotel?"

I chuckle. "It is, but I like the view from the top floor. I happened to be passing, I suppose."

She laughs. "You are funny, Toby."

"If you say so." A thought occurs to me. "Did you call the police?"

She waves a hand. "No, what was the point? I didn't see their faces much; it was dark, and we didn't get the car number. I don't think there were any cameras. Nothing was stolen …" She shrugs. "It would be more work than good."

I nod. "Yeah, I take your point." And I served justice in my particular way. The likelihood is that they won't come back to this car park again. Well, unless they come back specifically to shoot me or something. Cross that bridge when I get to it.

"So, what do you do?" She pauses. "I mean, when you aren't saving damsels in distress." That coy smile again.

When I'm not saving damsels in distress … well, not much, if I'm honest. That seems to be a big part of my life lately. "This and that, you know. I was in IT, but I'm taking a break for a while."

"A tech guy? Good to know." She grins.

"You could say that," I chuckle inside at the thought. I am a tech guy. Brain-flashed, I had my firmware upgraded. It's a field-upgradeable unit. Dynamic over-the-air updates from a long-forgotten program, written by a genius woman locked away in a government facility. She had the foresight to hide her work from evil eyes and hands, and I'm the accidental child of decades of research. A tech guy, for sure.

"I don't feel like going out, now we are here. Because of … you know. Would you mind if we have dinner in the hotel?"

I shrug. "Sure. That's fine with me. Never been here before. Looks fancy."

"I'm glad work is paying, that's for sure." She grins. "Are you hungry?"

"Starving, now you come to mention it."

Over dinner, Lorelei talks about her work and the conference here, and I'm surprised at just how similar her job is to Cassie's. I wonder if I should introduce them, but so far, I haven't mentioned it. I enjoy listening to her voice and accent, and as the delicious food is washed down with fine wine, I feel a warmth glowing in me. I'm drawn to this beautiful woman. I mean, why wouldn't I be? She's smart and witty as well as stunningly good-looking. She seems kind and well-mannered, gentle and calm. Her grey-blue eyes light up when she smiles. I'm already quite fond of her.

After we eat, we slowly meander back to the hotel bar, where I get us another glass of wine each, and we sink into sumptuous cushions on a low couch. Lorelei sits next to me. The furniture, as if conspiring with me, sucks her towards the black hole made by my body. I feel her warmth against me and her breath on my neck as she giggles, a little drunk from the wine and the wonderful evening.

"Hey, you know what?" She quietly says into my ear.

"What?" I turn to look her in the eyes.

"They have a steam room and sauna here at the hotel. After these drinks, would you like to 'get steamy'?" She grins at me with a mischievous twinkle in her eyes.

"Oh," I feel a pulse of adrenaline buzz through me unexpectedly. "Well, I didn't bring any appropriate sauna attire."

Lorelei leans so close to me that her breath tickles my ear as she whispers. She runs a hand down my chest, "Neither did I."

I CAN'T HELP IT; I know it's a cliche and ridiculous, but despite all the facts, I feel a spring in my step this morning as I walk towards the care home. Life, as they say, may not all be as bad as it seemed not that long ago. What changed?

I've had passion, lust, desire and blatant raw animal sex just for the hell of it plenty of times, especially of late, but with Lorelei that night at the hotel, something else was present. Something deep in my soul, stirring and firing up chemicals that have been AWOL for a long time. We made love. Joyous, rapturous, epic Hollywood-style love. It wasn't seedy, cheap or throwaway. It was special, life-changing, complete.

Emotional.

She felt it, too. I know she did.

Shit, I need to chill out.

Or is it too late?

Am I smitten?

Surely not … bloody hell.

Evelyn called me early this morning. Asked me to come to the care home as she had something to tell me. Given what she said the last time this happened, I feared the worst, but she wouldn't go into detail on the phone.

She sounded fine and said not to worry; all will be explained soon. She does love all the secrecy and big reveal. I suppose that's conditioned by her life of working on confidential government projects. I decided to walk in this morning as the weather was calm, and I felt like the stroll.

Lorelei Johannessen, Lorelei, Lolly … her name rattles around in my head along with the memories of the other night in the sauna. True to her word, she was naked as the day she was born when she took off her fluffy white dressing gown. Sweat was already beading on her incredible body in the blasting heat. She laughed at me and my British reserve, melting in my gown, then pulled at the belt, untying me and leaving me open. I shrugged the robe off and was glad that we were the only occupants of the sauna.

Thirty minutes later, we were in her room, showering together, and I couldn't help but laugh at my silly prediction coming true.

Wow.

The woman was as wild as a forest nymph, as unabashed as a Vegas stripper strutting in front of a room full of drunken men. She took the lead, wasted no time, pulled me into a kiss so deep I felt myself drifting out of reality, oxygen sucked away by her seduction, my soul throbbing through me, desperate for more. She teased, pushing me back when I hungered for her breasts. She gripped me tightly when I relaxed away.

Wet from the shower, we moved to the sumptuous bed, and she straddled me with a deft manoeuvre, forcing me inside her, still teasing with her body. She leaned down over me, tickling my chest with her nipples, running her tongue over my lips. "This is how we say thank you in Norway." She grinned and thrust her hips into me.

"Takk skal du ha!" I managed, and she laughed, clenching her muscles around me.

When I woke the next morning, Lorelei was already in the shower again. I tried to join her, but she got out and laughed me away.

"Good morning, Toby." She smiled, standing glorious and naked in front of me, not a care about her. "Sorry, I can't linger, I have a meeting to get to."

I had forgotten that she was on a work trip. I left her to get ready and slowly made my way home once she had gone to her meeting. I don't remember the walk home, only that it was on soft clouds of passion. I sent her a message when I got home.

> Can't wait to see you again. xxx

Then I felt weird about it and sent a follow-up.

> I mean, if you want to?

I got no reply for three torturous hours, but then a simple.

> Sure, I would love to! xxx

Since then, we've been messaging back and forth. The usual flirts of a new relationship, getting to know one another. I complimented her on her wonderful English. She told me she speaks five languages fluently. I resisted the urge to one-up her and say I know seven. Instead, I hinted that I 'knew a little Norwegian' but didn't go into detail about why.

She told me her father is German and her mother Norwegian. She's lived in Norway all her life but wants to travel more. This is her first visit to the United Kingdom, and if it wasn't for me she would have given it a low star rating so far.

'Attacked by thugs almost immediately, the rental car has the steering wheel on the wrong side. One star.'

I laughed and said I was glad I could be such a good ambassador for the realm.

She lives outside of Oslo and has a small flat. Single, no kids, never married, devoted to her work. Her last boyfriend dumped her a couple of years ago, saying he had met someone else more beautiful. I told her that was not physically possible in this reality, that he must be insane, blind, stupid or all three.

> He's a fool!

She sent me an emoji with love heart eyes and told me she was nothing special.

> I beg to differ!

But I stopped myself before I gushed too much about how Aphrodite and Freyja have nothing on her.

We are due to meet again this evening after her meetings are done. The conference starts properly tomorrow, but she has a lot of preparation to do.

This incredible woman fell from heaven into my life with an explosion of emotion and a splash right into the deep end of my pool. I'm shocked at the feelings welling inside me. Stunned by her beauty, and although I've only just met her, I feel like we have been lifelong companions. Connected and destined to meet. What is going on?

"Toby!"

I turn, shocked from my daydreams into reality, at the entrance to Cherryoaks Lodge care home.

"Cassie," Another beautiful woman who's a big part of

my life, holds the door open. "I suppose I should have expected to meet you here."

"Gran summoned you again?"

I nod. "Yup. But she sounded much better than last time."

"Yeah, that's what I thought, too."

"I wonder what she's got to tell us today?"

"Better go and find out."

I nod, and we enter the care home, sign in, and walk into the common room.

Evelyn sits in her usual spot, gazing out at the garden, her white hair neatly braided.

"Hi, Gran," Cassie announces.

Evelyn turns with a loving smile as she notices her grand-daughter. I wave a hello, and Evelyn nods back.

"Thank you both for coming so promptly."

"No problem," I bluster. "How are you, Evelyn?"

She looks very well, almost glowing. Far from frail and dying, as her age would suggest.

"Well, let's not get ahead of ourselves, shall we? Perhaps we can take a stroll in the garden, and we can chat."

I nod and fetch a wheelchair while Cassie and Evelyn embrace and catch up. I still feel like an intruder in their family so I take it slowly, meandering back with the chair, allowing them some time alone together to talk.

In the garden, we park Evelyn by a bench. Cassie sits on one side, and I sit on the other. I remark on how lovely the day is, and Cassie eyes me suspiciously.

"Are you okay, Toby?"

"Yeah, I'm great, thank you." I grin.

"You seem a bit cheerful today … did you win the lottery or something?"

"Ha. No, I wish." I shrug. "Just thought it was a nice day. Nothing wrong with that, is there?"

"No, not at all, if you aren't normally all aloof and mysterious."

I laugh. "I'll take that as a compliment."

Cassie grins and sticks out her tongue at me. "Not sure about that."

Evelyn clears her throat. "When you two have quite finished!"

"Sorry." We both say at the same time. Chastised, I bow my head in shame.

Evelyn pouts, but there's a smile in her eyes. "Now then. I have some news for you." She pauses for effect, looking both of us in the eyes slowly and silently. "It turns out that due to the incompetence and idiocy of the medical staff here, I am not in immediate danger of dropping dead, after all."

I feel my jaw drop and glance at Cassie, who has the same expression for a moment before she jumps up and embraces Evelyn in a hug. "Oh, Gran!"

"Now, now, dear Cassie. I'm still very old, but the immediate problem turns out to be a false alarm."

Cassie releases her gran and sits back down. I notice tears in her eyes, and I look away.

"What happened," I manage, stifling back emotion myself.

"Well, since we're all friends here," she grins, "what they initially thought was a cancerous lump was, in fact, only a build-up of gas."

"Seriously?" I burst out a laugh. "You just needed to f …"

Cassie interrupts me. "I'm so glad you are okay, Gran!"

"So, you aren't dying?" I feel it needs to be clarified.

"Not imminently, no," Evelyn states. "But don't forget how ancient I am, Toby."

"Well, that's amazing. I could kiss you!"

"Please don't."

"This is wonderful news!" Cassie erupts. She jumps up and dances around Evelyn in a circle, then grabs the wheelchair handles and gently wheels Evelyn around with her.

"Take it easy, Cassie." Evelyn laughs.

· · ·

"You didn't post yesterday or the day before." Cassie accuses me while Evelyn takes a powder room break, as she put it, back in her quarters.

"Oh, shit. Sorry."

Cassie raises an eyebrow. "Did you even check my posts?"

My face flushes with embarrassment. "Shit. No." I admit. "I'm really sorry. It slipped my mind."

Lorelei happened, and my world turned upside down. I genuinely forgot that anything else existed. Now, I feel like a fraud and a failure. A woman comes along, and I forget all my responsibilities? What kind of a person am I? Cassie could have been taken, and the system that I put in place would have failed us. I can't let that happen again.

"It's okay." Cassie laughs. "As you can see, I'm absolutely fine." She points both hands at herself. "But this was your idea … and you insisted it was necessary."

"Yeah, I know, I know. I feel like a total twat now."

Cassie rolls her eyes but says nothing.

"It won't happen again, I promise."

"It better not. I thought something had happened to you." She mocks me with a hand on her chest.

"Sorry." I offer again.

"I'm kidding!" She stares at me intensely and sticks out her tongue.

"Look, I know. I'm sorry. I believe in the system. I just got distracted, that's all." I look up at Cassie sheepishly.

"Oh, by what?" She squints at me. "Or, should I say, by whom?"

I sigh and hold out my hands to her together at the wrists in mock submission. "Yeah, you got me. I surrender. I met a woman …"

"Ooo." Cassie makes a childish playground sound. "Who is she? Come on, spill the beans."

I roll my eyes at her. "Just someone. Early days. Nothing to tell."

Cassie scoffs. "Bullshit! Obviously, there is something if you completely forgot about little old me."

I feel my cheeks flush again and a throb of adrenaline. "No, I didn't … oh, god. Cassie, I … ugh."

"Hang on, I'll get you a spade, and you can dig yourself a hole even faster."

I shake my head in horror.

"Toby, calm down. I'm still joking. It's okay, really. Maybe we should just stop the posts thing now. You proved a point, it isn't needed, everyone is fine, and we have better things to be doing with our lives. I'm fine."

"No, that's not right." I shake my head again. "You are extremely important, and the system is necessary, and I promise to do it every day no matter what. Same as you do because Evelyn wants me to make sure you are safe, and so that's what I have to do." I blurt out the words before I know what I'm doing. Evelyn chooses that moment to wheel into the room from her bathroom.

"Evelyn wants you to do what?" She stares at me, then at Cassie.

"Nothing, sorry, Evelyn."

Cassie flashes me a look, and I know I'm going to be grilled later.

"I hope you two aren't fighting again?" I don't know how she does it, but this frail old lady makes me feel like a naughty schoolboy being told off.

"No, it's fine, Gran. Toby was just overly concerned for my safety."

I nod.

"Good. That's his job."

"Yeah, well. I'm very glad you are okay, Evelyn. Thank you for letting me know, but I'll leave you to catch up with Cassie now." I flash a smile, then look at Cassie. "I'll talk to you soon, okay?"

She nods, "Yeah. Okay, Toby."

CHAPTER
TWENTY-THREE

I'VE BEEN able to cook myself basic meals since I was a young lad, taught by my mother. My brother wasn't interested, but I lapped it up. It meant getting snacks whenever I wanted, and I found it therapeutic, in a way. Peeling spuds is one of those brainless tasks that lets your mind wander, and I would spend ages daydreaming in the kitchen.

And being able to cook comes in handy with the bachelor lifestyle. If I didn't know how to make pasta and sauce, chilli, chips, oven pizza, eggs on toast and minimal-washing-up one-pot meals, then I probably would have starved long ago. A man cannot live on takeaway alone.

I've even cooked for women in the past, and sometimes they claimed to enjoy the food. However, since my encounter with Project Flash Gordon, it seems I'm a bit of a secret Masterchef. I suppose Evelyn added some cooking skills into the mix along the way as a bonus. I still wonder what else I'll find out about my new life randomly as I sink into the reality of it. Am I also a rocket scientist or a brain surgeon? I don't think so, but who knows? Maybe it just hasn't come up yet.

I haven't had much cause to use my culinary skills other than a couple of meals when Cassie has been here. She enjoyed my cooking and said she was impressed, but despite my attempts to make it romantic, it never was.

Cassie is an anomaly. Gorgeous, intelligent, funny and even flirty sometimes, but there's never been the spark from her that I desire. A shame, but I haven't completely given up. At least, not until I met Lorelei.

This dinner I'm lovingly preparing isn't for Cassie. Perhaps a tad on the keen side, I invited Lorelei to my home for dinner. It was a spur-of-the-moment thing, and I think I shocked myself with the question. Then came the fear when she immediately accepted. I had nothing in the house, so some urgent planning and shopping was needed.

Lorelei won't be here in my town for very long. She's only visiting for the green energy conference, so I thought I should make the most of the time. I don't know if I'll ever see her again after this. She'll go back to Norway, and I am stuck here, at least while the Department threat exists and Cassie requires my attention. I can't let her or Evelyn down. This isn't the sort of job a man can take a holiday from.

Cassie came over yesterday after visiting the care home. She pestered me into telling her about Lorelei, making cooing noises and raising her eyebrows accordingly. I left out the fact that Lorelei was being attacked by thugs when I met her. Instead, I said I happened to be walking near the hotel and bumped into her as she stepped out onto the pavement. From there, we got talking, and one thing led to another, yada-yada, and we ended up in bed via the sauna.

"Yeah, that just happens all the time, doesn't it?" Cassie mocked with an exaggerated eye-roll.

I shrugged and told her that she might like Lorelei as she's one of the delegates at the conference. Maybe she even knew her? She didn't but said she'd look out for her. She hadn't heard of the company, either, but said she'd look them up. I have a tiny, sneaky feeling that Cassie might be just a little bit jealous, but I didn't mention it.

She asked me what Lorelei looked like, and I had to stop myself from blurting out that she looked like the lovechild of a Botticelli angel and a Greek Goddess. "Blonde, petite, you know?"

Cassie rolled her eyes, shook her head ever so slightly, and muttered something that sounded like "Men …"

Well, what can I do? I'm only human.

I had a vague idea that Lorelei liked Italian food, but I also wanted to include something from her native Norway as a gesture. I spent some time online searching and planning and decided to make Krumkake from scratch—a big mistake. Krumkakes are sort of waffles rolled into a cone with cream and berries inside, but I didn't factor in that I don't have a waffle iron and my estimation that a toastie machine would do just as well was way off. Consequently, we'll be having ice cream for dessert. It's the thought that counts, isn't it?

Anyway, my pasta is to die for. My antipasto is elegantly dished and ready. There's enough wine for a party of six, candles, music, and ambience. I'm ready for her, but I'm also nervous in a way that isn't normal for my new augmented self. This dainty creature has set aside my smooth Bond-like persona. I'm like a teenager waiting for a prom date, wondering if this is the night I'll finally get laid.

The harsh ring of the doorbell stuns me from my last-minute preening in the bathroom, and I take a deep breath, swipe a hand through my hair and open the front door with a flourish.

My mouth drops open as I take in the seraphic vista. Lorelei with a delicate smile on her face, a hint of seductive-ness barely visible, but I feel it in my gut more than see it.

"Hi, Toby," she says in her singsong accent, melting my heart instantly.

"Hey, you look … amazing." She's in casual jeans and a blouse, but it wouldn't matter if she was wearing a green bin bag tied around with old mooring ropes. She's gorgeous. Simple as that.

I give her a brief tour of my home, and she settles down on the couch amidst a plethora of cushions that, for some reason, I have accumulated over the last few months. She fits in comfortably, and my mind drifts into future timelines where she's always there, a part of my life. Could she ever be my wife?

Jesus, I'm getting ahead of myself.

I shake away these ridiculous thoughts and open a bottle of wine, pouring us both a glass.

"Food whenever you are ready, Lorelei."

She smiles. "Come sit with me for a while first." She pats the couch next to her. I do as she suggests, and her warm body presses against me, stirring things deep inside. I take a sip of wine and feel the softness of Lorelei's lips touch my rough, stubble-covered face with a gentle kiss. I turn towards her and we engage in some moderate to heavy petting for a blissful few minutes before she gently pushes me away.

"Later, Toby," She grins, "you can't have dessert before main course, can you?"

I nod, "Well, you started it."

She runs a hand over my chest in a soft caress but then flicks me hard in the nipple with a laugh.

"Your home is nice," she changes the subject, looking around the room. "Not what I expected."

"Oh, what did you expect?"

"I don't know, but maybe more, you know, man stuff?"

Concerned, I glance around the room myself as if seeing it for the first time. I have a TV, couch, carpet, and bookshelves. Normal stuff.

"What do you mean?"

"Everything is clean and tidy, light and airy, you have healthy plants and all these, how you call it, pillows?" She motions to the couch next to her.

"Cushions."

"Yes, cushions." She laughs in her Nordic accent. "I don't know any men who live alone and have so many cushions."

"Oh," I don't know what to say to that. I suppose I do have more than normal, but I like to be comfortable when I relax here with a book or something.

"It's not bad!" She grabs my arm and pulls me close to her. "Just makes me like you more."

"Really?"

To prove her point, Lorelei kisses me again, long and soft. The cushion issue fades into obscurity as blood pumps through my veins, passion overwhelms me, and I lose myself in her pheromones.

Over dinner, washed down with plenty of wine, Lorelei asks me about my life, what I do for a living and what my future plans are. I can't give her solid answers to any of her questions; I bum around and help rid the world of scumbags in my own weird way. No, I can't say that, so I tell her I'm between jobs, but I work in IT mainly. My future, I don't know. For now, I am seeing how things go. Perhaps something in security or green energy?

In other words, I do nothing and have no plans. I know she sees right through my bullshit, but she doesn't complain.

"Maybe I can help you find something?" She offers with a smile, and yet again, my soul melts beneath her radiance.

"Really?"

"Yes, why not? My company needs tech people all the time."

"In Norway?" She nods, and I feel a frown creep over my

face. I can't leave Evelyn and Cassie here and swan off to Norway, not yet. "I'm not sure if that will work."

"Do you have reason to stay here? Wife or something you didn't tell me?"

"God, no." I laugh. "Just some commitments I need to keep for a while."

Lorelei nods but says nothing.

I change the subject to release the tension. "What exactly do you do in your company?"

"Renewable energy solutions, you know, we help companies stop burning coal and oil for their energy needs. We do some research and development, but I don't know much about that."

Weird that she does the same thing as Cassie.

"My friend works in a similar business."

"Oh, yes? Is he at the conference?"

"**She** is, yes." Lorelei raises an eyebrow ever so slightly.

"What's her name? Maybe I know her."

"Cassie Wright. She works at EverGreen Power."

She shakes her head. "I don't know the name. Should I?"

I shrug. "They do more or less the same as you do."

"Good to know. I will look for her."

A thought occurs to me. "Research and development, you say?"

"Yeah, you know, into new technology. We have some guys working on prototypes and machines." She waves a hand. "It's all very secret." She grins. "I shouldn't even tell you that."

I nod. "I think you do need to meet Cassie."

CHAPTER
TWENTY-FOUR

"HOW WELL DO you know this woman?" Cassie asks me with suspicion in her eyes.

"Well, not very well, I admit, but you can look up the company." I hand Cassie the business card that Lorelei gave me. I know her intimately, but I don't think she means that way.

"I will."

"Can't hurt to try, can it?"

Cassie absentmindedly taps the card on her chin and seems lost in thought. This morning, after Lorelei left my bed for her work meetings. After another night of steamy passion and lovemaking — enough to leave a burlesque performer speechless — I took a shower, downed a bucket of coffee to blast away the fatigue from multiple sleepless nights, and rang Cassie. I told her that I might have found a company that could help build her prototype. Lorelei was more than intrigued when I mentioned that my friend had a design she wanted to get made into a real device and that it was very much in the green energy domain. I was careful not to say much more, and Lorelei was keen to meet Cassie to discuss possibilities this afternoon once she is finished with her work duties.

I am a little concerned about having these two women meet — my lover and my ward. Sparks could fly, chaos could ensue, or, more likely, jealousy could rise from the depths and destroy everything. Still, I think this is worth the risk. Cassie wants to get her invention made, and Lorelei could make it happen.

"Yeah, okay. What did you tell her, exactly?"

"I said my friend had a design for a green energy device that she wanted to get made into a real prototype." I shrug. "No more than that."

Cassie nods. "And she was interested? They could do it? Build my prototype, I mean."

"She was definitely interested. Whether they can build it or not, I don't know, but only one way to find out."

"They are in Norway."

"Yeah. There's that, but it isn't out of the question?"

"Suppose not." Cassie looks away and down at the ground. I sense she is worried about leaving Evelyn.

"Meet her and have a chat and see where it goes? Take it from there."

"Fair enough." Cassie nods. "I'll see you later, then. I have to go set up my stand now."

"Need a hand?" I offer.

"Sure, why not?" She shrugs. "You are very keen, aren't you?"

"On what?"

"On this Lorelei."

My turn to shrug. "Yeah, maybe. She's nice."

"Nice? Must be more than nice."

"Well, okay. She's bloody amazing." I blurt out.

"Hmm." Cassie gives me a side-eye look.

"What?"

"Nothing, you do you, I suppose." She shakes her head and rolls her eyes mockingly. "Come on, then. Those tables won't shift themselves."

．　．　．

After helping to set Cassie's stand up as much as I could without getting in her way, I kill time by heading to the gym, followed by the pool for a few dozen lengths. I'm exhausted after three hours of it, so I drag myself home and fall into bed for a much-needed nap. Wiped out by passion. Not a bad way to be.

————

Another shower, and I'm on my way back to the Myatt to introduce Cassie and Lorelei to each other. For some reason, I'm nervous about the meeting. Ridiculous but true. I'd stop for a drink if I wasn't driving, but as it is I take a deep breath and open the window of the car, letting the wind blast away the thoughts.

I park in the multi-storey car park, and the memory of how I met Lorelei only a few days ago hits me like a boot to the head. Scumbag thugs. What were they doing there? Did they randomly attack Lorelei or was it a planned thing? Does she have a secret that someone wants? The Department? A Norwegian version of the Department? No, hired thugs aren't their style. They would send Brian or someone similar to lure her into a love trap, then wipe her brain. I get out of my car and walk over to where the patch of blood was. There's no sign of it now. A bleach-clean patch of concrete in its place. Did they return and tidy away any evidence, or was it the hotel staff? I have a feeling in my guts that something a little fishy is going on here, but what, I don't know.

In the hotel bar, I eye the Belgian beer taps but resist and sip at a coffee instead. Despite my busy day of exercise and sleep, I'm early, and I expect the two women will be late.

．　．　．

"Hiya," I turn and almost jump off my barstool. Cassie and Lorelei, together, beaming grins at me.

I stand, and Lorelei pecks me on the cheek, Cassie smirks.

"Hey! You've met already?"

"Yes, I saw Cassie at the conference, so we got talking."

I glance at Cassie, and she nods with a smile.

"Oh, right. Well, good. All okay, yeah?" I nervously ask.

"Yeah, all good, Toby." Cassie laughs. "What did you think was going to happen?"

"No, nothing. Fine, great!" I clear my throat. "Can I get you ladies a drink?"

Over drinks, I learn that Cassie and Lorelei have already had a heart-to-heart about her invention and prototype. Lorelei, trusted, was excited and amazed by the idea and was keen to get her company on board to start work on a prototype as soon as possible. She gushes about potential and world-changing possibilities as well as non-disclosure agreements, contracts, setting up calls with her colleagues back in Norway and before I know it, we're talking about the logistics of travelling over in the next week to get the ball rolling. Lorelei and Cassie both seem to assume that I'm coming too, and I'm not complaining. I can keep an eye on Cassie and be with Lorelei as well. I've never been to Norway, but my language skills should help. I start searching for hotels but Lorelei insists that I can stay with her and the company will put Cassie up in their apartment above the office.

Cassie is equally excited, and to my surprise, the two women are already getting along like a house on fire. Cassie isn't usually a touchy-feely type of person, but she's all over Lorelei with hugs and squeezes, laughing and joking. Champagne is ordered, and my plans to drive home are binned as Lorelei insists I celebrate with them and stay in her hotel room tonight. I don't need to be asked twice, and I'm glad of the nap I had earlier as tonight is going to be another hot and heavy one. I can feel it.

Cassie, excited, calls Evelyn and tells her about the plans to have her prototype built and a trip to Norway to start the process. We haven't even spoken to Lorelei's colleagues, and yet I know in my gut that this is the break Cassie has been waiting for. This is going to work. Cassie is going to change the world and be the mastermind that solves the world's energy problems once and for all. She'll be the most important person on the planet and it will all be down to a chance encounter with a beautiful woman who I happen to be sleeping with.

Bonus!

FRIDAY, 21ST OCTOBER, 2022,
10:00 AM. MYATT HOTEL, MILTON
KEYNES, BUCKINGHAMSHIRE.

"HEI, TROND, ER DU KLAR?"

"Ja, når du er det, Lorelei."

"Vi snakker Engelsk, ok?"

"Yes, sure, no problem."

A ridiculously handsome man beams at us from the huge video call projection on the wall of a hotel conference room we've commandeered for the meeting this morning with *GrønnEnergi Bærekraft Løsninger AS*, Lorelei's company in Norway. His blonde hair and shining head fill the wall, and a toothy grin dominates the camera frame as he leans forward to adjust something. It's a little scary, but he backs away and sips from a cup of coffee.

"This is Trond Nilsen, my colleague, and this is Cassie Wright and Toby Steele."

Lorelei motions to us in the room as she introduces us. Toby looks embarrassed to be here, but he grins like an idiot, basking in Lorelei's attention. It's a wonder men ever came to any power when all it takes is a pretty girl to knock them off the rails. I can't help but roll my eyes. She is beautiful, though. I must admit. I'd swing that way myself, given half the chance.

"Hey Cassie, Toby, hope you are doing good?"

Toby sticks up a thumb but stays silent. I nod. "Good, thanks, Trond."

"Great to hear." Trond flashes the whitest grin and seems genuinely delighted by our exchange of pleasantries. There's something a bit 'Max Headroom' about him. It's unnerving. Probably just the Zoom video signal on the dodgy hotel WiFi.

Trond gives us a quick overview of his job role in the company. He's the team lead of the research and development branch and has worked on many solar and wind power projects, including a quantum dot cell technology that I've barely heard of. Impressive. His accent is strongly generic Californian, but with the odd hint of Nordic thrown in. I expect he went to university at Caltech or Stanford.

They have an advanced lab with state-of-the-art aerospace and medical-grade metal 3D printing capabilities, which means they can go from idea to computer design to physical samples in hours instead of weeks or months. They can also design and print electrical circuit boards and have an advanced selection of modular 'chiplets' that allow them to quickly and efficiently put together almost any system.

An Aladdin's cave of treasure. With equipment like that, the only limits to what you can make are your imagination. I'm salivating at the thought of it. Give me a few days in that room, and I could build an Iron Man suit. Well, at least in my head, I could.

"Thanks for signing the NDA agreement so quickly, Cassie. It was a great help to get things moving here. You know, a lot of companies can take weeks with legal meetings and complications, but now we are free to talk about your invention."

I nod. But now, a bad feeling starts to brew in my guts. Was I too quick to sign over the details? I can't understand legalese, but the way Lorelei explained it made it seem all fine. I'm sure it is.

"No problem, Trond."

"So the good news is that we think you have something big here."

I feel a smile creep across my face despite my trying to be business-like. Lorelei beams a smile at me, and Toby nods and grins like a baboon in a 'told you so' way.

Trond holds up a hand. "Don't pop the Champagne too soon. We have a lot of work to do, and there are a few things in the design I don't quite understand yet. So we'd like you to come to our facility, Cassie, here in Oslo, as soon as possible so we can work together on this. How do you feel about that?"

I feel Toby staring at me, and I glance up at him. His face shows concern, but then he looks away and lovingly at Lorelei. She smiles at me, then towards Toby. There's a moment of silence. The image of Trond on the wall freezes for a second. He stutters back into life.

"Hey, sorry, I think the network went down. I was saying I think it would be beneficial if you could come over to our lab, Cassie. We'll fund it, of course, but I really think you have something here. Do you think this is possible?"

"I need to think about that. Check with work and things."

Trond nods. "Yes, of course. We have a slot in our lab schedule next week. I was hoping we could accommodate you then, but if you need some more time …"

"Oh, when would the next slot be?"

Trond shrugs, his huge image on the projector almost shaking the wall behind him. "I'm not sure. Maybe next year. I'll have to check."

"Oh. I don't …"

"Your friend can come with you if that helps?" I assume he means Toby. Trond flashes a grin at the camera.

Toby looks up the screen, tearing himself away from staring at Lorelei like a lovesick puppy. He shakes his head as if clearing away a daydream. He sits up and addresses the wall of Trond. "Yes, good. I'll need to come along."

I raise an eyebrow towards him. Is he concerned for my safety, or is this just an opportunity to stay with Lorelei?

Lorelei reaches under the desk and gives him a squeeze on his leg. Toby can't help himself and grins like a schoolboy finding himself in an unattended sweetshop. Men!

"I need to talk to my manager at work, but I think it should be okay." If there is a chance to get my prototype made sooner rather than later, then I need to take it. I want Gran to see my invention working. This could be my last chance.

Trond nods, then goes through some logistics with us. Apparently, there's an apartment above their office where I can stay. No doubt Toby will be staying with the lovely Lorelei. I notice that Trond just assumes we are all coming without any further discussion. He moves on to talk about the metal alloys and the resonant frequencies that my schematics called out. He has some ideas on how to improve efficiency and make the device less bulky. There have been advances in amplification and GaN; Gallium Nitride semiconductor technology that could help with the heat on the power circuit side of things. In the tank, the more heat, the merrier, but you don't want the power conversion to get too toasty.

Trond seems to know his stuff. I'm impressed. He's passionate, too. He's guarded. Anyone can see that. But he is open enough to see the possibility of what I've got. I don't mention that I was already taken hostage because of the same potential and that rogue government agents tried to wipe my brain and my invention off the face of the earth. No need to open that can of worms.

After the meeting, we adjourn to the hotel bar, and despite the tentative arrangements, Lorelei orders a bottle of bubbly and before I know it, we're looking up flight options and restaurants in Oslo. Lorelei knows a Michelin star sushi place that makes my mouth water just thinking about it.

It looks like we're going on a trip to Norway.

I wonder if I need a new jacket? In that case, I may as well get a matching bag and shoes; I'll need something comfy for the lab …

CHAPTER
TWENTY-SIX

AT THE BACK of my mind, waving and jostling to be heard, is a voice that tells me I'm being a bloody idiot.

I ignore it.

Not only do I ignore it, but I sometimes wave back at the voice with a stupid shit-eating grin and blow raspberries.

She makes me happy, what can I say?

The voice frowns, shakes its invisible head, sighs, and occasionally flips a middle digit at me. I still don't care.

And yet, deep down, I know the voice makes a lot of sense. I've lost the plot, fallen head over heels, gone bananas, all because of this woman I just met.

It isn't just the head voice, either. I'm sure that Cassie thinks I'm a fool. She hasn't said so in as many words, but I can see it in her eyes when she rolls them at me frequently.

Lorelei is back in Oslo already. Cassie and I are on the plane, heading there. The last three days without her have been torture, and I've catalogued the things I'll do with her when we get to be alone again. There are many pages in that catalogue, and most of them are *18-rated, mature audiences only*. Okay, all of them are. The things that woman can do would make a pornstar blush.

I grin inwardly only because if Cassie catches me 'lusting' again, as she puts it, I fear she will knee me in the nuts. Hard.

The voice that I'm doing everything I can to ignore is telling me that this is all ridiculous. I can't be so deeply in love with Lorelei after only a few days. I'm not like this. I'm smooth, casual, Flash Gordon cool. I'm not normally a lovesick puppy, salivating at the thought of a woman. I should fall back, ease off, chill out and act nonchalant. And yet here I am, besotted, and I don't care. It's wonderful. She's amazing.

I'm totally gone.

Cassie stirs in the business class seat next to me. She's been asleep most of the way here. I couldn't sleep. I've been on the plane WiFi messaging Lorelei every stupid thought that comes into my head. I'm sure she'll be sick of me soon, but so far, she seems to be just as in love as I am. She'll meet us at the airport in about half an hour, and I can't wait.

"Are you still texting?" Cassie rubs her eyes and frowns at me.

"Hey. Yeah, well, just making sure all is good, you know? Keeping in touch."

"We'll be there soon, Toby." Cassie rolls her eyes again, then stretches in her seat and disapproves of my actions with every crick of her neck and flex of her arms and legs. She's in the window seat, and she gets up and clambers out over me.

"Be right back. Try not to miss me too much while I'm gone." She sticks out her tongue and walks off towards the WC.

"Take your time." I snigger.

We went to see Evelyn to explain everything after the video conference with Trond at Lorelei's company in Oslo. Cassie was excited, and it seemed like Trond was, too. They are going to try and build a prototype of Cassie's invention. Finally, she'll have real evidence that it works. Trond is confident he has the equipment needed in the lab to at least cobble something together that proves the theory. From there, who knows what will happen. Cassie spouted like an Icelandic volcano with enthusiasm and stumbled over herself, trying to get all the words out. Evelyn was cautious at first, but as I was going with Cassie, she was eventually convinced all would be well. I do need to look after Cassie. I know that, but with Lorelei around, all I feel is safety and love. Nothing bad is going to happen. We're going to build a device that could solve the world's energy problems once and for all.

Well, Cassie is. I have to admit that I don't really understand the physics involved. I probably should. It's all about resonating frequencies and energy. Something I am familiar with these days. I suppose it's like being able to drive a car but not having a clue how the internal combustion engine works. I'm the driver of a souped-up Ferrari, but I don't own a toolkit or even know where the bonnet opener is.

We'll stay a week. It may not be long enough to build the prototype, but it's all Cassie could get off work at short notice, and it should be enough to get things started. We can always go back again soon if needed. Trond is going to lead the project, and Cassie was impressed with his technical knowledge.

The excitement was infectious, and Evelyn glowed with pride and admiration for her granddaughter. I could feel her emotions bursting out. Of course, we had no choice but to go and do this.

Not long ago Cassie's schematics and simulations were about to be destroyed and torn away from the world by the Department, and now we're about to right all those wrongs and blast it out into the universe. The world will know

Cassie's name soon, and she could be batting away Nobel prizes by the dozen. I'm proud to know her. Cassie is an amazing woman. I know that. Lorelei is equally amazing, but in different ways, mostly in the bedroom. I have to admit I don't know how Cassie performs in that situation. Hasn't stopped me from wondering, though.

She stumbles back down the aisle towards me with a grin. I can't tell if it's mocking me or just her being happy about what's happening. Bit of both, probably.

Back in her seat, Cassie nudges me, "All kidding aside, Toby, you do think this is the right thing to do, don't you?"

Taken aback, I turn and look at Cassie. "What?"

"Do you think it all seems a bit, I dunno, convenient?"

"How do you mean?"

"Well, you know. You meet the lovely Lorelei, and she just happens to work for a company that can make my prototype, and not only can but is willing to put money and time into it after only the briefest glance at all the research I've done."

"I wouldn't say it's convenient, flying to Oslo for a week." I laugh, "but no. I think it's serendipity, and you shouldn't jinx it with your cynical attitude."

Cassie raises a perfectly groomed eyebrow at me. "Says you!"

I laugh. "I admit, I have been known to be a bit cynical …"

"A bit?" Cassie guffaws.

"I have had cause."

"Yeah, well, what's changed?" She sighs. "Oh, Jesus, no, don't say it. You met Lorelei, and everything suddenly got better. Right? Birds sing, butterflies dance, yada, yada …"

I nod and stay silent, but my grin speaks volumes.

"Bloody hell. Men." Cassie mutters and turns back to the window.

The tannoy announces that we will be landing shortly and that we should return to our seats, stow our tray tables, buckle up, and do all that fun stuff.

"To answer your question, no. I don't think this is wrong. Of course, it's the right thing to do. You've been wanting to get this done for ages, and here we are, doing it. Be happy. You've earned this. You deserve it. It needs to happen for the good of the human race!"

She flashes a thin smile and gives a nod. "Yeah. I know, I keep telling myself that, but I don't know …"

"Look, we'll be there soon; you can see the lab, talk to Trond in person and all the rest of the staff, and get a feel for it all. If you aren't comfortable, we'll get back on the next plane to Heathrow and never speak of it again. Okay?"

"You'd leave the lovely Lorelei for little old me?" She pouts.

"I …" I almost blurt out that I would have no choice in the matter. My brain would make sure I looked after Cassie. Evelyn has made me promise I would. No amount of gorgeous Norwegian soft skin can divert me from that path, much as I would like it to. "Yes, Cassie. I promised your gran I would be there for you."

"Hmm." She eyes me suspiciously but then looks away again. "Okay."

"Good. Now chill out, enjoy it. We're going for a nice dinner tonight."

"Thank god. I'm bloody starving."

"Toby!"

"Lorelei!"

I rush forward and scoop Lorelei into my arms at the arrivals gate, spinning around and squeezing her close to me. I gently put her down and kiss her until I feel the head-shaking stare of Cassie's eyes on me. I pull away, only slightly embarrassed.

"Did you miss me?" Lorelei grins, then turns to Cassie and triple-cheek kisses her. They embrace, and we tell Lorelei how the flight was comfortable and fine, thanks. Courtesy of her company business class tickets and generosity.

"The least we could do." She smiles and takes the trolley I was pushing with our luggage on. "Come on, we have a car waiting."

In the car, between some more kissing and squeezing, I look out at the Oslo skyline. My first time in Norway, and I remember that I can speak the language. Road signs and billboards are legible. It's weird, and I drift into the familiar thoughts that often come up. How Evelyn's project Flash Gordon is so incredible and weird, and that it lives inside my head, somehow donating mad skills to me. I can travel to a country I've never been to before and understand everything. This fact is something I will continue to keep to myself, however. I can't give an adequate explanation as to why I should be fluent in Norwegian to Lorelei or Cassie.

Our first stop is the GrønnEnergi office building, where they have a courtesy apartment above. The office is closed now for the evening, but Lorelei takes us up in a plush elevator to the sixth floor and then opens a door with a keycard. Dim lights come on automatically around the room, and Lorelei shouts, "Lys på," and more lights fade quickly on in adjoining rooms. We enter into a huge open area that's so Scandinavian it may as well be singing A-ha's *Take On Me*. The place is virtually monochromatic in a tasteful beige that matches the perfectly smooth wood that covers the floor and makes up most of the walls. A heady scent of pine is rich in the air, and whilst the space is tall and open, there's no cold echo that you might expect. Outside is chilly, but the room is toasty warm. There's a kitchen — stark and pristine, a bathroom with a big Jacuzzi tub, two bedrooms and a vast living area.

"The view is amazing!" Cassie goes to the window. I follow, and we look out over Oslo city, evening setting in, dragging darkness with it to every nook and cranny of the diorama below.

"Yeah, not bad." I glance back at Lorelei with a wink.

"I hope you'll find everything you need. I made sure the fridge was stocked with drinks, snacks, wine, and beer. The WiFi password is on the fridge, the TV has Netflix, and a cleaner will call in the mornings and restock everything. The apartment is totally soundproofed, so you can blast some music if you want." Lorelei grins and I give her a gentle squeeze. She smells of vanilla and jasmine, and I yearn to be alone with her.

Cassie dumps her bags into one of the bedrooms and then heads straight for the fridge in the kitchen. "Ahh, now you are talking. A beer is just what the doctor ordered. Toby?"

"You read my mind." I open cupboards and find glasses. "Lorelei, would you like a glass of wine?"

"Why not?" She grins.

At dinner, which is delicious, we gush about the food, the drinks, the great company and the possibilities that are just around the corner. In the morning, Cassie will be taken to the lab and will meet the team who will be building her prototype. Lorelei has her normal work to do, and I think I'm free to go wandering around Oslo. I am not invited to the lab for company policy and secrecy reasons. I don't like the thought of leaving Cassie all day, but Lorelei will be at the office, and we can meet for lunch.

It will be fine.

. . .

After we are stuffed full of Oslo's finest fare, we take Cassie back to the apartment, then, finally, alone in the elevator to go back to Lorelei's apartment, not far away, I take the opportunity to show her how much I missed her these last few days.

Going down?

CHAPTER
TWENTY-SEVEN

I'M NOT PERMITTED into the office or lab, but I am given free access to the plush apartment three floors above. Lorelei and I somehow managed to tear ourselves from her bed this morning after far too little sleep, and after a short taxi ride, we met Cassie at the apartment, where she was looking rested and happy. Lorelei whisked Cassie away, and I took the opportunity to have a shower in the apartment's ample bathroom. I didn't have time this morning. Lorelei was showered and dressed in minutes and still managed to look like an angel.

I did look longingly at the Jacuzzi at the apartment, but it didn't seem appropriate and no fun on my own.

I didn't see much of Lorelei's apartment, aside from the bedroom ceiling, and I hadn't had breakfast. After the long, powerful shower, I made myself a decent breakfast of toast, eggs and smoked salmon and then a bucket of coffee to wash it down.

Now, I sit and sip, watching the world go by from the apartment window. Pondering on the nature of the universe. Of all the things I've done in the last six months, the people I've helped, the people I've disabled in whatever evil task they were engaged in. The one I've stopped for good, and the scammer guy who I took a chunk of cash from. Even the date-raping cufflinks prick; if nothing else, our revenge on him always gives me a chuckle to remember.

I wonder how Cassie is getting on. We should let Evelyn know everything is fine. I'll mention it at lunch.

———

"Wake up, sleepyhead!"

I open my eyes to see two beautiful women staring at me. One with a grin and one rolling her eyes, hands on hips.

"Didn't get much sleep last night, eh, Toby?" Cassie chides.

Lorelei laughs and reaches out a hand to pull me up from the plush couch.

"I just closed my eyes for a minute."

"Sure." Lorelei pecks me on the cheek, then slaps me on the arse. I don't object.

"Is it lunchtime already?"

"Yeah, well, some of us have been working all morning!"

I chuckle. "Sorry. Fancy a cuppa?"

"Go on, then."

"It's okay. I will make some *kaffe pause*." Lorelei chirps and heads towards the kitchen.

Cassie frowns at me. I shrug.

I change the subject. "Have you spoken to your gran?"

"No, not yet. They won't let me take my phone into the lab for security reasons, apparently."

"Oh. Well, we should let Evelyn know all is well."

"Yes. Good idea."

Cassie makes a video call to Evelyn and shows her all around the fancy apartment. I wave and say hello, and Evelyn smiles back. She has to find the right pair of glasses to see the little phone screen, but she's adapted to the technology very well. Not surprisingly, given her history.

"No problems in Norway, Toby?"

"None at all. Everything is great."

"Good to hear. Keep me posted."

"Will do."

Cassie goes to her bedroom to chat and finish the call. When she comes back, Lorelei brings us a tray with coffee, sugar, and a plate of little pastries.

"Oooh, what are those?" Cassie's eyes go wide at the sight of them.

"There's Kanelbolle, which are cinnamon rolls, and Skolebrød, sweet buns filled with custard and coconut on top."

"Yum!" Cassie grabs one of each. I do the same.

"Thank you, Lorelei." I smile at her.

"No problem."

"How did you get on this morning, Cassie?" I realise I didn't ask about the real reason we are here: the prototype.

"So far, so good." She smiles. "I haven't met Trond yet. Just been looking around the lab. Seems impressive."

"Oh, right. I thought he was going to be working with you?"

"Trond had to take care of some things. He'll be back soon." Lorelei tells us. "I hope Liang is taking care of you, Cassie?"

"Liang?"

"Yeah, Liang Chen. He's the main man in the lab, anyway. You should be in good hands."

Cassie cringes, "His English isn't the best, so it's been a bit strained, but I'm sure we'll get by."

"Did you get anywhere with the designs?"

"No, well, like I say, Liang seems nice, but I don't think he understood much, including who I was or why I was here. I think he was busy with his own work, so I didn't like to bother him."

"Oh. Was there anyone else around?"

Cassie shakes her head and shrugs. "Not really. The receptionist, and I think I saw someone in a corridor when I went to the bathroom."

"Right. That doesn't seem ideal." I look over at Lorelei. "Anything you can do to help?"

"Yes, of course. I will talk to him later." She smiles. "Where do you want to go for lunch?"

We settle on sandwiches, albeit strange ones, and they are delivered to the apartment promptly. None of us felt like going out.

"Toby, I am going to visit my mother and grandmother this evening. I won't be back until tomorrow. You can stay here this evening, okay?"

"Oh, right. Sure, no problem." I can't hide the disappointment, but I can't ask Lorelei to dump her family for me. I should probably get a good night's sleep, anyway.

"I will take the train to Larvik. It's about ninety minutes, so it's easier to stay over. I go every month to see them."

"Sure, well, I hope they are well. Say hello from me." I grin.

"Of course." Lorelei smiles, and my heart melts.

After lunch, Lorelei takes Cassie back to the lab, and I'm left alone in the apartment again. I claim the second bedroom, which has an en suite, a king bed, a 55-inch TV, and a work desk. It's like being in a Myatt hotel, fancy and elegant without being too much. I don't bother unpacking my bag into the wardrobe. No one ever does that, do they?

Rather than mope around for hours waiting for Cassie to come back from work I decide to go for a walk around Oslo. I grab my jacket and the apartment keycard and, without any idea where I'm going, wander aimlessly. I find myself walking along the docks where a huge cruise ship is moored, then an elaborate opera house building. Why does art always find itself near water?

As cities go, Oslo has its similarities and uniqueness in equal measures, anywhere that a lot of humans congregate has to have some basic features. Restaurants, shops, recreation, offices, houses, homeless people, cars, bicycles, and crime. It's that last one that draws me towards it every time. Not to participate but to try and cull it, especially if it involves harm to someone. Damsels in distress are my speciality, it seems. As I pass by a multi-storey car park I'm reminded of how I met Lorelei in the first place. She was being attacked by three thugs in a hotel car park. Would she have been raped, murdered even if I hadn't stepped in? Certainly robbed, at the very least. The thought gives me the shivers, and I hope the scumbags who did it are still suffering. One chap looked quite bad after my boot impacted his skull. Could be another one in a coma, or worse. They deserve it, though. All these scumbags who prey on the helpless for their own pleasure do not deserve the oxygen they breathe. It may not be legal in the traditional sense to serve my own justice like this, but if not me, who? I have the power to do something about the problems around me, so why wouldn't I use it? In a strange, indirect way, the powers I have were issued to me by the UK government, so doesn't that make me some kind of government agent? I can't help but chuckle as I think the words, but am I 'licensed to kill'?

Bloody hell. Who do I think I am; Agent Steele?

I climb to the top of the car park and walk to the edge, looking out over the city below, breathing in the cool air, consuming it, filling my lungs with the Norwegian tang of life, letting the frequencies of the city resonate around my body. The wavelengths are different here. Subtle, but noticeable. Stands to reason, I suppose.

After a few minutes of this, and before I blow too much smoke up my own arse, I shake myself back to reality.

I think I need a beer. I pull out my phone and find the nearest bar on the map.

I arrive back at the apartment just before Cassie. She gives off an angry vibe, and I let her change and wash before pouring her a glass of wine and silently handing it to her as she comes out of her room.

"Thanks. I need it."

"Want to talk?"

She sighs and slumps down on the couch. "Still no Trond, and this Liang guy is infuriating. I don't think he has a clue about my prototype at all, and anytime I try and explain something he can't seem to understand the words."

"Shit. Did Lorelei talk to him?"

"She said something, I presume, in Norwegian, and he smiled and nodded a lot, but nothing really changed after she went."

"Oh. What have you been doing, then?"

"I was allowed access to one of the 3D printers and I've been trying to figure out how to make some of the basic components for my prototype, but I'm in a bit deep here. I don't really know where to start with it. The software is complicated. At least it's in English, but it may as well be Swahili"

"I wish I could help, but that isn't really my area of exper-tise. Even if they allowed me into the lab."

"I'm starting to think this was a big mistake, Toby."

"Oh, do you want to bail?"

"I don't know. I'm just so frustrated. Not after we came all this way. I mean, they said they would build the machine for me. What's going on?"

"Give it another day, at least. Maybe Trond was called away for some family emergency. I'm sure he'll be back and will help you tomorrow. This Liang dude seems like he just hasn't been clued in yet. Maybe he doesn't have security clearance or something?"

"Yeah. Hope so."

Cassie looks so forlorn that I feel I should offer her a big hug, but I don't know if she wants that sort of thing from me. We've never been intimate like that. I sit down next to her and turn to face her. She is very pretty, but right now, she looks so vulnerable and open that it would be wrong on so many levels to assume anything. I bite my lip and focus on her emotions, feeling the raw frequencies pouring from her. Troubled, confused, frustrated and overall, sad and lonely.

I give in and spread my arms. "Do you want a hug?"

Her lip trembles and she throws herself at me, wrapping her arms around my neck. I squeeze her to me, feeling her warmth and tension.

I hear a muffled voice from somewhere in my chest area. "Yes. Thank you, Toby."

CHAPTER
TWENTY-EIGHT
FRIDAY, 28TH OCTOBER, 2022,
4:37 PM. GRØNNENERGI
BÆREKRAFT LØSNINGER R&D
LAB, OSLO.

THIS IS GETTING FUCKING RIDICULOUS. Pardon my French. I'm this far away from head-butting Liang and shoving a 3D-printed heatsink up his arse.

Gahhh!

We've been at this for days now and there's no sign of the mythical Trond. I'm starting to wonder if he even exists. Was he an AI-generated video projected onto that wall in the hotel a week ago? No one seems to know where he is or when he will be back. How do they run a business like this? There's barely anyone here, Lorelei disappears all day, the girl on reception is clueless, and Liang … don't get me started. Everything I say is taken the wrong way, no matter how clear I try to be. I explained that I was supposed to be building a prototype of my design for an energy-generating device. He asked me how it works. I explained the principles of resonating frequencies, quantum states, harmonizing fields, the natural vibrations of the various metals we'll need, and how a pulse of electricity at the right wavelength can be the catalyst to vast reserves of untapped energy. He looked at me like I was a goblin, and I'd just asked him for his firstborn son to make into a pie.

He told me such a device is not possible. I agreed that

until now, such a device was not indeed possible, but that's where my invention comes in and solves all the problems. I've proved it over and over, I know it works, if only I could figure out how to get these stupid machines to function. Every time I think I'm getting somewhere, there are another ten problems to solve. Liang doesn't seem to have any sense of urgency about him at all, and no amount of gesticulating and animated pantomime gestures seems to get through to him. One of the nozzles broke on a 3D printer, and when I asked Liang to fix it, he poked around for an hour, then said he would have to get approval to order a part, and it could take a month to arrive. I don't have a month! I have four days left in this stupid place, and then I have to go back to work in England. This was all a big mistake. I should never have come, never let myself get convinced it could work out by Lorelei and Toby. I got my hopes up, and now I'm just pissed off, sick of the whole thing. I should delete all the designs and forget it. It's already got me into so much trouble, kidnapped and almost brainwashed. Why do I continue this thankless task?

No. I know why.

I wanted Gran to see it working. That's all I care about. No matter the world-changing fame and fortune, I don't care about that. I just wanted Gran to be proud of something I had done with all the things she taught me. I know she loves me, dotes on me, and she is proud of everything I've already done, but it never seems enough.

If I could only get this bloody thing to generate a single watt of power and show it to Gran, then I could rest, knowing she had seen something I had created before she left me forever.

I feel like crying. I'm no further forward than I was a week ago. No progress whatsoever, and I'm wasting my time in this stupid lab. There's not even any windows to look out at the world. The internet is firewalled and limited. My phone is locked away. This is just so frustrating! It wouldn't matter if I was doing the work I came to do. Where is Trond? What the bloody hell is going on? I slam my fists down on the desk in anger.

Liang notices and waddles over to where I'm sitting at the computer terminal.

"You feel okay, Miss Wright?"

"Not really, Liang, to be honest."

"Maybe you want coffee?"

I take a deep breath. I guess this isn't his fault. But if I do ever meet the mythical Trond he will get a piece of my mind. "Yes, that would be nice. Thank you."

At least he knows how to do that. There's a machine down the hallway. All he has to do is press a button. Still, nice of him to offer.

Liang returns with a cup of black coffee. He tentatively sets the coffee down in front of me and then backs away.

"Thank you, Liang."

"You need anything else, miss?"

"Well, yeah. I mean, ideally, I would like to be building my prototype, as we've discussed."

He looks nervously around. "I cannot help with this."

"Yeah, so you said."

"Err, maybe Trond back on Monday?" He grins, hopefully.

"Right, well, I have a flight back to the UK on Wednesday, so … it doesn't give me much time left if he does."

"Finger crossed!" Liang holds up both his hands with a mess of crossed fingers.

"Indeed. Thanks."

He waddles away back to his computer and taps away at something. God knows what he's doing, but it isn't anything I can recognise.

Sod this. The prototype isn't going to get made. This was all a waste of time. If they want to actually make it, they'll need to work hard to convince me to come back another time. I'm not wasting any more time in this stupid place.

I'm going to tell Toby I want to go home. If he won't come, I'll go on my own.

I exit the 'super secret' lab, where they don't do anything at all, and go upstairs to the apartment. It's nice and quiet, cool and a pleasant scent of fresh linen and sandalwood fills the air. I flop down on the couch. No sign of Toby or Lorelei. Three guesses about what they are doing. If he was here, I would roll my eyes at him. Dirty bastard.

I'm not going to admit it, but I'm probably a tiny bit jealous of their relationship. Why isn't it me getting rampant sex and fun? With Toby or Lorelei, honestly. I don't think I care anymore.

I pick up my phone to take my mind off things. There's a message unread from Toby.

> Hey, L said she wanted to show me something in the city. Should be back soon, but don't wait up.

Oh, that's just great! Not only are they shagging 24/7, but now I'm dumped and left alone all night.

I don't bother replying and switch to the airline app and look for a flight home.

CHAPTER
TWENTY-NINE

"WAKE UP, SLEEPYHEAD!"

I feel my body shaken roughly. I open my eyes, or at least I try to open my eyes, but there's something different, wrong, painful. I feel tension around my wrists, ankles and chest. Senses tingle, there's something on my head clamped tightly. My eyes feel gummed up and crusty. They won't open.

I move my hand to wipe them, but I am restrained. My hand won't move.

I try to cry out, but there's something covering my mouth. Tape, I think. I inhale, but the taste of blood stings on my nose. My heart pounds in my chest, and a fog of blurry memories drifts just out of reach. Pain, tiredness, sadness.

"Wake up!" The voice again, but it isn't warm and loving now; instead, it is cold and disconnected. Different.

Adrenaline courses through me, spreading icy terror instead of warm blood. I tentatively force open an eye. The world is blurry and harsh. I blink several times and screw up my eyes, then open them both to a brightly lit room. A bare bulb is shining in my face from an anglepoise lamp. There are several figures, but they remain out of focus. Dark blurs that gently sway in close proximity but out of reach.

"Ah, there you are." The voice again, still different, still familiar. I look towards it. "Lorelei?" I try to speak, but the tape over my mouth makes it impossible. A muffled grunt is all that came out. But it is her; for some reason, she's wearing a bee keeper's hat, and her face is behind a mesh. I blink again because that can't be right, can it?

I realise that I'm also wearing a similar hat. The world is behind a mesh of wire.

I look down at my wrists, which still won't move. They are cable-tied to a wooden chair. I suppose that's why I can't move them. My ankles seem to be tied to the feet of the chair. What's going on?

"He's awake." Lorelei turns away from me and speaks to someone else behind her. I can't see who it is.

I strain at the ties, but there's no give at all, and the plastic cuts into my skin.

Where am I? What happened? Why is Lorelei wearing a beekeeper's hat? Why am I, for that matter? Who are the others in the room? Why am I tied up and gagged?

Questions buzz around my head, but no answers come. Focus, Toby. What's the last thing I remember?

We were at the apartment; we had some lunch and a bit of light petting once Cassie went back to the lab, and then Lorelei wanted to show me something in the city. An art gallery, I think? A surprise, she said. We left the apartment block, walked the usual way to the tram stop and waited. I remember holding Lorelei in a hug as it was quite cold out, then … what?

Focus.

Think.

Another thud of adrenaline courses through me. Where is Cassie? Is she okay? Is she also here and tied up? Worse? Shit. I wrench at the bonds again, but they hold tight. The chair creaks as I struggle, and someone steps forward in front of the bright light.

"Take it easy, now, Toby. Don't need any more violence, do

we?" I look up at the voice. There's something familiar about it. A man this time. He's also wearing a stupid hat. What the …?

My eyes adjust and I see the face now clearly. Shit.

Brian from the Department. Fuck, fuck, fuck! I've been lured into a trap. Where is Cassie? My heart pounds in my chest, and I strain and roar from behind the tape until the ties cut deep into my arms. Brian leans forward and lifts the mesh from my hat, then does the same with his and puts his cold, clammy hand on my forehead.

"Easy, Toby." He flashes a sickly grin, and I feel my eyes closing, so tired suddenly, I shake my head to get him off me, but he stays put, and the soporific wave hits me again like a tsunami, my limbs go limp, my eyes close and my head flops forward. Bastard!

Cold water shocks me from the induced slumber, I wake with a start. This time, my eyes are open, and my mouth is free, but my arms and legs are still restrained. I try to free myself, but there are even more ties now. Some thick metal thing around both wrists.

"Where is Cassie?" I demand. The bright light is gone, and now I can see I'm in a room that looks similar to the apartment above the lab, but it isn't the same place. Different colour walls and curtains, these are blue where the apartment was beige. A window looks out on the same skyline. There's a couch and some people in the kitchen. All of them are wearing bee-keeping hats. My mesh is replaced around me.

"Hello? What's going on? Where am I?"

I try to turn my head to look around, but I can't move more than a few degrees. Something like a motorcycle helmet clamps around me and holds my head in place. Someone moves over from the kitchen towards me.

"Now, Toby, no need for panic!" A man looms over me

and then sits down on the couch. "I do apologise for the … whatnot," he motions at me and then at his head. "All very necessary, I'm afraid."

"Who are you? Why am I here? Where is Cassie?"

He waves a hand. "All in good time, Toby, old boy. All in good time."

"Cassie is fine. She's safe and doesn't know about this. We don't need her anymore." This is from Lorelei, but her voice is not the same. Now Oxbridge English, no hint of the Norwegian accent. What the …?

"Lorelei?"

She shakes her head behind the stupid hat. "Not my real name. I'm sorry, Toby. I'm not who you thought I was."

"But …" Sadness suddenly fills me as if my mouth was thrust open and a wide funnel directed a torrential flow of pure emotion straight into my guts. It seems like I've taken a beating already, but now my stomach feels like it's filled with a black hole. My heart is ripped from my chest and torn into shreds, then tossed into the toilet. I would cry in any other circumstance. I've been lied to. I loved that woman, but … Oh, my god. She's part of the Department! She did this to me. Shit.

"We have met, rather fleetingly if I recall, back in Connemara, do you remember?" The man lifts his veil briefly and points to his face, then lets the mesh fall down again. It's Doctor Ian Davidson from the Department. I suppose the other person still in the kitchen, apparently making a cup of tea, is Cynthia. I should have killed them all while I had the chance.

I nod.

"Excellent, then we're all on the same page. Jolly good."

"No, we very much are not. Let's start with why on Earth you are all wearing bee-keeping hats?"

I glance around the area of the room I can see, and there don't seem to be any bees.

Ian shakes his head. "No, no. They are Faraday hats. To stop you from, you know, doing things to us with the frequency whatnot. Our invention. Rather dashing, don't you think?" He tilts his head from side to side.

They know I've run the Flash Gordon code. They know about my abilities. Brian was sneaking around in the server at Bio-Digi. He must have found the program even after it was wiped. This is bad, very bad.

The mesh around my head must be a double precaution or to stop me from manipulating things around the room.

I look around again for possible weapons, tools, or anything I can use. The kitchen has cutlery, but I doubt I could get to it quick enough, assuming I could get out of the chair. I can't see Brian, which makes me think he's behind me. He could have a gun. I know the apartment is soundproofed, so this place will be as well. No point in trying to call for help. I assume they have taken my phone, and I couldn't use it anyway. I'm screwed.

The other woman walks over, holding a cup of tea. "Look, if you co-operate and don't make a fuss, then we'll all be able to get back home before you know it." It's Cynthia, as I assumed. The bloody Department again. They regrouped and moved to Norway and, along the way, recruited Lorelei, or whatever her real name is, as a honeytrap for me. But why do they want me? What am I meant to co-operate with?

I won't be, obviously. I need to know where Cassie is, because I don't trust anyone in this room one iota.

"And to be honest, I'm quite ready to get out of this bloody place." Cynthia motions around the room with her cuppa. "So do be a good chap and play along, won't you?"

Emotions flood my body. Sadness, anger, frustration, but most of all, I can't believe I was taken like this. How could I be so stupid? I knew very well that's how the Department operates. They did it to Cassie, and to Tracy, now I think about it. Of course, they would do it to me. They just had to find a suitable woman to be the love interest. I have to hand it to them. The one they found was absolutely perfect.

I'm so stupid!

Cassie was right. She sensed this was all wrong, and I fell for it like a total newbie.

SHIT!

"What do you want from me?"

"Oh, isn't it obvious?" Ian gets up from the couch and wanders towards me. He looks behind and raises his eyebrows, then looks back at me. "We need the FSMI code, and you have it stored all nice and snug in your bonce, there." He taps the side of the helmet thing with a grin. "Can't have it out in the world, doing mischief, now can we?"

"What?"

"Oh, do keep up, Mr Steele!" Cynthia shouts at me. "Don't play the dummy, either. We know, you know, everyone bloody knows. Now let's get this done, and we can all go home."

Ian waves Cynthia away and continues. "We need to extract the code from you, Toby, and wipe that part of your brain. That code should never have left the factory, as it were. But your pal, Ms Greenwood, was a bit naughty, wasn't she back all those years ago? She hid it from us and saved a backup. We know you've run the Project Flash Gordon code on yourself. We know it was an accident, but nevertheless, it must be removed from the world for everyone's safety."

I squirm in my bonds. Thoughts flood my brain. They know Evelyn hid the code. They know everything, somehow. I have no advantage.

"Evelyn … you better not have done anything to her!"

Ian shakes his head. "Lord no, old son. We aren't murderers! Good old Evelyn is a bit long in the tooth to be a threat anymore. Yes, we know she ran the code, too. My stochastic analysis predicts that Evelyn will not cause any problems now that she's into triple digits."

I grit my teeth. "You all have it, too." I look at all of them in the room that I can see in turn. Ian, the old man who looks like he wouldn't hurt a fly; Cynthia, who is as much a battle-axe as she always was, from Evelyn's memories in my brain. And the woman I thought I loved, Lorelei, who is just an actor, another stooge in the Department. Every time I see her is another stab into my guts.

"Ah, well spotted! But, no. What we have is something altogether different, something I've worked on for a long time. You see …"

"Ian, just get on with it!" Cynthia cuts him off.

"Yes, sorry, right." He grins from behind his mesh. "We know you have the original FSMI code. Our Brian went tinkering around in your servers. I'm sure you know that by now. He was able to piece together traces of the code. Enough to prove it was Evelyn's original version. Not the cheap knockoff she fed to us. She kept the good stuff for herself. Naughty, naughty!" He wags a finger at me. "Still, no matter. We'll have a quick tidy-up, flush it all out, so to speak, and we can all get back to doing what we do. You are in technology, yourself, aren't you?"

I ignore him. My brain cycles overtime, trying to find a way out of this. They are going to wipe the code from me? Is that possible? Am I going to end up as a vegetable? The Flash Gordon program is part of me now. I'm not the same Toby I was before. What will happen if they 'flush it out' as he says? This is likely death for me, at the very least for the Toby I am now. I can't let this happen. I also need to know that Cassie is safe, and Evelyn, too, while I'm at it.

"What are you going to do?" I force myself to keep calm. The code that still runs in my brain knows how to handle situations like this. That's the whole point of it. I should be able to get myself out of this mess, no problemo, and yet, as I sit here firmly bonded and incapacitated with this stupid hat on, I can't think of anything I can do. I need to stall and come up with a plan.

"Well, I'm delighted you asked!" Ian claps his hands together as if he's been waiting for this moment. He looks over my shoulder again. "Brian, if you will?" He nods towards me.

I feel a rough grip on my chair, and I'm twisted around to face behind. Where there would be a bedroom in the twin apartment to this one, there is instead an array of technology laid out like a spacecraft control panel. Unlike in the old Galway operation, the place I burned down, where it was all ancient tech that they had removed from Evelyn's old lab at Porton Down, the Cray-1 being the most obvious item, this desk is covered in brand new equipment. Modern screens, tower computers, a small server rack, networking switches, and cables in their dozens. Lights flicker on and off all over it, and a screensaver drifts over the three large monitors. It seems they have upgraded their system.

At the centre of the mess of cables is a helmet that is very similar, if not identical to the one they put on me in the room in Galway. This one is connected into the network with what looks like fibre-optic cable. On the desk next to it is something like a VR eyepiece.

"You've been busy," I note.

"Yes, rather!" Ian is loving this part. He's finally getting to talk about his dastardly plan like a Bond villain, and he's going to milk every drop out of it. I'll keep him talking as long as I can. "It turns out you did us a favour back in Connemara with the old incendiary devices you planted. Insurance covered the whole lot, and we were finally able to upgrade."

"My pleasure. Perhaps I can do it again?"

Ian laughs. "Ah-haha, you are a wag, aren't you, Toby? No, no. This lot is quite safe, and soon, there won't be any threat at all." He walks over to the desk. "You see, we've rigged up the goggles to project the visuals directly, which eliminates any data loss, and coupled with the enhanced speed of the helmet, the whole thing only takes a couple of minutes. Quite remarkable. Isn't the advance of technology quite wonderful?"

"But why Norway?"

"Good point. It's all down to old political agreements and protocols. I don't pretend to understand it all myself. Cynthia takes care of that side of things." He turns to face her, but I can hear her back in the kitchen clashing around, and she ignores him. "But we have certain assistances with the Norwegian government that make this an ideal location. It's all about location, isn't it? I must say, I do miss the Connemara air, lovely and fresh." Ian's eyes focus off into the distance, and he genuinely seems upset about having to leave Ireland. "Still. Change is as good as a rest, so they say."

"I thought you lot were against the advance of technology. Isn't that your stupid remit or something? The Department for the Prevention of World Changing Technology."

"Ha. There's a difference, Toby old son, between this stuff." He waves a hand towards the desk full of kit, "And the world-changing thingy that your friend Cassie was cooking up. These computers have evolved slowly over the last fifty years to what we have now. A gradual change that the population can handle, little steps, small advances. They only add up to something world-changing if you skip ahead a generation or so. These machines we have now are wildly more powerful than my dear old Cray but only marginally more so than, say, last year's models. That's the nub of it, old son. We have no issue with the normal, gradual progression of things. Society can swallow that without choking." Ian holds up a finger as if he's just remembered something. "By the way, you may as well tell Cassie; the invention she came up with … it doesn't work. We tried it. So we're all quite safe there as well. All a bit of a false alarm, I'm afraid. Interesting ideas, but no."

He shakes his head. "It will never do as she claims. Still, without all that fuss, we would never have found you or the real FSMI code. So swings and roundabouts, eh?"

I bite my tongue and stay silent.

"Now, then. Without further ado, let's get the show on the road, shall we?"

"Before you do anything, I want to talk to Cassie to make sure she's safe. I don't trust any of you one bit, I'm afraid."

Ian nods. "Stands to reason, I suppose." He looks over at Cynthia with a raised eyebrow. "Very well, we will make arrangements."

CHAPTER
THIRTY

FRIDAY, 28TH OCTOBER, 2022,
6:28 PM. GRØNNENERGI
BÆREKRAFT LØSNINGER
BUILDING, OSLO.

THE EARLIEST FLIGHT back home I could get was Sunday, and it's at crazy o'clock in the morning from Oslo airport, but it will have to do. The sooner I get out of this stupid place, the better. I've tried calling Toby over and over, but there was no answer; then it just went straight to voice-mail, so I gave up. If he's too busy screwing Lorelei, then he can bloody well stay here. I'll be fine on my own. I don't need a chaperone to fly back home. I'll tell Gran when I get back safe. No need for her to worry.

I may as well try and make the best of the day I've got left to explore the city. So far, all I've seen is the inside of that stupid lab and the odd restaurant. I pull out my phone and scroll around, looking for things to do in the local area.

There's a big fancy Opera house nearby, but that isn't really my thing.

You know what I really fancy all of a sudden? Good old greasy fish and chips. If there was a chippy nearby, I'd demolish a plate. I don't suppose they have that here, though.

Either way, I'm hungry, and I don't fancy cooking in this unfamiliar but pristine kitchen. I'll have a quick shower, change, put my face on and go out into the world and find something resembling chips. Then, back here, Netflix binge until I fall asleep. That's the evening sorted. Sod them all.

I've wasted an hour doom scrolling on my phone, forgot all about the shower and going for a walk to find some food. My bladder prompts me back to the real world. I get up and wonder why I bother looking at the absolute drivel that Instagram shows me, and I suddenly remember the equally stupid protocol that Toby came up with to ensure my safety. We were meant to post a phrase containing certain words every day to a Facebook group he made up. I knew that was ridiculous, and yet, for a while, I played along. Seems that is all forgotten now, once he was busy with the new woman in his life. Oh, well. I'm safe, nonetheless. Pissed off, yes, but quite safe. As I sit in the bathroom, there's a faint knocking sound. I think it's coming from the apartment's front door. I finish, flush and wash, then quietly move towards the door. Who would knock? Toby has a keycard, as does Lorelei. It's too late for a cleaner now. Has something happened? There's a peephole on the door, so I peer out into the corridor. A short man waits there. I think it's Liang, but the lens distortion makes it hard to be sure. He stands near the door with a nervous expression, hands behind his back.

I open the door.

"Hello?"

"Ah, yes. Hello, Miss Cassie. May I come in?"

It is Liang. Well, this is weird. "Err, I suppose so. I was just about to go out, actually."

I move aside and Liang comes in, slowly, carefully, as if he's expecting the place to explode if he makes a wrong move.

"Would you like a drink or something?" Liang awkwardly stands in the living area.

"No, thank you." He stands, waiting, making no move to explain his reason for visiting. Strange chap.

"Okay, what can I do for you?"

"Miss Cassie, I must apologise." Liang fidgets and flicks his thumbs against his fingers. "I looked at your designs again after you left. Now I think I can help you to build this system." He grins wide.

I pause for a second, shocked. "Oh? But you said it was impossible before."

"Yes, much sorry. Before, I misunderstood. Now I see potential." He smiles and nods, almost bowing.

"Oh, right. I'm not sure what to say. I booked myself a flight home, I'm afraid. I thought this was a big waste of time."

"No, no. Not waste!" He holds his hands up. "We can make it. I know what to do now."

"Really?" Liang is bouncing around, excited. He's changed his tune. What happened in the last couple of hours? "Well, okay. I'll come to the lab tomorrow, if you can be there on a Saturday?"

"Err, not tomorrow. Come now. Yes!"

"What?" I check my watch. It's almost eight o'clock in the evening now, and suddenly, he wants to start working on a prototype that could reasonably take weeks to build. I thought I would make a start on this trip, show Trond what he wanted to clarify, and set things in motion. Instead, I've wasted days doing absolutely nothing, and now, on a Friday evening, this weird little man wants to reset and start again. Something doesn't sit right. "It's too late now to get anything done. I'm tired, just want to eat and go to bed."

"I make 3D designs already. Want to show you before start machine." He mimes turning a handle. "It work overnight, then we look tomorrow. Only take ten minutes now."

"Oh, right."

He nods enthusiastically. "You look now. Back to bed in twenty minutes. Very quick."

"Did Trond return?"

"No, he has family emergency and cannot come, but I speak to him, discuss the model."

"Oh … right, well, I suppose I'll come take a look, then."

I wonder if I can sneak my phone into the lab because the receptionist will likely be gone home, and I'm only staying in there for five minutes to see whatever this thing is that Liang has made. I'll feel safer knowing I at least have some method of communication while in their lab.

"Give me a minute." Liang nods again so hard I think his head might fall off, and I slip back into the bathroom. I wash my face, brush my hair and pull my phone from my jeans pocket and slip it into my bra. Uncomfortable but unlikely to be searched. I step back out, grab my keycard, and turn back to the waiting Liang.

"Let's go see this wonderful thing, then."

"WHAT'S YOUR REAL NAME?"

While the Department muppets set about making whatever arrangements they need to make so I can talk to Cassie before they possibly wipe my brain forever and turn me into a walking parsnip, I take the opportunity to indulge my sadness and try to find out if Lorelei, or whatever her real name is, actually cared for me one tiny little bit, or if it was all fake, acting, Department fuckery. She might be able to turn off the love without any problem, but I can't. Gut-churning torment fills me; thoughts swirl in my brain. My limbs, if they weren't already restrained, would feel like they are made of lead. I've felt this before, but not so soon, so binary. On / Off. It's not natural.

The sex we had was amazing. I know she didn't fake that, did she? Not all of it? I would sense that, wouldn't I? Or was I so smitten and overcome that I ignored any signs that would have given the game away? She's a good actress, that's for sure.

Even now, under the ridiculous bee hat, double-crossing and no doubt deep down evil, she's bloody gorgeous. There's no denying that. And we had a relationship, even if it was all in my head, one-sided, planted by her weird version of the FSMI thing that Ian has developed over the decades.

I felt it, triggered by wavelengths, perhaps, but the reaction is real.

A weird way to take the research, if you ask me. But perhaps he had his reasons. Dirty bastard. Can't have been much use to him in the wilds of Connemara, though, unless he's into sheep … best not go there.

Even now, strapped into a chair, knowing my life as I know it might be over in a few minutes, I would kill everyone else in this room to be alone with Lorelei again. Not the fake, stooge Lorelei honeytrap, but the girl I thought I was in love with. The real, *fictional*, Lorelei. The beautiful woman who was equally in love with me, who giggled when I tickled her just so, whose breasts rose and fell with her breathing when we lay together, whose heart I could feel thumping next to me when we embraced. Cliches and romantic rubbish, I know, and yet … it's there churning in my head despite the situation. I need to focus. I have bigger problems right now, but try telling my heart that.

All this mess to satisfy the desire, no, *need* that my body had to be with her. I became an addict, and she was the drug. I can see why Cassie was lured to her capture and how Tracy was driven to leave her husband. This skill that Ian crafted into his version of FSMI is perhaps more powerful than any I possess. I can shatter glass, speak languages, and fight crime, but Lorelei can speak the language of love and shatter hearts with nothing more than a fleeting glance. That overpowers everything. Wars have been fought and all that.

"I shouldn't say."

"Come on. What does it matter now? You are going to wipe my brain in a minute."

She frowns. "No, that's not what it is. They only want the PFG frequencies."

I raise an eyebrow. "You must be new to the Department?"

She says nothing, but the empty expression gives it away. She wasn't in Galway, and she's far too young to be part of the original crew, which was apparently just Ian and Cynthia. I wonder if she's their daughter, and a shiver comes over me. No, there's no resemblance at all. She's probably a government agent, recruited for this job because of her looks. After I'm flushed, she'll go back to her office at GCHQ, Cheltenham or wherever, armed with these extra new skills she's picked up. She'll go on to do amazing things. Maybe evil things, certainly she'll break more hearts than mine.

"Please?"

She bites her lip and glances around at the others who are busy tinkering away on phones and laptops. She's tasked with watching me. Protected from my talents by the weird hats we all wear. I haven't even tried to break through whatever shield they provide. I assume they know it blocks whatever wavelengths I output. Maybe I should give it a go, anyway? I focus on Lorelei behind the gauze, sending out feelings of trust and safety, adding into the mix some of the love that still lingers in my gut for the girl she never was.

She leans closer, "My name is Laura, but that's all I can say."

I smile. Did my frequencies get through, or was it just me and my smile that made her realise she does care for me in some weird way? "Thank you, Laura. It was a pleasure doing business with you."

She can't help but smirk, and it's the same genuine face she made when I made a stupid joke while we were together. "Likewise, Mr Steele."

"What are you doing when this is all over? Wanna get a drink or something?"

She chuckles. "No, I can't, but thank you."

"Is it because I'll be a dribbling pot plant?"

"No! You'll be absolutely fine, just how you were before."

"Ha!" I exclaim. "How I was before was not absolutely

fine by any measure. I was a night shift nobody with no friends and no prospects. I was bullied, always angry, and never able to do what I really wanted. Never had the confidence to do anything real. This thing changed my life. Maybe saved my life."

She looks away. Once this job is finished, maybe they will also take away her skills. I imagine her life has changed since she was upgraded, too.

"What do you know about Evelyn?"

"I was briefed on the history of the project."

"Did you ever ask why they cancelled the project back in the 80s?"

She shrugs, "None of my business. I wasn't even born, then."

"No, but all that work, all that energy and talent, all to be just thrown away at the last minute. Why?"

"Well, she didn't throw it away, did she? She hid it, and now we have to delete it."

"That's another thing I don't understand. Why do you have to delete it?"

"It's too dangerous to be out in the world."

"It isn't out in the world, only in me and Evelyn, and she's over a hundred years old."

"And look at the damage you have done, Toby Steele."

"What damage?"

Laura, Lorelei, whatever, looks at me, then shakes her head just a tiny bit, then looks away. What does she know?

"What?"

"We keep an eye on things, Toby."

"What things?"

"Things. Just be careful. This is why we need to remove the code. You think you are so smart, so able, but you leave a mess behind that others have had to clean up in case certain information got out."

She raises an eyebrow at me.

I say nothing, taken aback. Have they been watching me the whole time? Do they know about the brothel cop? The scammer? Jenny and Oleksandra?

Laura folds her arms and gives me a look like I'm a naughty eight-year-old schoolboy caught with his hands in the sweetie jar.

I feel my cheeks flush. I thought I was being careful. Is it possible that I'm absolutely useless at everything, even being an augmented superhero? On top of the heartbreak, the danger, the worry, now I have imposter syndrome, big time.

The Department stooges have set up a green screen and portable lights in a corner of the room. They place a laptop on a coffee table in front of a couch. The green screen behind the couch. Laura sits down with Brian, and they adjust the lighting and position, fiddling with settings and tweaking the lights.

Once they seem satisfied, Ian and Brian move over to me. I've been restrained this whole time, and genuinely, I'm going to piss myself if I can't use a toilet very soon. I'm sure no one wants that to happen.

"Cassie will be in position shortly. You can speak to her via video call." Ian motions to the couch where Laura still sits. Laura takes off the beekeeper's hat and adjusts her hair. "However, there are rules." Ian looks to Brian.

"Cassie is in a controlled location with one of our operatives. She's perfectly safe, but if you break the rules, she won't be for long. We will monitor the call, and at the first sign of subterfuge, the signal will be sent."

"You harm a single hair on her, and none of you will leave this building alive." Anger courses through me, not just from me, but from Evelyn, via the code that runs in my head. Cassie is as precious to me as life itself. I can't let anything happen to her. I try to keep calm. They want me to be agitated. Brian ignores my threat and continues.

"You will casually call her from Lorelei's laptop in her apartment. Your phone battery died, that's why you haven't answered her calls or messages. The green screen will allow us to put up a backdrop on the video stream. You and Lorelei will appear on the camera together on the couch. You'll talk about how her day went, how you ended up a little too drunk, and you'll stay with Lorelei tonight, but tomorrow, you'll go back to the apartment. Everything is absolutely fine and normal." Brian flashes a smarmy grin. "Agree?"

"Yes, sure. Whatever."

"You keep the call short, you just wanted to check in with her to make sure all is well, no funny business, no mention of the Department, the equipment, the FSMI code. Got it?"

"Yes. Got it." I grit my teeth, holding back the urge to pummel this twat into the carpet.

"Obviously, we will need to remove your restraints and Faraday hat for the duration, but again, if you try anything, make any wrong moves, try to harm anyone in the room, then the signal will be given to our operative and your precious Cassie will be … taken care of."

I stare at Brian, knowing that if I wasn't restrained and wearing this kryptonite hat, he would be flying through the window, plummeting to his messy death seven or eight stories below. I assume this apartment is directly above the one Cassie is staying in. The view from the window is the same, and the building has only eight floors.

"Her fate is in your hands, Toby. Don't fuck it up."

Cynthia comes over. "Thank you, Brian. That will do." She turns to me. "Really, Toby, we just want this over with as soon as possible, with no one getting hurt, no trouble, and no problems. If you just work with us, we will do what we need to do and be out of your lives forever."

I nod. "Yes, okay. Fair enough."

"Good." Cynthia flashes a smile at me, which is the first time I've ever seen her release the resting bitch face scowl. "After the call, Cassie will be free to go. We'll order a pizza to be delivered to the apartment and she'll spend the evening watching trashy romcoms on Netflix and possibly having a bath. Honestly, I'm quite jealous, but we have work to do first. Now, can we get on with it so we can all have some peace?"

"Yes, but I really, really need to pee first."

Cynthia sighs and shakes her head. "Right, untie him, take him for a wee-wee!"

I'm on the couch, being watched by Brian and Ian from behind the laptop and its camera. Out of sight, Cynthia produces the scene like we're shooting a movie. A half-drunk glass of beer is placed on the table in front of me; Lorelei is changing in another room and will appear during the call, casually draping herself over me and thereby indicating that the discussion should quickly end. If I try anything or say the wrong thing, they will do God knows what to Cassie, and I will then be forced to spend the rest of the night cleaning up dead bodies from this apartment. It won't be pretty. Let's not go there. Once the call is made, I am to proceed back to the electric chair, and they will run the FSMI flush on me using the weird helmet and eye goggles they have rigged up. I am told it will take only a few minutes, and I'll fall asleep after. When I wake up in the morning, I will never have to see them again, nor will I have any memory of what exactly happened in this room or any remnants of the PFG code left in me. They claim I will go back to how I was, but I can't quite understand how that can work. Still, I don't really understand how Evelyn's code worked, either, so I'll have to trust that they know what they are doing. Last time they tried something on me, I was able to feedback into their system and overpower it, then firebomb the house and escape. They assure me they have built-in protection for that sort of thing this time, and I will not be able to prevent the procedure.

Can I go back to how I was? Lose all my self-esteem and languages, the ability to manipulate things and people, smash glass with thoughts and wavelengths, burn out circuits, and change people's minds. Can I go back to a normal day job and churn away my life in a dull IT support role?

No, I don't think I want to lose any of those things, but at this stage, what choice do I have? I can't let anything happen to Cassie, and if that means I sacrifice everything I gained from the PFG code, then that's the price I have to pay.

"Are we ready?" Cynthia looks around the room. Everyone is in position, wearing their ridiculous hats. They nod and Cynthia gives the signal to go ahead. I take a deep breath.

"Hey, Cassie, how are you?" The call was answered by an Asian man, presumably Liang, and he then called over a very angry Cassie to the screen. Her face fills the laptop in front of me, scowls and confusion spreading over her pretty features.

"Toby! Where the bloody hell are you, I've been trying to call you all fucking evening. What are you doing?"

"Cassie, I …" She cuts me off. Maybe she didn't hear me?

"This absolute fool, Liang, called me back down to the stupid lab saying he had figured out how to build the proto-type, and I had to come see, but all he's got on the screen is the same design I had hours ago and gave up on. Is he actually stupid or something? What is wrong with them here?" Cassie throws her hands up. "I'm leaving, Toby. I've booked a flight home early. If you don't want to come, then that's up to you, but I've had enough, this was a big mistake, sod them and their promises. I'm done with the whole thing!"

"Cassie … please, listen."

"And so much for you being around to watch out for me. Where have you been all day? Are you drunk? Where are you?"

"I'm at Lorelei's apartment. We had a couple of drinks and …"

"Oh, lovely. You know, I've been patient, I've given you the benefit of the doubt, I know what men are like, blah, blah, but come on, Toby, we are adults here, and you are behaving like a stupid teenager."

"I know, sorry. Look …"

She rubs at her forehead. "Sorry, I didn't mean that. I'm just fed up, and I want to go home."

"Okay. I understand." The Department glare at me from three sides, Lorelei I can't see, but she will join me shortly and I'll have to wrap this up. Cassie seems a tad agitated. I don't know what's been going on in that lab, but now I know this is all a scam to lure me here, rather than Cassie, it makes sense that they aren't actually building her prototype at all and that they've been fobbing her off with lies and distractions. I'll have some explaining to do once this is all over. She will be as disappointed as me, if not more so. I know why she wanted to build her invention so urgently. It's because Evelyn might pass away anytime, and Cassie wanted to make her proud of her. "Cassie, I just wanted to make sure you are okay, that's all. Why don't you just go chill out, get some food and take it easy? I'll see you tomorrow, and we can talk about going home, okay?"

"You'll come back?"

"Yeah, of course." I smile, avoiding any glances at the stooges around me.

"Right, okay." Cassie seems to calm down a little. "Well, I only booked a flight for me. I didn't know if you would want to leave."

"No problem, I'll sort something out tomorrow."

"Okay, well, good. I'll see you tomorrow, then?"

"Yeah." I smile again, and as I see Cassie return the gesture, an idea pops in my head like a balloon caught on a holly bush. "Oh, by the way, you know you lost that earring?"

A flicker of confusion flashes over Cassie's face. She starts to speak but then stops, her face flushing. Then, she smiles back at me. "Oh, right! Yes. Did you find it?"

"Yeah, I did. Upstairs. You know, in the apartment. I left it by the window."

"Great, thank you. I've been looking for that."

"It's the one that looks like a little sun, isn't it?"

"That's the one." She grins.

"It never hurts to keep looking for sunshine." I chuckle.

"Well, that's true, for sure."

Lorelei/Laura takes her cue and comes into the camera's field of vision. "Hey, Cassie, how are you?" Back with her fake accent and she sits down next to me, close and warm. Every inch of contact is torture, but I keep up my grin for the camera.

"Oh, hi Lorelei, good, thanks."

"I'm so sorry. I took Toby away, and we left you alone. I thought we would come back this evening, but you know, we had some beers, bit of wine, you know how it goes."

Cassie waves a hand. "I do. No problem. I'm just going to chill out for the night, anyway. Tired, you know?"

"Good idea. Hey, I'll send some pizza for you. Put on Netflix. There should be some wine in the fridge."

"Sounds great, thank you." Cassie grins convincingly.

"Okay, we let you get comfy. See you tomorrow, yeah?"

"Sure, cool. Thanks, Lorelei. See you, Toby."

"Bye, Cassie."

The video is cut off. The room falls to silence. I sit and wait. Did they notice my signal?

Laura is the first to move. She gets up and walks away, her warmth dissipating with every step. For a brief moment there, I almost believed that everything was as it was before, that all this Department rubbish never happened, and I was really at Lorelei's apartment, drunk on love and lust. But, no. I am motioned to get up by Brian and pushed back into the chair. Restraints re-applied.

"Very good, Toby. Thank you for cooperating. You know, it's a shame you are on the wrong side. You could have made a good operative." Cynthia says, looking down at me in the chair of doom.

I grunt a response. At least I know Cassie is safe, and maybe she understood my message. What she can possibly do about the situation, though, I have no idea. Cassie might know I am in danger, but realistically, what can she do about it? She doesn't know the details or what is going to happen in just a few minutes. She isn't exactly going to break into the room in the next thirty seconds armed with guns and explosives, take out all of the Department stooges, destroy their equipment and rescue me, is she? How could she?

Well, at least I tried.

CHAPTER
THIRTY-TWO

FRIDAY, 28TH OCTOBER, 2022,
9:18 PM. GRØNNENERGI
BÆREKRAFT LØSNINGER
BUILDING, OSLO.

TOBY IS IN TROUBLE. That much is obvious. He used the code phrase 'lost earrings,' and for some reason, he called from a fake apartment on a laptop to the lab. I could see fringing around Toby's hair where they had set up some kind of fake background using a green screen. When Lorelei showed up, the camera refocused on her, and there was a flicker of the green itself while the software adjusted. Just a frame or two, but I saw it. They weren't in Lorelei's apartment, but they wanted to make it look like they were. Why?

How did Toby know I'm in the lab? Why didn't he call my phone from his phone? He's being made to pretend all is well when it very much isn't well. That stinks of the Department.

What I don't know is exactly what kind of trouble he's in or why they want him and not me. What has he done?

Liang closed the call after we had said goodbye and then locked the laptop and walked away out of sight. This was a setup. Liang has not figured out my prototype at all, despite his raving. All he did was open my original 3D CAD file, move some things around, and save it under a new name. He's not very good at bullshitting, and I can smell it a mile away. When I questioned his design changes he went back to the blank looks and kept repeating that now it would work. How stupid does he think I am?

Why did they want me here, in this lab, for the call? I need to get out of here. Fast.

I know the exit to this room requires a keycard, and I don't have it. Liang does. Could I overpower him with something? I look around for anything I can use as a weapon. There's a lot of large equipment, but all much too heavy for me to throw and probably bolted down. There are fire extinguishers. That could work. I check the ones closest to me, and they are freely moving on their holders. They look new, CO_2 ones. A quick blast of those in Liang's face should do the trick, and if not, then the canister over the head definitely will. If it comes to it.

I pull one of the extinguishers off its wall hook, remove the pin, and stash it under the desk where I'm still sitting. It's out of sight but quickly available if I need it. I still have my phone, but a quick check reveals there is no signal. It's useless. I squeeze it back into my bra and wait for Liang to make the next move.

Promptly, he comes back with a big smile and a jaunty composure. I smile back at him.

"So, I will start the 3D printer now, then we can look in the morning, okay?"

"Yes, it looks fine, Liang. Thank you." I yawn. "After a good night's rest, we'll look at the results."

He nods frantically, almost bowing. "Very good, Miss Cassie." And he motions towards the exit. Lucky for him, he's letting me go, or he'd be defrosting his nose until morning.

My heart thuds in my chest, but I try to keep calm. Liang opens the door, letting me out and the relief is almost overwhelming.

"Thanks, see you tomorrow."

"Yes, goodbye."

He closes the door and I immediately run for the stairs up to the apartment. I'm safe and free, and I have zero intention of ever going back to that bullshit lab. I get to the apartment and rush over to the window, but there's no sign of anything. I wasn't expecting an earring; I haven't lost one, and I don't even own a sunshine earring, but that's what Toby said. I was expecting to find a clue here. Nope. Nothing.

Must be something else. I try to recall exactly what he said.

'It's upstairs. You know, in the apartment. I left it by the window.'

Upstairs in the apartment. I look around, but there's nothing new here. My bag, Toby's bag, a drink where I left it from earlier. Gah. What does he mean? I peer out of the window, trying to look above, but I can't see anything of interest.

'It never hurts to keep looking for sunshine.'

That's the phrase I used on the postcard to Gran when they kept me prisoner in Connemara. Now, here we are in Oslo, and Toby slips that same sentence into the conversation. That wasn't accidental; he was telling me that he was being held against his will. Upstairs? I know there are more floors above this apartment, but if he's being held prisoner somewhere upstairs, there must be more people around than him and Lorelei. How can I do anything about that? Should I call the police? Tell them what? That my friend said he found my lost earring? Obviously, that won't work.

Toby got me out of my kidnapping by starting a fire, but that was in a farmhouse, not a tower block. I can't burn this whole place down, can I?

No, but maybe I don't need to.

In the kitchen, I flip on one of the stove rings to max and find a frying pan. I pour in a little extra virgin olive oil — this place is really well-equipped. Then, wait for it to heat up. Just in case, I also grab a slice of bread, pop it in the toaster and turn it up full. Toasters always set off smoke alarms, don't they? I need to trigger the building alarms. That will force everyone to get out. The kidnappers surely won't want to burn to death in a tower block. My heart thuds again as I wait for the oil to heat or the toast to burn. Which one will be first? Both seem painfully slow. In the meantime, I grab all my things and bundle them into my bag. I'm obviously not staying here tonight, no matter what. I take the initiative and throw Toby's things into his bag while I'm at it.

Could it be the Department here in Oslo? Can't be? Who then? Lorelei must be in on it, or she would have said something. She's a baddie! I bloody knew it, but Toby was blinded by her beauty. I have to admit, I was a little, too. The bloody bitch! Toby must be heartbroken.

I peek over at the kitchen, and the oil is starting to smoke a little now. I look up. There's a sensor on the main room ceiling and sprinklers here and there in each room. That should do it. If I'm wrong and Toby isn't in trouble, then I suppose I can just say I fell asleep while cooking something. Toby better bloody appreciate what I'm doing for him.

Okay, what next? Should I go up to the next floor and look around? The corridors on this level are plush, softly lit, mostly beige and newly decorated. There's a lift, but I won't risk that. The fire escape is the concrete stairway. No, I'll wait until the alarm goes off before leaving the apartment, or it will seem strange. The smoke is getting noxious now from the oil and the smell of toast is making me hungry. I haven't had dinner yet. Bloody starving, actually. Time for a quick cheese on toast? No, I suppose not.

I zip up the bags and leave both near the apartment door.

An air conditioner flips on, blowing away my smoke. No!

There's a control panel on the wall, so I rush over and switch the thing off. There's a beep, and then the fans slow and stop. I glance over at the kitchen. Now, there's a plume of nasty dark blue smoke coming from the pan. It won't be long.

On cue, there's a screeching siren sound splitting my eardrums, followed by darkness as the lights go off, and two seconds later, dim red lights flicker on. One at each end of the apartment. I rush to the door and open it as sprinklers come on, drenching everything in the room. Excellent.

I leave the apartment and head upstairs, grabbing another fire extinguisher as I pass it in the corridor, then go through into the stairwell. It's dark, with only a red light to guide me where I should be going down, but instead, I go up, bravely facing who knows what to save the captured Toby Steele! I can't help but chuckle, but I know it isn't funny. He could be in real danger. My heart pounds again, adrenaline floods my veins, and I get to the top of the stairs to the next floor. I pause, looking through the glass panel in the door into the dim corridor beyond. Aside from red lights and sprinkler water, there's no sign of anything or anyone. I wait for a few more seconds but then carry on up to the final floor above, brandishing the extinguisher in front of me like a shotgun. I skip two at a time up the stairs to the top floor and once again pause behind the door. Less than a minute has passed since the alarm started. I go through the door into the corridor. Here, it splits off into two. Which one do I take? There's one that mirrors the floor where my room is downstairs and another that goes off acutely. I hesitate, but then a door bursts open ahead of me. Shit!

I duck into the other corridor and flatten myself against the wall behind a fake Chinese rubber plant that's taller than me. My heart now thudding so fast that surely someone will feel it amplified through the building.

I wait. Now I can hear voices, yelling, confusion and anger, but nothing clear over the siren wails. A moment later three figures pass by the end of my passage towards the stairwell door, then one last one. It was Lorelei, I think. Hard to see in the dim red light, but I'd know her golden locks anywhere. They all slam down the stairs, and I hear their footsteps dissolve into nothing. That's it? Was Toby with them?

Tentatively, I edge back to the other corridor and slowly move towards the door which they have left open. I peek inside, and the room is flooded with sprinkler rain, dimly lit in red like everywhere else. I see the green screen set up behind the couch where they called me from not fifteen minutes ago, and then I turn and see a scene from some kind of sci-fi movie. Toby is slumped in a chair, a weird mesh thing and a helmet on his head and something over his eyes. Behind him are banks of computers, all dark apart from two laptops that are still lit up, showing a trippy screensaver pattern. Toby doesn't move.

"Toby!" I run over to him. I shake him by the shoulders, but he doesn't stir. I can see he's tied down to the chair. They just left him to burn? Bastards!

"Toby, wake up!" I check his pulse. He's breathing and heart beating.

I pull the goggles from his face, and his eyes remain closed. I look around for something to cut the ties on his arms, finally finding a pair of scissors in the kitchen area. I cut the plastic and then undo the strap around his chin that is keeping the helmet on. This is the same thing the bloody Department used on me in Galway, so it is them.

"Toby, wake up!" I repeat, to no avail.

Water pours from the ceiling, and the alarm is getting annoying now, piercing and ridiculously loud. If this isn't enough to pull Toby from his slumber, then my yelling isn't going to help.

What do I do? I can't carry him out of here. Surely, the police or fire brigade will show up here shortly. Don't these big tower buildings have a direct link to the authorities?

Panicking, I hop from foot to foot. What do I do? Just wait for help? The culprits have fled the scene, but once they realise it isn't a real fire, they'll be back. They won't leave all this equipment here. No, we need to leave, and fast.

"Toby!" He vaguely stirs, and suddenly, I have an idea.

Without pause, I lean down and kiss him hard on the lips, sliding my tongue into his mouth, then reach down and grab hungrily at his crotch through his jeans.

That does it, and his eyes spring open. I pull back and stand up.

"Toby, are you okay? What happened?"

He blinks, looks around at the red-lit rain and chaos, and then up at me. "Cassie?"

"We need to leave, NOW! Can you walk?"

"The Department... they did something. I ... Oh, no. Oh, no!"

He stands up, then immediately falls over, and the chair tips over on top of him. Shit. His ankles are tied to the chair legs.

"Sorry, hold on." I reach down and cut the ties and he slowly stands up, brushing himself down.

"It's all gone, Cassie. They wiped it. I didn't think it would work, but it has."

"What's gone? What did they do to you? What is this stuff?"

"Flash Gordon, it's all flushed!" He coughs out a cry of anguish and almost bursts into tears, then doubles over and rests on the chair.

"What?"

"They fucking took it from me! The bastard Department."

"I'm not sure I follow, but we need to get out of here now. Come on. You can explain later."

"Yes, right. Okay." He turns to look at the equipment behind him, grabs his phone from inside a little cage on the desk, then pulls out all the cables from one of the laptops and closes the lid, picking it up. "Maybe Evelyn can get something from this. Let's go."

"Gran? What's she got to do with it?"

"Err, nothing. Forget it."

"Is she safe?"

"Yes, absolutely. They told me they don't see her as a threat."

He strides towards the door but then stops and turns to me, eyes wide.

"Hang on, did you just kiss me?"

Men!

CHAPTER
THIRTY-THREE

JE NE PARLE PAS FRANÇAIS. *Ich spreche kein Deutsch.* I had to look those up on my phone. Why? Because those statements are now fact. Not only French and German, but I can't speak Polish, Norwegian, Italian, Spanish, Dutch or Russian. I suppose I'm lucky I can still speak English. This was brought to my attention when checking into a hotel in Oslo and I could no longer understand signs or conversations as I passed by natives. Those memories or pathways in my brain are dead, like forgotten dreams. Eroded, wiped and flushed. When I try to force the memories forward, I get a load of nothing. Buzzing emptiness, no through road, turn back, dead end.

They killed Toby Steele and left me in his place. The old Toby who was pathetic and normal, shy and bullied. Toby Steele who chose to work the night shift in a boring job, because it meant not having to deal with people.

They took away the Flash Gordon code and left me like an empty shell.

I don't remember much about what happened, but I suppose that's part of it. Cassie found me unconscious, strapped to a chair in a room two floors above the apartment she was staying in. She said I spoke to her on a call just before and I sent a help message to her, encoded. 'Lost earring.' I don't remember the call, but I know we set up that system a while ago. It was meant for her to tell me she needed help, but it turns out it was me who needed Cassie to rescue me. Ironic, as I was meant to be looking out for her. Now I'm some normal dude with no special abilities, no confidence, no speed.

Soaking wet, we left the building. Cassie triggered the fire alarms and sprinklers. Smart girl. But it was too late. The Department had done their evil work already, and my brain was flushed away. They scarpered and left me to burn to death. Bunch of tossers!

Cassie flagged down a taxi and asked to be taken to a hotel near the airport. That's where we are now. She's showering. I'm sitting on the bed lamenting all I have lost in the last twenty-four hours. Love and life. Lorelei … that golden-haired temptress made me fall in love with her as a honeytrap.

It hurts, I have to admit. Deep down pain in my guts that constantly taunts and nags. Did she really care for me at all? I will never know.

Cassie comes back into the room, a cloud of steam framing her in a white fluffy dressing gown, hair wrapped up in a towel. "Your turn, Toby."

I nod, but don't move.

"Great shower, and the soap smells gorgeous."

Cassie checked us into a double room. She has a flight booked for Sunday morning. I suppose I'll book myself onto the same flight, but I can't face it yet.

"Go on, then." Cassie flops down on the bed next to me. It won't be the first time we've shared a bed. I remember waking up next to her in Connemara in a similar situation.

"Yeah, give me a second."

"You okay, Toby?"

"No, not really, to be honest."

"Want to talk about it?"

A good question. I'm sure she will want to know what the hell is going on and why the Department flushed something out of my head, but I'm not supposed to tell her about the Flash Gordon code. Maybe it doesn't matter anymore now it's gone. Wiped from the planet because those fools think the world isn't ready for it yet. Ridiculous. The world benefited from it already. I've done good, haven't I?

"I don't know, Cassie. I'm not supposed to say anything."

"What do you mean? Who said that?"

I look her in the eyes as she takes the towel off her head and tousles her hair dry. She's all fresh and clean, flushed from the hot shower. So pretty. "Evelyn."

Cassie wrinkles up her nose and pauses for a moment. "I won't tell if you won't."

I sigh. "Okay. I suppose it doesn't matter anymore, but let me have a shower first."

When I exit the steamy bathroom, having pummeled away some of the stress with the admittedly excellent shower, Cassie is cross-legged on the bed in leggings and a t-shirt that proclaims 'I'm not a morning person' with an angry cat holding a cup of coffee. I'm now wrapped in a fluffy white gown that's many sizes too small for me, but I also have a towel wrapped around me to protect the innocent. Cassie has procured food and drinks in the form of pizza and a bottle of wine. She pats the bed and motions to the half-empty pizza box. "I didn't know what you wanted, so I got pepperoni. Everyone likes that, don't they?"

"Thanks." I nod.

"Wine?"

"Fuck it, yeah. Why not?"

She hops off the bed and pours me a glass of white, then hands it to me as I slump down on the bed.

"Cheers." I take a sip, and the cool grape juice goes down nicely.

"Feeling any better?"

I shrug. "I guess so. But … ugh. I don't know."

She sits down next to me and reaches over, pulling me into a quick hug. "I know. It happened to me, as well."

"I know, but she was … so perfect."

"That is true. Lorelei isn't really an equivalent to Brian. Was that him running away from the scene earlier?"

I nod. "Yeah, slimy twat. He's shaved the dodgy moustache, though. Wise move."

She chuckles. "You'll get over it. She wasn't perfect, was she? She was a double-crossing government agent honeytrap!"

"Yup. Seems so."

"Bitch!"

I laugh. "Real name is Laura, she told me. Don't know much else. She's English, though, not Norwegian."

"Why are we here, then, in bloody Oslo?"

"Good question. I asked that, something to do with historic political situations." I shrug. "I don't understand that sort of thing."

"So … want to tell me how my Gran is involved in all this?"

I take a deep breath and run a hand through my hair, which still drips water from the shower down my back. "Right. Buckle up." I grab a slice of pizza and take a bite. "And you might need a top-up of wine."

I start my story sometime in the 1960s, when Evelyn was approached by Spencer Jenkins of GCHQ to start work on a super secret project, codenamed Project Flash Gordon. The mission; to take any simple man and rapidly make him exceptional. Strong, intelligent, quick and effective. Remove all his fears and cowardice and replace them with bravery and confidence. They thought this was possible by means of applied technology. And, as it turns out, they were right. It took Evelyn, working alone for decades, to bring it to fruition, but she did it. The problem was that her project was cancelled before she could finish her work. The Department stepped in and took it over when the government changed its mind about where funds should be directed. Evelyn hid her code, then was retired off with a healthy pension, and Cassie knows her story from there. After decades of lying dormant, on Evelyn's 100th birthday at 22:22:22, that code activated accidentally, and I happened to be in the room where it ran. My brain was flashed, augmented and vastly upgraded with the frequency-shifting memory implantation process. I suddenly had speed, agility, languages, skills and abilities I had never even dreamed of. I could manipulate things and people, and above all, I had an absolute loyalty to Evelyn. I was driven to find her, and it turned out that she was in a care home not far from where I live.

I told Cassie how I set off the incendiaries at the house in Galway by igniting the lithium, overwhelming the batteries with a resonant frequency that would start them burning. For the last eight months or so, this has been my life. I've been trying to do the best I can with it. Fighting crime, basically, in my own way.

This is what the Department really wanted, and that's why we were lured here. They knew I wouldn't leave Cassie, so they dragged her along with a fake story about building her prototype.

"Oh. I should tell you something that Doctor Ian Davidson said to me."

"What's that?"

"Bear in mind that the Department are a bunch of cheating, lying, manipulating arseholes, so this may be a load of nothing, but he said that they tried to build your prototype already, and it didn't work. Won't ever work, he reckons, so they were no longer trying to wipe your memory."

Cassie's jaw has been hanging open for most of my story, increasingly far with each revelation, but now she looks dejected and down at her glass of wine.

"As I say, they are likely lying."

"If they were, then they would still have tried to wipe the designs. They obviously found out I had a backup of everything, so all that hassle in Connemara was a waste of time."

"True, but still, they may just be incompetent. Have no idea how to build it properly. Messed it up in some way?"

Cassie shakes her head. "Maybe they are right. I was thinking I should forget it, anyway. I don't need all this hassle." She waves around at the room we're now cosy in. "Perhaps it's better that I know it doesn't even work before I waste any more energy on it." She laughs. "Pun not intended."

I nod, not knowing what to say. We sit in silence for a moment, each pondering our disappointment.

"What now, then?" Cassie looks over at me.

"I don't know, to be honest. I've got a bit of money left. I suppose I'll have to get a normal job again. Boring IT support is all I'm qualified for." I groan. "What about you?"

She shrugs. "I'll go back to work, tell my boss I had a lovely holiday, thanks, and pretend none of this happened."

"Fair enough. I'm sorry, Cassie, for getting you mixed up in all this."

"No, it sounds like I was always going to be mixed up in this. If what you say about Gran is all true."

"Every word, I swear."

"Well, then, I'm sorry you got mixed up in it when that code thing ran on you. I can't believe I finally found out what Gran worked on her whole life, and it's something so utterly ridiculous that I would never have believed it if she told me."

"It is kind of amazing what she did. Evelyn is an incredible woman."

"I know that much." Cassie nods. "And it's definitely all gone, out of your head? How is that possible?"

"Yes, all wiped. I feel empty, like a shell. Something huge missing from me. I don't know how to describe it, but when I try and use those skills, it's like a memory that I know I had, but can't quite pull to the surface. A dream lingering for a moment, then dissipating into nothing. It's bloody frustrating, actually."

"I can imagine."

"I'm a normal, boring, and I have to emphasize that word — BORING, bloke again. Don't know if I like that."

Cassie laughs and pokes me in the ribs. "Nothing wrong with boring every once in a while. I think I've had enough excitement to last me a long time."

I hold up my wine glass. "I'll drink to that."

We clink glasses and take a gulp of wine.

"Shall we get another bottle sent up?"

"Fuck it, why not?"

YESTERDAY WAS A WRITE-OFF. I don't think I've been that hung over in a while, and I'm attributing a good chunk of it to whatever the evil Department did inside my head. I'm sure that couldn't have helped my headache.

Yes, the two, three, then four bottles of wine we drank could possibly have been a contributing factor, but that's beside the point. We got tipsy, drunk, then silly drunk, and after that, it was everyone for themselves, total shit-faced ridiculousness. Thankfully, neither Cassie nor I can recall much of what happened after the third bottle, but we woke up on Saturday afternoon with four empty Chardonnay bottles in the room, and both of us with pounding headaches, so two and two … I was still wearing the fluffy dressing gown that didn't fit, but the privacy towel had long since vanished. Cassie was still wearing her leggings and t-shirt; the angry anti-morning coffee cat was far more appropriate. However, it was inexplicably inside out. Did we do anything other than sleep? Well, I can't be sure.

Anyway, we had a sedate early Saturday night and a very early start this morning. I slept the whole flight, and now we are back in good old England, heading to our fate or doom. I'm dreading telling Evelyn all that's happened. I know I got

PFG by accident, but now I sort of feel guilty and responsible for losing it. I still have a loyalty to Evelyn, and there was no point in putting it off. Cassie wants to see her, anyway, so may as well get it over with. Is she going to be upset or relieved that it was taken, especially that it was the same Department people who took it from me. How many times will they take the same project away from Evelyn's reach?

Plus, I've screwed up my only chance of saving something of my programming, and I really should have known better as an IT professional, but as I said — major hangover. That probably wasn't the best time to start fiddling around with the laptop I took from the Department. I managed to get into the OS, not Windows or anything I recognised. It must be some custom front end to a Linux variant. Anyway, it was going sort of okay, not that I found anything useful, but then I connected it to the hotel WiFi. Big mistake. Less than a minute later, a red screen flashed up before a lot of fan hissing and heating up, followed by a totally dead brick of junk. It wiped itself in a spectacular way. Totally fried. It wouldn't even boot to the BIOS. I threw it in the bin.

I assume the Department had remotely wiped it as soon as they realised I had taken it. So, that's that.

Short of tracking Doctor Ian and Cynthia down and somehow forcing them to undo what they did, if that's even possible, it seems my augmentations are all lost forever. I doubt that Evelyn can rewrite the software she made decades ago with no equipment and being as fragile as she is. I couldn't even ask her to try. I know the code was wiped after it ran at Bio-Digi, and Brian was able to retrieve some parts, but that's far from something I could download and run on my home PC. I have to accept that it has gone.

As with Lorelei, I had fun for a while, and now it's all over. Doesn't stop it from hurting, though.

Cassie has been quiet on the journey. She won't say it, but I think she's upset that the Department told us that her invention won't work. She's been scribbling things and tapping away at her phone. I think she's trying to check calculations or theories or something, but it's all over my head, especially now. I'm as much use as a fart in a hurricane. Yes, Ian said that they had tried the prototype, and it didn't work, but I have no evidence of that, and they could very well be lying. They are good at lying, as I've found out.

Cassie put a lot of work into that design, and I know in my heart that if she says it works, then it does. Screw the Department and their lies.

Back home from the train after a boring and long journey, we dumped our bags, used the bathroom, and then hopped in my car to drive the short distance to the care home. It isn't visiting time, but they know us very well by now and we seem to have free access. Evelyn isn't expecting us back so soon. Cassie didn't want to worry her, so we didn't mention anything that happened.

I pull up in the car park, and we go into the building, sign in, and tread the worn path towards the common room. Nurse Rosie informed us that Evelyn had been arguing with another resident over a game of chess this morning. Sounds like her.

"Hi, Gran." Cassie goes over, and I stay back, allowing them to say hello before I step in.

"Cassie, darling! What are you doing here?"

They hug and Cassie flops down in a chair next to her grandmother. I shuffle over.

"And Toby, too?"

"Hello, Evelyn. Yes, I'm here as well."

"What's happened?" Evelyn looks shocked and worried. "Are you all right?"

"We're fine, Gran. The trip was just a bit of a waste of time, that's all."

Evelyn looks between both of us, then motions for me to sit down. I do. "Well, you had better tell me what happened, then."

"I …"

"We …"

Cassie and I both start speaking at once. I pause and let her go first. She does the same. Evelyn shakes her head and then points to her granddaughter. "You first, Cassie."

"Perhaps we had better go somewhere more private?" Cassie glances around the room at the other residents, who, in fairness, probably wouldn't hear if a bomb dropped in the back garden. Still, one never knows.

We adjourn to Evelyn's room and find water and chairs. Cassie starts again.

She takes a deep breath, then shakes her head. "I don't really know where to begin, so I'll just jump in. It was the Department."

"Oh, my god!" Evelyn's hand flies to her chest. "What did they do to you?" She turns to me. "Toby, did you protect Cassie?"

"Gran, I'm fine. It wasn't me they were after."

"What?" Evelyn looks between us, confused.

"It was me they wanted, " I say, holding up a hand. They wiped me, Evelyn. They knew I had the PFG code, and they lured me to Oslo and took it away from me." Pent-up emotion suddenly hits me like a stone wall at a hundred miles per hour, and I can't help it. Tears burst from my eyes, and I cry out. I quickly hide my face and turn away, but Cassie comes over and wraps her arms around me before I can move.

"It's okay, Toby."

"No, it really isn't."

"My god. Please tell me exactly what happened. Cassie, fetch a cup of tea for him. There's a good girl."

I take a moment and wash my face in Evelyn's en suite

bathroom, then sit back down, taking a sip of the tea Cassie brought from somewhere. Then, I start the story from the beginning. Evelyn listens in silence.

Once I'm done, I sit back and feel the emotion pricking at my eyes again, but I take a breath and clutch the warm cup. "I'm sorry, Evelyn, but I had to tell Cassie everything, too. Since I no longer have the code, I figured it didn't matter anymore."

Evelyn ponders for a moment, then looks at me with a kind smile. "I understand. What's done is done. There's no changing that, now." Evelyn turns to Cassie again. "What he's told you is all absolutely true, Cassie, and I hope you know that I kept it a secret all these years only for your safety."

"Yes, Gran. I know. I mean, I still wish you had told me, but I understand."

"I'm sorry, Evelyn, for falling for their trap and ruining everything and potentially putting Cassie at risk. It was stupid of me. I should have realised it was too good to be true."

"Nonsense. They knew exactly what they were doing, and don't forget the manipulation. You didn't stand a chance with those odds. They used their methods on you the same as they did on Cassie. You didn't love that woman. They just made you think you did."

"Well, yes, but she is very attractive."

"You didn't know her, Toby. You don't love with your eyes. You love with your soul." Evelyn scolds and wags a finger.

I nod and bow my head. "Yes, you are right."

"Now, Cassie dear, fetch my computer, will you? It's in the drawer there. The bottom one." Evelyn points to a chest of drawers, and Cassie retrieves an ancient-looking laptop. "Good. Now, plug it in. I'm afraid the battery is long since dead. There's a plug down here somewhere."

"What are you doing, Gran?"

"Nothing until I find my other glasses. Ah, here we are. Now, then. You children go for a walk or something and come back in half an hour. Yes? I need some peace to think things over."

Cassie and I look at each other, confused.

Evelyn makes a shoo motion with her hands towards us. "Off you go, don't just sit there like potatoes. Go get a sandwich. It must be lunchtime."

"Right, okay. Do you want something?" I stand up to go.

"No, no. just some peace and quiet. Half an hour, please."

Cassie and I leave, a bit puzzled, and do as Evelyn suggested, finding a café nearby to the care home.

"She took it well, I suppose." I break the silence.

"Wonder what she's up to?"

I shake my head. "God knows. Maybe she's hacking into the Bank of England or GCHQ." I chuckle, but I'm also wondering.

"Coffee?"

"Yeah, I'll get it."

I fetch two coffees and muffins from the counter and sit down opposite Cassie. She's still tapping away on her phone. She looks up and smiles as I sit.

"I know you were only looking out for me because of the code thingy, the Flash Gordon project, but I hope you don't just disappear now."

"What? No, of course not."

"You are a good man, Toby, with or without the superhero stuff."

I chuckle. It sounds so ridiculous. "Thank you, Cassie. I don't feel like a good man, though. I feel like an idiot."

"Hush. You got tricked, so what? It happened to me, and you came to my rescue. I did the same for you. Now we're even."

I laugh again, "Fair enough. But you managed it without any special skills. Just your brain and talents."

"It was me who got us caught up with the bloody Department in the first place, remember."

"No, it was … never mind. Thank you, Cassie. I have no intention of vanishing, anyway."

"Good. I thought we made a good team out in Oslo, and you've always been there for me, even when you didn't need to be. I appreciate that."

I nod. "Thanks for coming to my rescue. I don't think I've said it yet."

"A little too late, huh."

"Yeah, well. They had some fancy gear and speeded up the process. What took hours back in Evelyn's original system took less than five minutes now. They've had a long time to hone the process."

We finish our drinks and check the time. Roughly half an hour has passed. "Think we should go back, now?"

"Yeah, let's see what Gran has been up to."

"Just in time. Very good." Evelyn beams a grin as we come back into her room.

"In time for what, Evelyn?" I try to look at her screen, but it seems to be off.

"Sit down, Toby." I do as she says. "Now, then. I need to ask you a question, and I don't want you to answer immediately. You take as much time as you want to ponder. Come back tomorrow if you fancy. This is not a simple thing."

"Okay." I look over at Cassie, and she shrugs.

"I think you underestimated me, Mr Steele." Evelyn chuckles.

"How so?"

"Did you think I spent decades working on a project and didn't plan for any countermeasures and contingencies? Did you really think I could be beaten by those imbeciles at the Department!"

"I … well, no, I mean. I don't know?"

She turns to Cassie. "Remember when they tried that helmet on you in Connemara?"

"How could I forget?"

"But it didn't work, did it?"

"No, I've always wondered why."

Evelyn taps at the laptop in front of her. "This is why, Cassie. Countermeasures. Precautions."

"Sorry, I don't follow?"

"Me either." I'm very confused now.

"You remember when you stayed with me all those years ago, and there was a screen in your bedroom showing soothing patterns."

"Yes, like a screensaver. You said it would help me sleep."

"I said it would help you sleep and keep you safe."

"Oh!" The penny drops, and Cassie springs up. "You ran some of that code on me, as well? To prevent anyone … err, hacking into my brain?"

"Precisely!"

I sit up. "You have the PFG code?"

"No, Toby, that is long gone. What Cassie saw all those years ago was something much smaller and simpler. A firewall, if you like. A barrier. I was developing the process towards the end of my time at Porton Down, and it was fresh in my head. I kept working on it once I could buy something powerful enough to run my code."

"So … you can put that barrier in my head, too?"

Evelyn shakes her head. "No, Toby. There's no need. Now, back to my point." She pauses for effect. "You were brought into this by accident, dear boy, and I have always felt bad about that. You didn't ask for this. It fell on you from a great height. I have to say, I think you have handled it well. A better man I could not have found. Well done, and

I thank you for all the things you have done. I don't need to know the bad things. I'm sure there are some. But I know you have done good, and you have protected my Cassie gallantly."

"It has been my pleasure, Evelyn."

"Now that you are free from the burden, you need to make a choice."

"Oh?"

Evelyn taps at her laptop again. "The original code that you ran, Toby, had the same safety countermeasure process as I gave to Cassie. A different version, granted, but there nonetheless. No one knew about this, not even Spencer. It's a shutdown feature. A lockout. If the code detects an attack, it burrows down into a hole and hides like a mole, preventing any damage."

My heart thuds in my chest as Evelyn explains, "So, let me get this straight: You are saying the PFG code is still in me, but it's just turned off and hiding?"

"Bingo!" She points at me with a bony finger.

"Oh, my god."

"And so my question to you, Toby, is now that you are free of this duty, do you want it back again? Now, remember what I said. I want you to think about this before you answer."

I nod. "Evelyn, I've thought of nothing else since I woke up in that tower building. I feel empty and useless like this. What you gave me was the most amazing thing in my life. Toby Steele died up in that room, and now you are saying you can resuscitate him! Yes, I want it back!"

Cassie stands up, clapping her hands. "Gran, are you sure it will work?"

"Quite sure, Cassie, dear."

"Hit me!"

"Toby, you understand what this means? You will have to keep your skills even more secret this time, because if those fools in the Department hear about it again, then I'm afraid of what they will do. If they know they can't take it away from you, then perhaps they'll have to take you away from … life."

"I'll take that risk. Sod them and their stupid policies. I understand, and I'll do what it takes."

"Very well, if you insist."

"What do I need to do?"

"The code will run on this screen. It will take about an hour, and after that, you'll be asleep for a while. When you wake up, you'll be back to your augmented state."

"Simple as that?"

Evelyn shrugs. "I mean, I spent decades creating the process, if you can call that simple, but yes."

"Wow. Okay. Let's go, then."

"Not so fast. Cassie and I can't be in the room when it runs." She taps her finger to her chin. "I think you had better take this home with you and do it there. I can't have you asleep on my bed here. The staff would get the wrong idea!"

"Ah, good point."

Cassie and I take the laptop with strict instructions from Evelyn on what to do. It must be a quiet and dark environment with no distractions. I'll set it up in my bedroom, and Cassie will stay in the house to make sure nothing happens while it runs.

I tap in the code that Evelyn wrote down. She's made an executable file that I can run. It gives me a thirty-second countdown, and I position myself on my bed, ready to fall backwards safely.

"Good luck, Toby." Cassie waits at the door, showing me her crossed fingers.

"Thanks. See you in a bit, I hope."

She closes the door, and I'm in darkness, apart from the green numbers counting down on the screen.

10, 9, 8, 7, 6, 5, 4, 3, 2, 1

The black screen is replaced by bright white, harsh on my eyes. At the same time, a blast of noise bursts from the tinny speakers. Like scratching and screeching mice in a blender. A pattern emerges from the white screen: blue, then green, then red, swirling and undulating, twisting and spinning, growing bigger, shrinking back, then flickering at high speed, the noise changing to pulse with the images. I'm mesmerised, my eyes fixed on the screen. I try to move my fingers, but no signal gets to the nerves. I'm paralysed, staring at the twisting patterns. A warmth bursts in my chest, and a calming sensation floods my veins. I watch as the world changes for me once again, and Evelyn's ancient code changes the very core of my brain.

———

I wake up with a start. A jolt of electricity passing through me. I look up, and the laptop now shows a black screen filled with the words **SYSTEM RESTORED** in large green text. I don't feel any different. Did it work?

I fumble for the light switch and find I need to visit the bathroom urgently. After, I have a mad thirst, so I go down to the kitchen for a glass of water. As I go down the stairs, I hear the television on. I forgot Cassie was here.

In the living room, she sits on the couch, legs folded under her. She sees me and yawns.

"Oh, there you are. How are you feeling?"

"Not sure. How long has it been?"

She checks her phone. "Four hours and a bit. I was going to check on you soon."

"Thirsty. Be right back." I grab a water bottle from the fridge and come back, sitting next to Cassie.

"Did it work?"

"Dunno yet."

"What happened?"

"Sound and patterns, like the screensaver thing you saw before. I only remember the start of it; after a minute or two, I have no idea."

"Well, do you feel any different?"

"Err, not sure." I try to probe my mind from the inside, but it isn't as easy as it should be.

"Well, try one of your augmented skills or whatever?"

"Yes, good idea." Of course, my mind goes blank, like scrolling through Netflix, trying to find something to watch. I can't think of anything. Then, a flash of inspiration hits me like a frying pan in the face. I feel the wavelengths lapping around me, I can taste the frequencies in the air, smell the sensations and hear the buzz of life. I focus on the light bulb above us and, with my mind, travel the circuits that send power to the LEDs. I harmonize with the copper, resonate with the power, and flash a spike of energy into the mix. The light dims, then comes back to full brightness, and then flickers off. I laugh as the energy flows through me; the language of life once again fills my brain, and I ride the wavelengths like a surfer. I take a big gulp of water from the bottle, then turn to Cassie. "Je suis de retour, bébé! Pardon my French."

DO ME A FAVOUR?

I genuinely hope you enjoyed this story and I'd love to hear about it. So would other readers. I would be eternally grateful if you would leave a review on Amazon for me.

I don't have a big-name publisher or agent, or any marketing help. I rely on the kind words of readers to spread the word and help others find my books.

In a world of constant rating requests from everything you buy, I know it's a pain, but it does make a huge difference and it encourages me to keep writing.

Thanks!
Adam.

www.AdamEcclesBooks.com

ALSO BY ADAM ECCLES

In order of publication:

Time, For a Change

The Twin Flame Game

Who Needs Love, Anyway?

Need a Little Time

The Soul Bank

System Restored

22:22:22 Frequency Shift

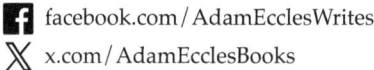

facebook.com/AdamEcclesWrites
x.com/AdamEcclesBooks

NEED A LITTLE TIME - AUDIOBOOK

Need a Little Time
Unabridged audiobook.
Narrated by Mark Rice-Oxley

SYSTEM RESTORED - AUDIOBOOK

System Restored
Unabridged audiobook.
Narrated by Mark Rice-Oxley

22:22:22 FREQUENCY SHIFT - AUDIOBOOK

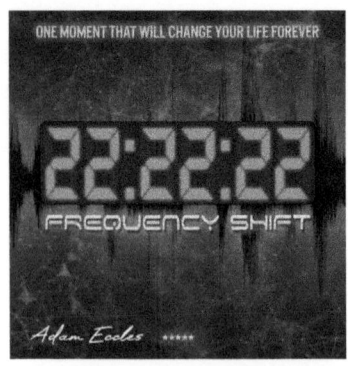

22:22:22 Frequency Shift
Unabridged audiobook.
Narrated by Mark Rice-Oxley

SIGN UP FOR NEWS

Scan this code with your phone

Did you know that I have a very low volume email mailing list where I'll occasionally send out information about upcoming books, offers, and maybe even some free short stories and terrible puns?

Or join here:

`www.adamecclesbooks.com/subscribe`

TIP JAR

If you are a fan of my work, and you'd like to support me with a donation to help fund ongoing writing and publishing, a tip no matter how large or small is much appreciated.

Scan the code to donate on Ko-Fi

Thanks a million!
   — Adam.

https://ko-fi.com/adameccles

CYPHER FUN!

Just for fun …

Somewhere, hidden in this book there is a clue encrypted in a cypher.

The first person who can email me with details of what it is will win a signed paperback copy of the book!

Scan this code to send me the answer.